SARA REINKE

AN UNEXPECTED ENGAGEMENT

Best wishes :
Sara Reinke

Jewel Imprint: Sapphire
Medallion Press, Inc.
Printed in USA

DEDICATION:

This book is dedicated in loving memory of Dorothy Howard, my grandmother and avid romance reader.

Special thanks to Joyce Scott, who graciously read through my first draft, and to my grandmother, Thel Brady, who told me romance novels could "never be too steamy."

Published 2007 by Medallion Press, Inc.

The MEDALLION PRESS LOGO
is a registered tradmark of Medallion Press, Inc.

Typeset in Adobe Garamond Pro
SecesjaPL typeface designed by Bartek Nowak
Printed in the United States of America

10 9 8 7 6 5 4 3 2 1
First Edition

AN UNEXPECTED ENGAGEMENT

SARA REINKE

CHAPTER 1

Essex County, England
October, 1748

"STAND AND DELIVER!"

At the cry, Charlotte Engle snapped awake with a startled gasp. Her eyes flew wide, the last vestiges of sleepy disorientation whipping from her mind as a sharp, booming report of gunfire ripped through the air outside of the coach.

She had been on the road from London and into Essex County for little more than an hour and had not meant to doze off. However, the sun had set, leaving the carriage to darkness along the highway, with only the dim, golden glow of interior lamps for illumination and the droning, inane gossip that passed for her aunt,

Maude Rutherford, the Dowager Viscountess Chelmsford's idea of conversation for company.

Charlotte yelped in bewildered alarm as the carriage lurched and she plowed gracelessly into the side of the coach belly. She could feel the wheels skitter for uncertain purchase along the edge of the rutted highway. The horses screamed, and the carriage shifted again, listing to the right before sliding to a jostling halt. She stared across the carriage cab at Una Renfred, her maid, her eyes wide in alarm, her hand darting instinctively for the muff against her lap.

"Highwaymen!" she gasped, even as Lady Chelmsford uttered a low and horrified moan, her hands fluttering about her bosom.

Charlotte heard footsteps hurriedly approaching the left side of the coach, and she jerked out the loaded pocket pistol she carried tucked within her muff. Lady Chelmsford caught sight of the weapon and moaned again, nearly swooning. Charlotte drew the doghead back against her thumb and leveled the petite weapon at the carriage door just as she heard someone outside take the handle in hand. The hinges creaked and the door opened wide; Charlotte caught a glimpse of a shadow-draped figure beyond, moving as if he meant to lean into the coach, and then she squeezed the trigger.

The pistol bucked against her palm, the barrel seeming to explode in a sudden, bright shower of sparks and a thick, pungent cloud of smoke. She heard the man at the doorway cry out, but could not tell if she had hit him or not. The door bounced closed as he fell away, and the smoke from the gunfire filled the coach cab, choking them.

"Come on!" Charlotte cried, whooping for breath, tears springing to her eyes. She groped about blindly in the thick smoke and caught Una by the wrist. She punted the door open and sprang from the coach, dragging Una in tow. She shoved the older woman toward the trees beyond the edge of the road.

"Run, Una!" she cried, choking on smoke, struggling for breath. She turned, reaching into the carriage and seizing Lady Chelmsford by the outstretched, flapping hand. She nearly toppled backward and onto her rump as her aunt came stumbling gracelessly from the cab. "Run!" she cried again, snatching Lady Chelmsford's redingote in her hands and offering her a hearty push in the direction of the forest. "Into the trees! Go! Go!"

Charlotte turned to run as well, and yelped when she felt a strong arm catch her firmly about the waist. "Let go of me!" she yelled, ramming the heel of her shoe firmly against the top of her captor's foot, drawing a surprised, pained yowl. His arm loosened about her, and she shoved her elbow mightily into his gut, knocking the breath from him. She wriggled from his grasp and tried to run again; the man caught her by the sleeve, whirling her around.

"Turn me loose!" Charlotte cried, closing her hand into a fist and sending it in a wicked arc from the fulcrum of her shoulder. Her knuckles slammed into the man's cheek; she could see he wore a black tricorne hat and a heavy black greatcoat, his face obscured by a drape of black fabric. His head snapped toward his shoulder at the impact of her fist, and again his hand loosened from her coat.

She turned to bolt for the trees, and plowed headlong into another highwayman. This one grabbed her firmly by the wrists; when she tried to draw her knee up into his crotch, he pivoted his hips, struggling with her, blocking the proffered blow with his thigh. She looked up into his face, also hidden by a scarf, and screamed at him. "Turn me loose, you rot damn bastard!"

She could not see his eyes above the edge of his scarf because of the heavy shadows cast by the brim of his hat, but he stiffened all at once, as if startled. She heard him draw in a sharp, hissing breath and his fingers slackened about her wrists. She wrenched herself free and staggered away from him, nearly tripping as her heels settled unsteadily in the soft loam at the road's edge.

Before Charlotte could regain her footing, much less her wits, she heard Lady Chelmsford utter a high-pitched, warbling wail. "Aunt Maude—!" Charlotte gasped, turning in time to see a third highwayman tussling with Lady Chelmsford. He had caught her by the arm, and she proceeded to swoon. Lady Chelmsford was a well-endowed woman, and when her legs failed her, she tended to take anyone not observing a safe margin of space down with her. She crumpled as Charlotte watched, and the highwayman yelped, his hands flailing as she knocked him beneath the broad basin of her pannier frame and the ballooning swell of her skirts.

"Do not move, my lady," said another highwayman, the first to have grabbed her. He had recovered from her blow, and managed to give Una chase. He dragged the older woman ahead of him, holding a dagger blade pressed beneath the shelf of her chin.

"Una!" Charlotte whimpered. Her brows furrowed, and she closed her hands into fists, squaring off against the highwayman. "Let her go, you coward rot."

The stern measure of her voice, the baring of her fists, seemed to give him pause, because she saw the edge of the knife against Una's throat momentarily falter.

"Charlotte, do as they say," Una said quietly. She was remarkably calm for a woman in her circumstances, and she held Charlotte's gaze evenly. "Do not fight them. Let them take what they want and leave."

"Let her go," Charlotte said again to the highwayman. She stepped toward him, and when the one behind her caught her shoulder, she pivoted, drawing her fist back to strike.

"Charlotte, stop it," Una said, more sharply this

time. Charlotte's fist paused, and she held it cocked, glaring at the highwayman.

"Step against the coach, my lady," he told Charlotte. His voice was hoarse from gun smoke, tremulous with uncertainty. Charlotte doubted the lot of them had ever before encountered a woman who would resist them. She could not see his face or eyes, but she could tell from the angle of his head, the hoist of his chin, that he was eying her readied fist with appropriate caution. "Please," he said. "Stand against the coach."

Charlotte and Una stood together with their backs to the carriage, watching the three highwaymen set to work. While one held a pistol on them, the other two bound Lady Chelmsford where she had fainted, with her hands trussed behind her back. Next, they dragged the driver, Edmond Cheadle—apparently unconscious—from the front of the coach.

"What have you done to our escort?" Charlotte demanded as they began to bind Cheadle. "You bastards, did you shoot him?"

The highwayman with the pistol trained at them stepped forward. "Do not fret," he said. "Your man is clumsy, not shot. He pitched off the driver's bench when the horses started. Knocked the wits from himself." He studied her for a moment and then chuckled. "He did not prove much of an escort, if I do say so, my lady."

Charlotte glared at him. "Bugger off."

"Such foul words from so lovely a mouth," the highwayman said, and he laughed. He held a small black sack out to them, not lowering his pistol. "Your jewelry and coins, my ladies," he said. "Kindly tender them, if you will."

Una poked her elbow firmly into Charlotte's arm, a mute but plain admonishment: *Do as they say.* Charlotte opened the front of her redingote, her motions sharp and angry. As Una removed her modest and inexpensive necklace and rings, Charlotte jerked at her dress ornaments, snatching the small, diamond-studded brooches each in turn from her stomacher. She shoved them unceremoniously into the pouch, and reached for her earrings, glowering all the while at the thief.

"You must feel like such a man," Charlotte told him. "Holding a pistol on a pair of unarmed women. How magnificently bold of you."

The thief paused; to judge by the canted angle of his head, he looked at Charlotte with surprise. "I beg your pardon?" he said.

"I would have thought the hanging of Dick Turpin would be enough to keep the likes of you cowed," Charlotte said, lifting her chin and pinching her brows.

"The likes of me?" the highwayman said, and then he shook his head and laughed. "Have we met before, my lady? Do you know me so intimately?"

"I would as soon be intimate with a corpse,"

Charlotte said, and when he laughed again, it stoked her outrage all the more. "I have read about you. You are the Black Trio, a rotten lot of scoundrels preying up and down these highways."

The highwayman chuckled, shaking his head again. "I think 'prey' perhaps is a bit strong a word," he remarked. "I would have you know I am a proper gentleman. The gazettes favor saying so, at any rate."

"You have been misinformed by the gazettes," Charlotte told him. "You, sir, are no gentleman."

"And you, my dear, are no lady," he replied.

Charlotte stiffened at his challenge, and Una uttered a soft groan.

"You have without question the most abrasive tongue I have ever heard from a woman," the thief said pointedly. "You throw a punch like a man in a gin-prompted brawl. You damn near scattered the brains from my associate's head with that little Bunney pistol you packed."

"How dare you," Charlotte challenged. "How dare you imply that because I do not swoon before you, quaking and pleading for mercy as you strip me of my valuables, I am not a lady."

"I am implying nothing," he said. "I am simply making an observation." He stepped closer to her, drawing so near she could see the faint glow of lamplight from inside the coach reflect from his eyes, winking beneath the shadow of his hat brim. She shied reflexively, feeling the back of her pannier frame press against the carriage, and as her eyes left his face, her gaze finding the barrel of his pistol still aimed at her, Charlotte felt the first inkling of anxious fear. Her throat tightened, her breath hitching softly, and any retort she might have offered faded from mind and tongue.

"You missed one," he said softly, tapping the barrel of his pistol against a small brooch holding her fichu closed at the swell of her bosom. Charlotte blinked, glancing down at it, a small rosette of diamonds.

She looked up. She could see the glint of his eyes; she could discern the outline of his nose and mouth beneath the drape of silk covering the lower quadrant of his face. "I . . . the clasp is broken," she said. "It . . . it is difficult to put on, much less remove once in place."

When he smiled, she could see the wry uplift of his mouth beneath the scarf. "Take it off, please."

"I told you, the clasp is broken," she said. "I do not know if I can."

"Why do you not give it a go?" he suggested mildly, rekindling her ire.

"It belonged to my grandmother," she said. "I would as soon keep it, if you do not mind. It is an heirloom, one of few reminders I have of her."

That aggravating measure of his smile, only hinted at beneath the scarf, widened. "Then I assure you, my lady, I shall hold it dear to my heart."

Charlotte blinked at him. "You are reprehensible," she whispered. She reached for the brooch, struggling with the clasp. She could hear one of his fellows rummaging through the luggage stowed against the back of the coach. The other tromped toward them, taking Una by the arm and forcing her to sit by the wheel, where he promptly set about tying her hands to the spokes.

"You are taking too long," he growled.

"It is not my fault, I assure you," the highwayman before her replied. "Our unladylike lady is distracting me."

His friend finished with Una and stood, moving toward the rear of the carriage. "Get her jewels and come on," he said.

The highwayman looked at Charlotte, and moved the pistol slightly. "You heard the gentleman," he said. "Move your hands aside. I will get it."

Charlotte did as she was told, watching as he tucked the pistol beneath his coat, under the waistband of his breeches. He stepped near to her, close enough to feel the weight of his hips buckle her pannier inward slightly. He reached for the brooch and tried to wrest the pin loose of the clasp. After a moment's futile effort, he glanced at her. "You were not lying."

"No," she said, scowling. "I was not."

His fingertips slipped unexpectedly down the front of her stomacher, delving into the slight margin between her breasts, beneath the top of her stay. Charlotte's breath caught against the back of her throat, and her eyes flew wide. She had never so much as kissed a man before; the delicate friction of his gloved fingers slipping against her flesh stoked something immediate and unexpected within her. She felt her heart thrum suddenly, frantically, and she slapped at his hand, knocking him away. "Do not touch me," she said.

"I only meant to try from the other side," he said. "I meant no disrespect."

"Then you should not offer it," she said. "Do not touch me."

He looked at her for a long moment, until Charlotte realized he understood her innocence and was amused by it. "Am I the first to do so?" he asked. "Have none ever ventured before me, then?"

"None with teeth remaining intact."

He laughed. "There is a blessing and a shame," he remarked. "A blessing for the man who is fortunate enough to be the first in full, and a shame for the rest of us. I told you I am a gentleman. Do not worry. Your virtues are secure."

"You will forgive me if your reassurances bring me little comfort at the moment," she said, and he laughed again.

"If you were as you claim—a gentleman of some meritorious character—you would not resort to highway robbery," Charlotte said, shrugging against the back of

the coach to draw away from him. She hoped to bait
him again, get his tongue wagging, and his attention di-
verted from her brooch. She had not lied; it was her
grandmother's, and an heirloom. It was the most precious thing Charlotte owned, worth far more within her
sentiments than any price it might fetch at a pawn shop,
and she had no intention of surrendering it to him.

"How do you know I do not need the money?" he
asked, feigned injury in his tone. "How do you know I am
not pressed into such circumstances by dire poverty?"

Charlotte frowned. "This is your eighth robbery—I
have read the gazettes. You have made more than enough
to cover any costs of your own subsistence and beyond.
You wear the fine clothes of someone with a well-padded
purse, and I am sure you did not walk to this site to greet
us. Undoubtedly you have a horse near at hand—a horse
you must feed and stable. You should be ashamed that
you would offer such an excuse as need or poverty. You
are greedy, nothing more."

"Greedy?" he asked. "You speak as though I run
amok, robbing tithe bowls or convents. I am pilfering
spare change and paste jewels from aristocrats so bloated
by their own perceived self-importance they can scarcely
sometimes fit through their carriage doors. If I did not
take it from them, they would only squander it at card tables or on courtesans—or perhaps in your circumstance,
my lady, on season tickets to Vauxhall. That seems more

your fare than a brothel."

Charlotte blinked, caught completely off guard by his rebuke. Her surprise proved only momentary, as her fury restored and her brows narrowed again. "The operatic season is scarcely a squandering of money," she said. "And it is my money to spend as I please. I did not steal it from others."

"Oh, no," he said with a laugh. "You get it from your parents, I am certain. A modest allowance so you might enjoy that fair lifestyle to which they have seen you so accustomed."

"I earn my own money," Charlotte snapped, balling her hands into defiant fists. "I do not need any allowance—I write essays for what is mine."

"Essays?" he scoffed.

"Essays and chapbooks, yes," she replied.

"And let me guess—flowery verses of delicate prose," he said. "Something inane and idle, chirping about true love and rose gardens."

Charlotte planted her hands against his chest and shoved with enough force to send him stumbling back a step. "I write about social ills," she said. "About how people suffer needlessly in our society because of scoundrels like you who think wealth is something one is entitled to—whether by birth or force—rather than something attainable through hard work and education. Things you obviously know nothing of—you have likely never tendered a day's effort at anything in your life, save for crime. The only greater shame you should know is that the gazettes have made heroes out of you—and there are poor children who learn of it, and aspire to nothing greater than your pathetic measure."

He stepped near to her again, pressing himself so closely she could draw his fragrance from his coat against her nose, an intermingling of pine sap and wood smoke. She struggled to lift her chin, to offer him some challenge with her eyes, the set of her brows. "If you were a man of any merit, even one somehow forced into crime at the start, you would take the proceeds outside of your own subsistence, and you would give them to those in need," she said.

"And who might that be, my lady?" he asked. "These poor children upon whom I am such a bad influence?"

"Exactly—yes," she said. "England is full of charity schools. There are some that are splendid—St. Bartholomew's in east London, for example. They are good people doing God's work and helping poor children learn to read, write, cipher. They impart skills that will help them find work and make wages to see them out of poverty one day."

"That would please you?" he asked. "If I gave my proceeds to a charity school?"

She raised her brow. "That would shock me," she said. He reached for the brooch again, and Charlotte jumped, bewildered, when she felt him draw the flaps of her redingote together against her bosom, hiding the pin. "Do not let the others see," he said softly, little more than a hushed breath.

He stepped back from her, leaving her blinking at him, confounded. "Sit down, my lady," he said. "Against the coach wheel, if you would be so kind."

Charlotte lowered herself warily to the ground, the skirt of her manteau swelling about her pannier and hips. The thief genuflected before her, drawing a length of rope from his coat pocket. He leaned toward her, and began to bind her wrists together behind her back, lashing them to the wheel. She did not say anything as he worked; she did not know what to say. She was again acutely aware of his breath against her skin as he leaned over her shoulder. She could cant her head ever so slightly and feel his hair, protruding from beneath his hat, brush her face.

He leaned back once her wrists were securely bound. Charlotte tugged on her ropes, feeling the bonds draw against her skin. She realized he had left her some wiggle room; not much, but enough that with a few moments of concerted effort she would be able to work the knots loose and free herself. "I suppose you think I should be grateful to you," she said.

"For what?" he asked innocently, rising to his feet. He shrugged his shoulders, drawing his greatcoat off.

She blinked in new surprise as he offered it to her, tucking it about her shoulders to help hide the fact her brooch remained in place. She felt his residual warmth in the wool; she could smell his fragrance in the fabric.

"I suppose you think this offers amends," she said. "That you have proven yourself a gentleman to me, that I should feel all aflutter at your kindness."

He laughed, stepping back from her. "Aflutter," he said. "I like that. Are you not?"

"Not in the least," Charlotte replied, her brows drawn.

"You would make me try more than this?" he asked. "All right. Fair enough. I will donate my money to St. Bartholomew's." She stared at him, startled. "Would that demonstrate some caliber of character in your regard?"

"I . . . I cannot see how my regard should scarcely matter," she said.

"It matters to me," he replied, and she blinked at him, puzzled.

"Why?" she asked, frowning.

He was quiet for a moment, his mouth outlined in a smile beneath his scarf. "Because you are quite possibly the most extraordinary woman I have ever met," he told her, and her frown deepened. He was taunting her; no different than any other man with whom she had ever shared her opinions.

"You should venture outside of Essex County more often," she said, trying in vain to punt him in the shin.

CHAPTER 2

"GOOD MORNING, CHARLOTTE," UNA SAID as she drew back the heavy draperies and allowed a sudden, searing spill of sunlight into Charlotte's bed chamber at Darton Hall. "Time to rise."

The relentless, bright light snapped Charlotte almost immediately from asleep to awake, and she groaned, opening her eyes a squinted half-mast to blink at Una. "It cannot possibly be," she mumbled, her hand pawing clumsily for a pillow. She drew the pillow atop her head, damping the incessant glare, and burrowed beneath the dark sanctuary of her blankets.

"It most certainly is—and well beyond," Una said, and Charlotte heard the rustling snap of more draperies drawn wide. "It is nearly ten o'clock. Up now, Charlotte."

She felt Una's hand hook the pillow, trying to ease

it away from her head, and she clutched it fervently. "I
have been victimized," she moaned. "Leave me be. I am
entitled to sleep in."

Una laughed as she snatched the pillow away, leaving
Charlotte bathed and cringing in the sunshine. "Victimized," Una said, shaking her head and laughing again. "I
was more concerned for the poor highwayman you ver-
bally accosted than I ever was for your well-being." She
slapped her hand against the swell of Charlotte's rump.
"Up with you, Charlotte. Your mother and father are
waiting, and you have guests."

"Guests?" Charlotte asked as Una walked away from
the bed. Charlotte sat up, blinking dazedly, her long,
blond hair drooping into her face. She shoved it back
and glanced at Una's daughter, Meghan, who stood patiently at the end of the bed. "What guests?"

"Your sister, Lady Harlow, has arrived," Meghan
said, to which Charlotte's shoulders hunched and she
groaned aloud. "And Lord Roding has been here since
well before the dawn."

Charlotte stared at Meghan in desperate plea. "Run
me through," she said. "I beg you. Right this moment.
Take that iron poker by the hearth and jab me with it."

"Now you stop that," Una scolded. She was standing before Charlotte's opened wardrobe, drawing out a
cream-colored dress dappled with large, printed roses.
"They are both worried for you. Lord Roding was nearly

frantic when he arrived."

"How did he know to be frantic?" Charlotte asked. James Houghton, Baron Roding, was older brother to Lady Margaret, whose forthcoming wedding was the pretense for Charlotte's return to Epping parish from London. James had tried so long and so futilely to claim Charlotte's hand in marriage, his efforts bordered on pathetic.

"His man, Mr. Cheadle, the coach driver seems to have recovered from his rapped head," Una replied, draping the dress over the crook of her arm and collecting petticoats from the wardrobe. "Meghan said he remained here at Darton less than an hour upon our arrival last night before heading northward for Dunmow."

Charlotte walked over to the porcelain washbasin. She cupped her hands together and let water pool into her palms. She splashed her face, gasping softly as the cold dousing wiped the last cobwebs of grogginess from her mind. "How did my sister know?" she asked, glancing over her shoulder at Una as she reached for a linen. "Mother did not send her word, did she? She should not do that; she knows Caroline gets all excited about such things and with the baby so near . . ."

Charlotte's older sister, Caroline Prescott, the Viscountess Harlow, was in her ninth month of pregnancy. The occasion of a first grandchild for Charlotte's parents had not brought the reprieve from their scrutiny Charlotte might have hoped; if anything, it had only seemed to bolster Lady Epping's resolve Charlotte should, in short measure, find everything that Caroline possessed and she was lacking: a suitable husband of status and title, a home and a soon-to-be family.

"Lady Harlow would have heard of it whether your mother sent word or not," Una said, trundling the heavy load of Charlotte's clothing to the bed. The mountainous pile of dress and crinolines rose to nearly obscure her head from view.

This was true. Caroline, ever the proper aristocratic wife, kept her fingertips pressed to the pulse of the rumor mill. Even though her pregnancy had left her swollen and hobbling, Caroline had continued her rounds of social engagements—and occasions to gossip—with a determination that was nearly admirable.

"Breakfast has been laid and the tea poured already," Una said. "Come, Charlotte, before it is all cold."

Charlotte braced herself while Una and Meghan helped wrestle her into her corset. She curled her hands about the bedpost and grunted breathlessly as they jerked the ties to excruciating tautness, cinching her already slim margin of waistline to an even slighter circumference. "Are you all right, Una?" she asked, grimacing when Una wrenched the stay ribbons and fettered them fast to keep her breasts shoved upward toward her chin, her stomach shoved inward toward her spine, and her waist pinched to miniscule proportions.

"Yes, lamb," Una said, turning her about and tugging on the front to affect the appropriately stylish, solitary, lumped-bosom look. "None the worse for the wear. And you?"

"My hand hurts," Charlotte said, looking down at her knuckles. They were somewhat swollen and discolored; no real bruising, only a distant hint, but there was soreness nonetheless. "I suppose Mother will scold me when I tell her what happened. Ladies are not supposed to throw punches."

"Your mother has already heard an account of things," Una said, turning Charlotte around once more. Charlotte glanced over her shoulder, her brow raised inquisitively. "Lord Roding has spoken at some length of it."

"How would James know what happened?" Charlotte asked. "He was not even there."

"I would assume that Mr. Cheadle relayed events to him," Una replied as she and Meghan began to overlap buoyant layers of crinolines atop the bowing circumference of Charlotte's pannier.

"Mr. Cheadle was unconscious," Charlotte said. It took her a moment before she realized, and she looked at Una, groaning. "What role have I been relegated to in his account? Tell me not the hysterical girl quivering against the carriage belly, weeping and sniveling."

"Not precisely," Meghan said. She knelt beside Charlotte, helping her mother settle and fluff each petticoat atop the other. "I do believe you were the complacent female, wide-eyed with fright and offering no resistance when the highwaymen accosted you."

"Splendid," Charlotte muttered, rolling her eyes. "And the lump on Mr. Cheadle's head?"

"The result of a beating received when he engaged the three bandits at once, and was overpowered," Una said.

"The brooch incident?"

"A shocking display of perversion when the thief plunged his hand down your bodice and groped you," Meghan told her, as she fussed with the arrangement of Charlotte's jupe underskirt atop the crinolines.

Charlotte laughed. "Obviously Mr. Cheadle has never tried to plunge his hand down the front of a corset."

"As Mr. Cheadle has already offered his account, it is probably best to keep to that version," Una said, reaching around Charlotte's torso to settle her embroidered stomacher in place against her corset. Her hands moved to the ties at Charlotte's back, and again she tugged. "Lady Epping is already distraught enough, and as you said, if you tell her it was you swinging punches and cursing like a landsman . . ."

Charlotte understood her meaning. "She will throttle me."

"Precisely," Una said.

Charlotte shrugged her shoulders as Una helped her settle the bodice and skirt of her dress into place atop her underpinnings and jupe. She stood patiently while Una jerked and tugged to fasten the back of the dress closed, and Meghan turned back the sleeve cuffs to tie her ruffled engageantes into place just below her elbows. She lifted her chin and Una drew a slim ribbon about her throat, tying it in a bow beneath the angle of her jaw. "Sit down," she murmured, tilting Charlotte's head down to be sure the bow was in proper place. "I will bundle your hair."

"What should I do with this?" Meghan asked, as Charlotte settled herself comfortably on an upholstered stool, and Una ran a brush through the waist-length hair. Charlotte glanced toward her bed and found Meghan holding the highwayman's black greatcoat pinched in her fingertips, her nose wrinkled slightly, as if she had stumbled across a dead mouse. "Shall I burn it?" Meghan asked, looking at Charlotte.

"No, Meghan," Charlotte said, shaking her head. "No, just drape it against the foot of the bed, if you will." Meghan raised her brows in surprise. "I should like to keep it, I think," Charlotte said. "A souvenir of sorts."

When Charlotte's hair was arranged, Una and Meghan stepped momentarily from the room. Charlotte stood and walked over to her bed, looking down at the highwayman's coat. She reached out and brushed her fingertips against the heavy wool. She picked it up and drew the broad lapel flap toward her face. She could smell his fragrance lingering in the wool. Why this would please her, as it seemed to, why it stoked some unfamiliar, but not entirely unpleasant warmth within her, Charlotte could not say, but she smiled softly and in spite of herself.

She laid the coat on the bed again and studied it for a moment. She patted her hands on the deep outer pockets, and blinked in surprise when she felt something within one. She drew out a silver snuff box and turned it over between her palms. The top had been engraved, a pair of initials set into the silver: *W.S.*

It is likely nothing, she told herself. The Black Trio had made eight robberies, including her own. The snuff box might simply be a keepsake from another heist; something functional enough the thief had decided against pawning it. "Or it could belong to you," she whispered, trailing her fingertip against the inscribed initials. "Who are you, W.S.?"

❀   ❀   ❀

Charlotte could hear James Houghton's voice booming along the corridor, even before she joined her family and guests at the breakfast table.

". . . an outrage, nothing more!" he declared, and Charlotte hunched her shoulders at the sound, groaning inwardly. "I assure you, Lord Epping, such offense will not go unanswered within my father's lands. I have sent word to him. These scoundrels will be brought to bear—by my breath, my lord, I will see to it."

"It is not your fault, Lord Roding," Charlotte heard her aunt, Lady Chelmsford say. "You did all within your power to keep us safe. You even hired that brave Mr. Cheadle, a thief-taker no less, to escort us in proper fashion."

"Aunt Maude, a thief-taker is generally a thief himself," Charlotte said, forcing a smile of unconcerned good cheer and steeling herself mentally for the onslaught she was about to face as she walked into the room. "One with even less scruples than most, I might add, as they mete out a living in between thefts by turning in their fellows for rewards."

Her mother, Lady Epping rose to her feet to see her, and Charlotte struggled not to grimace when James stood quickly, beating Lady Epping in her advance and hurrying around the side of the table in her direction.

"Charlotte, darling!" he exclaimed. She despised it when he called her *darling*; even now, when he affected overwhelming concern for her, he uttered it in a condescending tone that made her bristle. He spoke to her as though she were a small child, and no matter how often, how sweetly, or even firmly she had asked him not to, he remained oblivious and insistent.

James took her hands, nearly drawing her into a

stumble as he pulled her near, his brows lifted. "Darling," he said again. "Here you are at last. My heart has been seized with such worry for you!"

"Lord Roding, what a surprise," Charlotte said, trying to dislodge his hands. "How kind of you to come, though I scarcely see need to worry."

"Need?" James asked. "My man, Cheadle, comes to me in the night to tell me my lady has been ravaged and robbed, and you see no need?" He leaned toward her, kissing her brow. "My brave darling," he murmured. "Feigning such nonchalance, lest the rest of us fret."

"You know me well, James," Charlotte muttered, abandoning the polite pretense of gentle tugging and jerking her hands away from him. Lady Epping had followed James, and Charlotte turned, allowing her mother's arms to enfold her.

"Did you sleep well, darling?" Lady Epping asked, kissing Charlotte's cheek, cradling her face between her hands. Before Charlotte could offer reply, her mother's brows pinched slightly. "Look at these shadows . . . no, you did not. I am sure you tossed and turned all night, overwrought and filled with fright. I will call for Una. Some powder should disguise—"

"I am all right, Mother. No cause for a fuss," Charlotte assured her, smiling.

"Only you could be so dismissive in light of such an assault," her sister Caroline said, waddling forward, her breasts and belly nearly distended into one indiscernible swell. Charlotte leaned precariously over the broad hump of her womb to accept her kiss.

"It was scarcely an assault, Caroline," Charlotte said. "More of an inconvenience than anything, truly . . ."

"Do not play coy—James has told us of Mr. Cheadle's account," Caroline said. She blinked at her sister, wide-eyed and flushed with excitement, her mouth unfurled in a delighted smile. "Accosted by highwaymen—by the notorious Black Trio, no less! I cannot begin to fathom! How your heart must have fluttered!"

"It was not precisely an accosting . . ." Charlotte began.

"They were savages," Lady Chelmsford declared from her seat at the table, flapping her hand at her face as if she felt overcome. "Dreadful men, those scoundrels, laying their hands upon our darling Charlotte and frightening the lot of us terribly!"

"They lay their hands upon you?" Caroline asked Charlotte, grinning all the more.

"Not precisely," Charlotte said, growing aggravated. "And not *they*. It was only the one, and he wedged his fingers down my stay, that is all. He was trying to—"

Lady Epping and Caroline led Charlotte to the table, where a plate of breakfast had been set for her. All at once Charlotte's appetite—which before entering the room had been fairly well stirred—waned, and the sight

of the poached egg and sliced cheeses left her vaguely
nauseous. "None of this would have come to pass if you
had been properly married," Lady Epping said.

Charlotte struggled not to frown. "It is not as though
we traveled with a broadside tacked to the coach declar-
ing my marital status, Mother," she said.

"My lady," Charlotte's father, Lord Epping said, just
as Lady Epping had drawn breath to continue. "Do you
not think it might be distressing for Charlotte to recount
such a harrowing experience so soon after the suffering?"

Lady Epping blinked at this and a servant drew her
chair back for her, allowing her to lower herself in a swell
of skirts.

"Perhaps," Lord Epping suggested gently. "Charlotte might enjoy hearing of some more light-hearted
matters this morning."

"Well, I . . ." Lady Epping said, as the servant draped
her linen napkin over her lap. "I suppose, yes, my lord."

Charlotte glanced at her father, grateful for his intervention, and he met her gaze briefly; long enough to
drop her a wink and make her smile.

"I know what will keep her mind from such un-
pleasantries," Caroline said brightly, as she, too, resumed
her seat. She leaned toward Charlotte, even as a servant
struggled to find enough lap around her swollen belly
upon which to deposit her napkin. "You can expect
to find a familiar face at all of Margaret's pre-wedding

festivities," she said. "Lord Woodside has emerged once more into our social circles after all of these months of seclusion."

"Lord Woodside?" Charlotte asked. "You mean Lewis Fairfax's father?"

Lewis Fairfax had been a childhood friend to their older brother, Reilly. Charlotte remembered countless summers when Lewis would come to stay at Darton Hall and play with Reilly, or Reilly would in turn be shipped east to Woodside Hall, the home of Lewis' father, the baron. In adulthood, Reilly and Lewis had enlisted as officers in the Royal Navy together; most recently, they had been sent across the Atlantic to the English colonies.

"No," Caroline said, and her brows lifted in sudden dismay. "Oh, lamb, has no one told you? Baron Woodside died six months ago. A terrible fever came upon him. Lewis received an honorable discharge from His Majesty's service and came home to Essex. He is the new Lord Woodside. He has mourned awhile, of course, but emerged again these past months here and there. They will be so pleased to see you again, Charlotte. Truly, it has been ages."

"They?" Charlotte asked, puzzled.

Caroline smiled. "Yes, the Fairfaxes are back in full, the both of them," she said. "Is it not delightful?" When Charlotte still looked perplexed, she said, "Do not tell me you have forgotten Kenley Fairfax? He and Lewis came to visit Reilly nearly every summer for a time—along with that little stable boy of Lord Woodside's . . . what was his name? Anyway, the four of them as fast as thieves. Surely you recall."

Lady Epping snorted softly and sipped her tea. "We are precious few in the entire county, then, who can claim recollection of the boy," she said. "He has kept from our circles rather neatly all of these years."

"Mother," Caroline said patiently. "He has been abroad—a Grand Tour in Germany and Italy all the while. He only returned when Lewis sent word to him of his uncle's grave illness."

"And it does not take a scholar to know why the former Lord Woodside dispatched him so," Lady Epping said, her mouth turned disagreeably, as if she had tasted something unpleasant. "The boy was a ruffian and a scoundrel. I never approved of Reilly's time spent with him. He never saw a moment's discipline or instruction in proper manners. His uncle allowed him to behave as boorishly as he pleased. Though what should one expect, sired by the likes of Lord Theydon?"

"My lady . . ." Lord Epping began, trying to quiet her.

"Baron Theydon was a drunkard and a brute, my lord," she said, frowning. "He hung himself rather than face debtor's prison. His poor wife suffered so with his character. It is no small wonder the strain of childbirth drove her to her grave, as taxed as she was married to that man. He gambled away his lands until he had nothing left, not a haypenny to his purse—Kenley Fairfax only has the Theydon title and acres to call his own because Lord Woodside bought and held them. Why is beyond my understanding. Fruit never falls far from the tree that bore it—you can mark me at that. Kenley Fairfax has always been no more than trouble, and will prove no less than—"

"My friend, Mother," said a voice from the doorway. "One of the dearest I have ever known, and I would thank you kindly not to disparage him within my ready earshot."

Charlotte turned, her eyes flown wide, her mouth spreading in a broad, sudden grin. "Reilly!" she cried, nearly toppling her chair when she leaped to her feet. She rushed toward her brother, her arms open, and he laughed when she fell against him, throttling him in a fierce embrace. "Reilly! You are home again!"

"I have been here awhile, lamb—it is you who are home again," Reilly said, lifting her from her feet and squeezing her against him. He set her daintily on the ground once more, and she stared up at him, wide-eyed and delighted.

"I have missed you, you bloody yob!" she cried, slapping the sleeve of his justicoat. "How dare you return to England and not send me as much as a jotting to let me know!"

"Charlotte, do not hit your brother," Lady Epping said. "And your mouth! Where have you learned such dreadful—"

"My return was meant to be a surprise," Reilly said to Charlotte, leaning down and kissing the corner of her mouth. "How many times in the last six months has Mother written to Aunt Maude, asking you to visit? You have proven obstinate in your excuses not to come back to Epping. I damn near had to marry Margaret Houghton myself to bring you home."

Charlotte laughed and hugged him again. It had been nearly two years since she had seen Reilly; only an occasional letter in the meanwhile had proved he was even still alive. She clung to his neck as though she was afraid to ever let go of him. "You do not know how wonderful it is to see you," she gasped in his ear.

He had always been her staunchest supporter, Charlotte's advocate against her mother's efforts to force her into proper thought and marriage. As he held her, Reilly's eyes swept the table, settling momentarily upon James Houghton, and he laughed softly. "I can just imagine," he said.

❀ ❀ ❀

After breakfast, James invited Charlotte for a walk through her mother's garden. Charlotte did not want

to go, but she was in Lady Epping's house, and any disregard of courteous protocol would be unaccepted. She
did her best, however, offering the excuse of the damp
morning chill, but neither James nor Lady Epping proved
dissuaded.

"Darling, draw a redingote on and tuck your hands
in a muff," Lady Epping said. "It is only October, not
the dead of winter."

Charlotte hunkered her shoulders in miserable resignation. As she drew her redingote about her in the
foyer, she spared Reilly a glance. *Help me*, she tried to
impart with her eyes. The corner of his mouth hooked in
a smirk that conveyed, *Would that I could, Charlotte.*

James offered his arm genteelly to her, and she rested
her hand against the crook of his elbow as they strolled
together along the cobbled pathways twining through the
garden. Most of the flowers and decorative shrubbery had
already been uprooted or trimmed back in anticipation of
winter months, but Charlotte pretended even leaf-barren
nubs or overturned patches of soil absorbed her attention.
He accepted her silence for awhile without interruption,
but she could feel his gaze upon her and knew he would
not let her so easily escape for long.

"Do you know how precious you are to me, Charlotte?" he asked at length, pausing in midstride, and
drawing her to an obliging halt alongside of him. "Do
you know how desperate with worry I was?"

She looked up at him and tried to find something polite to say in reply. "That . . . that is very kind of you, James."

"When I think of that scoundrel highwayman touching you," James whispered, his brows pinching. "Laying his filthy hands against your soft flesh, the innocent swell of your bosom in such savage fashion, I. . ." He lowered his face to the ground. "You do not know what swells within me to think of it, Charlotte."

Charlotte had her ideas, but kept them to herself.

"This would not have happened if I had accompanied you properly," he said quietly, looking at her. "If, in addition to Mr. Cheadle, I had seen a full appointment of grooms to escort you."

"James, there is no way to have anticipated what happened," Charlotte told him. "It was unfortunate that we encountered the Black Trio—and blessedly, none of us were hurt or killed for the incident. No one is to blame, least of all you."

He turned to her, draping his hands over her muff. "Your words make sense to my mind," he said. "But not to my heart, Charlotte. I promise you, I will spend the rest of my life making it up to you, if only . . . if only you will let me."

Charlotte blinked at him. She knew what he was saying, even without him uttering the words. "James," she said. "We have spoken of this before."

"I know," he said, nodding. He moved closer, drawing very near, and his hands moved from her muff to her shoulders. She felt his palms slide over her throat, and she tried to shrug away from him.

"James . . ." she said, frowning.

He cradled her face between his hands and leaned toward her. "You are so beautiful, Charlotte," he whispered. "Do you know how much I long for you? How mad you drive me with need?"

His mouth lowered to hers, poised to settle in a kiss. "James, stop," she said, ducking her head. "My mother can see plainly through the windows, if she wishes."

She pulled away, and he let her go. "Must you always be so insufferable in your persistence?" she asked.

"If it will yield me your hand, yes," he replied.

"It will not, James," she said. "I have told you."

"And I have told you," he said. "It is not right that you should refuse me. We live in a society unsuitable for a woman on her own."

"I am hardly on my own," Charlotte said.

"You are unwed," he said. "And of an age when such a status is no longer considered proper or agreeable. You are meant to be married—that sweet chamber of your womb is meant to welcome a husband's seed, to bear him children. Your days are meant to be spent without the pains and tribulations of worry or complicated thought. You busy yourself with such nonsense all the time, Charlotte—

and being unaccustomed to it, you work yourself into a state whereby rumors peg you shrewish. It is not ill-temper that causes such within you, Charlotte, and I know it. It is confusion, and you need not burden your sweet, delicate mind with such bewildering matters. That is not your place, Charlotte. Your place is with me, by my side as my wife. Can you still not realize this? I would present you proudly as my bride, a magnificent adornment on my arm."

"I am not a cufflink, James," she said, her brows narrowing. Her ire amused him, and he chuckled.

"It is only your stubborn resolve that keeps you refusing me," he said. "You have not even stopped to consider that marrying me would be for your own good." I am the son of the Earl of Essex," he continued. "Any noble daughter would grovel to see my attentions turned to them. And yet, mine remain fixed upon you. You are pristine and proud; your beauty takes my breath."

"And you know nothing else about me, for all of the years we have been acquainted," Charlotte said.

He blinked at her in surprise. "What else is there to know?" he asked. She frowned at him and he laughed. "Oh, now, unknit that threatening, unkind brow," he said. "I was teasing."

"No, you were not," she said. She turned and walked back toward the house. "Charlotte . . ." James called, his tone of voice suggesting he humored her while she pitched an unnecessary fit. "Charlotte, darling, come back. I am sorry. I meant no disregard—I spoke in fun."

"Some fun," she muttered. "And do not call me 'darling'!" she snapped without turning around.

"Charlotte, of course I know more about you than your beauty. It is just your beauty that strikes me the most—is that such a crime? If so, I plead my guilt gladly. I throw myself willingly on your gallows—throttle me from your sweet Tyburn tree."

She did not turn. She followed the path back to Darton Hall. She could hear him laughing behind her, as one might at the histrionics of a malcontent child. The sound made her fume, and she balled her hands into fists.

❀　❀　❀

Charlotte stood in Reilly's bedchamber on the second floor, watching James and her mother speaking in quiet counsel in the front yard. James was preparing to leave, and Charlotte knew before he went he would undoubtedly broach the subject of marriage with Lady Epping. While Charlotte's own room afforded a view of the front grounds, it was obstructed by the wide boughs of an oak tree. Reilly had the best chamber in the entire house for peering on visitors unaware upon their arrival or departure, and she had been standing at his window for awhile, wishing she could hear the conversation below.

Reilly was not in his room. His door had been ajar, a lamp lit and a book opened on his bedside table, as if he had recently been about, but Charlotte had entered anyway. She doubted Reilly would mind the intrusion; more than anyone, he was the most fond to point out she was too incessantly curious for anyone's good.

As she crossed his chamber for the window, she noticed a rather thick stack of letters bundled together on his writing table. She had paused, glancing down at the first page atop the pile, and had seen the words, *My darling Reilly* and had nearly forgotten her interest in James and her mother.

Reilly was at an age when noble sons began considering marriage, but he had been at sea for so long, Charlotte was surprised he might have kept in contact with a prospective bride. She was also surprised Reilly had never made mention to her of any love or lover in his occasional letters, but here, apparently, was evidence of one, the other, or both.

She had skimmed the opening of the letter. *My darling Reilly,* it read. *I cannot tell you of the joy and sorrow your last letter brought to my heart. Joy to simply read your words set to parchment and imagine your voice within my mind, to lay my fingertips against a page yours had only so recently abandoned—and sorrow to know this tender proximity was the closest I could hope to enjoy for the moment. I miss you and long for you—your caress, your embrace, the*

*measure of your smile that always brings me such comfort
and companionship.*

As she stood at the window, watching James' mouth
flap soundlessly, telling Lady Epping God alone knew
what, she wondered about the letter. She had a difficult
time imagining Reilly in love. He was very handsome
and certainly a prize as the heir of a viscount and a Lieutenant in the Royal Navy, but the thought of a young
woman somewhere longing for Reilly's caress or embrace
left Charlotte blushing, near to giggling for reasons she
could not quite explain.

"Has your walk with Lord Roding ended so soon?"

Charlotte whirled, startled, and laughed breathlessly
to see Reilly enter the room behind her. "You gave me a
fright," she said.

"That is what you get for sneaking into my chamber," he said. He carried a gazette folded in his hand; as
he walked toward her, she did not miss the casual way he
dropped the newspaper on his writing table—and atop the
bundled letters—as if he did not want her to notice them.

"I was hardly sneaking," she said, pretending to
frown. "Your door was standing open. That is practically an invitation."

He laughed, coming to stand beside her. He looked
out the window, and arched his brow thoughtfully when
he spied James. "Is he still pestering you to marry him?"

Charlotte crossed her arms, frowning at James in the

yard. "Of course. He is relentless on the matter. That is why Mother summoned me back from London, I am sure. There was no polite way to decline Margaret's wedding invitation. Mother will agree to see me marry James."

"It is not so bad," Reilly remarked, and she blinked at him as if he had been struck daft. "He is the Earl of Essex's heir."

"Marrying James simply because he stands to inherit a good title is no different than him marrying me simply because he finds me beautiful," she said. "Neither should be the sole reason for wedding."

"Neither hurts, though," Reilly said.

Charlotte looked away from him, out the window once more. "He has never read my writings," she said quietly. "Not because he does not agree with me—that would be welcome, even. He does not read them because he does not care. Not about what I think or how I feel. He told me in the garden I am confused. That was his word for it—confused. I am confused about the workings of the world because I am only a woman, and I am asking too much of myself by worrying over complicated matters best left to men."

"Oh," Reilly said after a quiet moment. "I imagine that settled well with you."

"He is going to use the robbery to prove to Mother that I am ill-suited without a husband," Charlotte said, the warmth of her breath frosting in a dim haze on the cold window pane.

"Yes, I heard about the robbery," Reilly said. He raised his brows gently. "Are you all right?" He brushed the cuff of his fingers gently against her cheek, and she nodded.

"I am fine," she said.

"Do you promise?" he asked, and she smiled for him.

"Yes, truly. It was not so horrible. And I was scarcely accosted. Grandmother's pin would not come loose of my fichu, and one of them stuck his fingertips down beneath my corset to try and work the clasp open. I am sure I will recover from the trauma."

Her expression grew troubled. "He let me keep it," she said quietly. "Grandmother's brooch. In the end, he tied my hands to the wheel—loosely, so I could squirm free without much work—and he draped his coat over me to hide the pin against my stomacher. He said, 'Do not tell them' and that was all. It was . . . nearly gentlemanly of him."

"So I would assume James Houghton's secondhand recounting of events is inaccurate, to learn of this," Reilly said, and Charlotte laughed.

"Mr. Cheadle has a remarkable memory for a man who spent most of the robbery trussed and fainted dead away," she said.

"Leaving you alone to face the highwaymen," he murmured. He shook his head. "Those poor bastards did not have a hope."

She laughed again. "Not much, anyway. Look, I punched one of them." She held up her hand proudly to show him her wounded knuckles. "And the one who gave me his coat told me I had the most abrasive tongue he had ever heard on a woman."

"Well, there is something to hold dear," Reilly said, and she snickered. He cradled her hand against his own, examining her dim bruises. "You will not tell Mother of this?"

"Of course not," Charlotte said. "She would have a fit to know."

"You are right," Reilly said. "She would want to know where you learned to throw a proper punch, and then you would see me in trouble along with you."

Charlotte smiled. She hooked her arm around his neck and rose onto her toes, embracing him. "I am so glad you are home, Reilly," she whispered. "I have missed you so much."

"I have missed you, too, lamb," he breathed.

"Please tell me you will stay awhile," she said.

"I do not know," he said. "At least until January, and then I will probably be sent back to the colonies." He kissed her ear. "But do not worry for that. It is mine to consider."

He held her for a long moment and then drew away. "I have read your essays, Charlotte," he said. "Do not pay James Houghton any mind. I do not think you are confused."

"You have read them?" she asked, surprised.

"Of course I have," he said. "My sister is a published author—that makes me very proud. Father sends them to me."

She blinked at him, pleased and dumbfounded. She was completely unaware Lord Epping had ever seen— much less purchased—one of her chapbooks.

"They are very good, Charlotte," Reilly told her. "I especially liked the one where you criticized arranged marriages. What did you call it? 'An antiquated notion pairing couples based on their merits as breeding stock, rather than any common affections.' " He smiled. "I thought that was very insightful."

He looked out the window again, and she smiled at him. "Thank you, Reilly," she whispered, pleased beyond measure, her bosom pressing against the confines of her stomacher as her chest swelled with stoking pride.

"Perhaps Mother should read it," he remarked. "She might understand your point of view better. I know I do . . . and I do not blame you at all for not wanting to marry, save out of love."

A melancholy shadow crossed his face as he said this; his gaze grew distant, his eyes somewhat sorrowful. Charlotte noticed, and her thoughts turned to the letters she had seen. Again, she wondered who Reilly might be in love with, and why the notion of marrying out of that love would bring him sorrow.

CHAPTER 3

THE NEXT MORNING WHILE DRESSING, Charlotte noticed an unfamiliar traveling bag on the floor by her wardrobe. "What is that, Una?" she asked, grunting as Una jerked on her corset ties, crushing the wind from her.

"Your father's valet had it delivered upon our arrival," Una said. "There are some books and gazettes inside. I did not know if you would want them unpacked." She cocked her head, looking around Charlotte's shoulder, her brow raised. "It is not yours?"

"No," Charlotte said. "I have never seen it before. It must be Aunt Maude's."

Una snorted quietly and returned her attention to the stay. "Not unless Lady Chelmsford has suddenly taken interest in Isaac Watts' *Improvement of the Mind*," she said. At Charlotte's inquisitive glance, Una said, "That is what is in the bag. A copy of *Improvement of the Mind*; Voltaire, I think—*Letters on the English Nation* and *The Pleasures of Imagination*, I do believe, though that author escapes me."

"Akenside," Charlotte murmured, puzzled.

"Yes, thank you," Una said, wrenching back on the corset again and managing to fetter the ties. "Very good. You can breathe now, Charlotte."

"That is a matter of opinion," Charlotte said, somewhat breathlessly, and Una laughed.

"At any rate, I did not consider the fare in the knapsack to be of your aunt's . . . preferences . . ." Una said as Charlotte turned to her.

Charlotte laughed. "Not at all."

"And I assumed it was yours," Una said. "It is not mine. That leaves few to choose from."

"It must be Mr. Cheadle's," Charlotte said, still perplexed.

Una met her gaze, raising an interested brow. "Mr. Cheadle is well-read, it appears."

"He certainly is," Charlotte said. "I will bring it with me this afternoon, and see it is returned to him."

Charlotte and her family were due to attend a midafternoon party in honor of Margaret Houghton and her fiancée, Frederick Cuthbert, at nearby Chapford Manor. James would be in attendance. Charlotte genuinely meant to bring the knapsack with her, but in the hustle and bustle of her preparations—spurred to a nearly frenzied pace by Lady Epping's harping and fretting over tardiness—she forgot. They were well underway, and almost through Warliss Park before she realized she had not brought the bag along, and by then it was too late to turn back.

"Damn," she muttered. Cheadle had not noticed the missing bag yet, but it was only a matter of time. She figured opportunity least presented was least encountered, and knowing James, he would only return to Darton to claim the sack and pester her mother again.

"Charlotte, your mouth," Lady Epping said, poking her elbow firmly against Charlotte's arm. "Wherever did you pick up such atrocious language? Not in our house, that is for certain."

Charlotte glanced at Reilly, seated across from her with their father. The corner of Reilly's mouth hooked, and he drew his hand to his face to muffle a quiet snicker.

"Well, she did not learn it in London at my home, either," Lady Chelmsford said, her shoulders stiffening, and the abundant swell of her bosom shoving forward in prim indignation.

"You will display good manners today, young lady," Lady Epping said, waggling her forefinger at Charlotte.

"Yes, Mother," Charlotte said, forcing a pleasant smile for Lady Epping.

❀ ❀ ❀

At Chapford Manor, Charlotte followed her parents and aunt across the expansive grounds toward the house. Reilly accompanied her, with his elbow cocked politely so she might drape her hand against his sleeve. Servants took their coats and Charlotte's muff in the front foyer, and then they were swept into a parlor where they were promptly surrounded by a massive crowd of guests. Charlotte immediately recalled why she despised social engagements. Between the din of overlapping laughter and conversations, the jockeying for ample space with other ladies' panniers, and the endless barrage of unfamiliar, powdered and painted faces, she was soon shied fiercely against her brother, clinging to the broad, embroidered cuff of his justicoat sleeve lest she be jerked away from him and lost forever in the throng.

"Lieutenant Engle, by my boot heels, here you are!" someone bellowed with almost deafening good cheer from behind them. Charlotte turned in tandem with Reilly, and her brother laughed.

"Lieutenant Fairfax, you bloody bastard! They will let anyone pass for society these days!" he cried.

Charlotte blinked as Reilly pulled away from her, clasping hands with a tall, burly young man. Though his face was vaguely familiar to her, it was his voice, the resounding, booming sound of it, that registered first. Lewis Fairfax had always been very loud and good-humored.

"Look at you!" Lewis exclaimed, his mouth extended in a wide, handsome grin. He was a strapping man, with thick limbs, a broad chest, and large hands. When he clapped one of his palms against Reilly's arm, he nearly sent Reilly stumbling. "I almost did not recognize you, what with you dressed all prissily like a proper nobleman!"

His gaze settled upon Charlotte, his brows lifting. "Surely, this is not your little lamb sister?" he asked. "It cannot be! She was only hock-high to a pony when last I saw her."

"You are old, Fairfax, and she has grown," Reilly told him, making Lewis shudder the floorboards beneath them with laughter. "This is Charlotte, indeed. Charlotte, do you remember Lord Woodside?"

"Not likely as Lord Woodside," Lewis said. He offered Charlotte a quick, courteous bow. "Splendid to see you again, Charlotte, to discover a rose has bloomed in the Darton garden in my absence."

Charlotte laughed, feeling color stoke in her cheeks as she dropped a curtsy. He was flattering her, which normally aggravated her witless; however, there was something so endearing in his smile, she could not help but be charmed. "And to see you again, Lord Woodside," she said. "I am terribly sorry to have learned of your father's passing."

"Good men go to good places in the end," Lewis said, his smile faltering slightly. "I find comfort in that, if not some hope for the rest of us." The dimples cleaving his cheeks broadened again, his momentary sorrow gone as quickly as it had come. "Reilly, you remember my cousin, do you not?" He pivoted to look behind him, flapping his hand. "Kenley, come here. Look what I have found."

He drew a young man forward, disengaging him rather rudely from a conversation by pulling him in tow. The young man blinked at Reilly, and then smiled. At the sight of him, Charlotte felt her breath draw to an abrupt and unexpected halt.

She remembered Kenley Fairfax by name, but not by face. As recollection of Lewis' features dawned on her with their reintroduction, she assumed that as his cousin, Kenley would be of similar form and feature. To her surprise, he was not.

He was tall, like Lewis, but as lean in his build as Lewis was broad. He was not handsome in the conventional, haughty fashion of noblemen; he had delicate features framed in unusual contrast by a long brow, strong jaw line, sharp cheekbones, and tapered chin. His large, dark eyes were accented by angular brows; his nose was long and narrow, his mouth delicately shaped.

His clothing was well-tailored to his form; the long, embroidered flaps of his justicoat and underlying waistcoat accentuated his long legs and slim hips, while the arrangement of his cravat, the lapels of his jacket drew one's gaze to notice the length of his neck, the full breadth of his shoulders. He wore a fashionable campaign wig dyed a few shades of brown lighter than his own true hue, to judge by his brows.

He was quite possibly the most striking man Charlotte had ever seen.

"Lord Theydon," Reilly said, offering his hand. "You look marvelous. My God, it has been . . . what? Five years?"

"Six, sir," Kenley said, accepting Reilly's proffered clasp. "You are looking splendid yourself. Lewis has written fondly of you, and often, sir."

Though he addressed Reilly, his gaze had averted to Charlotte and remained fixed there. When Reilly declared, "Lies. Naught but lies. Do not believe a word that bloody yob wrote," Kenley laughed, but kept his eyes upon Charlotte, his expression softened as though with wonder.

"And what is this 'sir' nonsense?" Reilly asked. He put his hand on the back of Kenley's neck and drew him close in a brief but fond embrace. "You have run off to Italy and learned manners on us, rot you. How was your trip?"

At last, Kenley looked away from Charlotte, and when he did, her knees nearly buckled. His gaze had held her immobilized. She felt her breath sigh from beneath the confines of her stay and she blinked, as though emerging from a reverie.

"It was splendid for the time spent, Reilly," Kenley said. "But wearisome besides, and I have never been more grateful to be home once more."

"Do you remember my sister, Miss Charlotte Engle?" Reilly asked, sidestepping to present Charlotte. "Charlotte, this is Kenley Fairfax, Baron Theydon."

"I remember the name, but not her face," Kenley said. "I must be daft, surely. How do you do?"

He bowed before her, and as he straightened she held his gaze, offering a slight curtsy. "I . . . I am well, my lord," she said. "And pleased to meet you."

"Hoah, the pomp and circumstance of social introductions," Lewis said, clapping Reilly and Kenley on the shoulders, jostling them both. "Dropping nods and bending over. I am aching already, sorely out of practice. Where is the brandy? That would help."

❅   ❅   ❅

Charlotte would have preferred to have spent the day in the company of Reilly and his friends, but such was not to be. Within moments of her introduction to Kenley Fairfax, Lady Epping caught hold of Charlotte and led her away. Charlotte glanced over her shoulder as Lady Epping led her through the crowd, chattering about retiring to the ladies' parlor for tea. She had a last, momentary glimpse of Kenley before the throng closed between them, obscuring him from view behind a forest of shoulders and wig-capped heads.

Ladies and gentlemen began to part company, the women retiring to gossip in one parlor, while the men gathered in another for brandies and hands of cards. Charlotte was forced into the insufferable company of Essex County's aristocratic daughters and wives, and as the most recent victim of the Black Trio highwaymen, she found herself the unwitting center of attention amidst a swarm of eager chatter.

"Well, I, for one, fully intend to begin keeping jewels tucked down beneath my stay just in case my carriage is stopped, and the thieves should decide to fondle me," declared Payton Stockley, one of the parish's most notorious gossips. She was a perfectly lovely young woman—until she opened her mouth, and then she was prone to ramble nonstop, and to the delight of her fellows, with juicy tidbits about everything and everyone.

"I would make their efforts worth the while," Payton said with a wink that left the other ladies around her giggling and fluttering their fans.

Payton's notoriety as a rumor-monger paled only in comparison to her older brother's reputation. Julian Stockley, Baron Stapleford, was a cad whose character was brought into question all the more by whispered rumors he had murdered his own father. The former Baron Stapleford had died after eating spoiled meat two years earlier. Although no evidence was ever discovered to implicate Julian in his death, it was no tremendous secret Julian had inherited a sizeable quotient of lands and funds, or that he had not mourned too long or terribly for his father's untimely passing.

Charlotte was seldom inclined to lend much credence to rumors. Whether Julian had seen his father dead to his own benefit was irrelevant to her. Like his sister, she had always considered him unbearable either way.

"Miss Engle, darling, prithee tell," Payton cooed, leaning near her and tapping the folded spines of her hand fan against Charlotte's wrist, much to her aggravation. "Were you not simply trembling at his touch? I mean, the terror of the moment not withstanding, did you not find even a fleeting thrill as that ruffian set his hands against your breasts?"

"Miss Stockley, if I found passing fancy from every moment of unintentional friction against my breasts, I could scarcely draw breath against my corset," Charlotte said, wishing she had thought to bring a fan of her own, that she might reach out and whap Payton against the cap of her head with it.

Payton blinked at her, and then exchanged a sideways glance with another lady close at hand. "I must say, if I was faced with such a thrilling prospect, I doubt I could draw breath in full," she said. "A man who would dare touch a lady in such fashion must surely possess some worthwhile skills to back his mettle."

"Are you prattling yet again about the Black Trio, Miss Stockley?" asked a young man from behind them. He paused, making his way among the ladies toward the adjacent parlor, and looked at Payton with the corner of his mouth and his brow raised in amused tandem. "Someone might mistake you as in love, as loudly and often as you mention them."

Payton turned and spared him a cool glance. "Why, Lord Hallingbury," she purred, her lips lifting in a thin, icy smile. "What a surprise to discover you tucked among the ladies, rather than at the card tables. Someone might think you have not a haypenny to your purse, as obviously as you are avoiding them."

When Payton spoke, Charlotte put a name to the young man's face: Camden Iden, Baron Hallingbury. He was attractive in a doe-eyed, effeminate sort of fashion; his innocent appearance belied a rather improper penchant for wooing young noble daughters. By rumor, many a lady's unsullied virtues had been lost to his bed. Charlotte had heard once that he kept a rather distasteful collection of garter ribbons in his highboy as testimony to his conquests. Payton Stockley was one of his most recent. Caroline had told Charlotte the pair carried on quite a conspicuous and reckless affair over the summer, and when Camden had broken it off abruptly to pursue another, it had apparently not settled well with Payton's heart, mind, or pride.

Camden glowered at Payton for a long moment and then tromped away, leaving the women to fold together, whispering and wide-eyed.

"He does not have a cent to his name, you know," Payton said, and as her friends all offered fluttering gasps of appropriate shock, she nodded grimly. "His gambling has grown well out of hand. His debts are great enough now that they speak of debtor's prison and Lord Hallingbury in nearly the same breath."

"It is disgraceful," one of the young ladies lamented, her pretty, powdered face scrunching into a frown. "Almost every eligible noble son in the whole county seems encumbered by debt anymore. How can any of us hope to find a suitable husband among them, if they all keep gambling away their purses?"

"What possible appeal does debt hold to them?" whispered another, shaking her head.

With this, their gossiping resumed, their chattering voices overlapping eagerly. Charlotte rolled her eyes and turned away, abandoning them. She had done her part to be the proper noble daughter for the day, but her patience was taxed. She glanced around to make sure Lady Epping and Lady Chelmsford were both occupied with their own conversations, and then she followed Camden

Iden to the gentlemen's parlor.

It was unconventional for women to venture among the card tables, although not uncommon for them to cluster about the doorways, if only to keep themselves visible to those eligible bachelors whose affections they hoped to garner. Charlotte wasted no time lingering uncertainly upon the threshold and walked inside. She lifted her chin and squared her shoulders, poised as if she had every reason and right in the world to pass among the men. She looked and found Reilly sitting at a table with Lewis on the far side of the room, and strode purposefully in his direction.

Kenley Fairfax stood in a corner nearby, watching his cousin play cards without joining. He looked at Charlotte as she approached, and she felt warmth flutter through her, snatching at her breath as his mouth unfurled in a smile.

"Are you going to play, Miss Engle?" someone asked, and she blinked down at Julian Stockley, beside whose chair she had happened to have drawn to a faltering halt.

Charlotte glanced at Kenley again, and then toward Reilly. He arched his brow at her, perfectly aware that if Lady Epping discovered her playing cards with the men, she would pitch a fit. Charlotte looked back at Lord Stapleford. "Have you room for another?" she asked.

Julian laughed. "I should dare say for so lovely a distraction, we might all scoot our chairs a bit in accommodation," he said. He lay his hand of cards face down on the table and motioned to his mates. "Make room, lads."

The men rose, scooting their chairs closer to one another. Charlotte was so distracted by Kenley's presence she did not even notice James Houghton at the table until he was upon her, darting like a spider toward a hapless moth caught in its web. He drew a chair behind her, offering her a seat beside her brother, and Charlotte nearly groaned aloud.

"What a pleasant surprise, darling," James said with a smile.

"Thank you, James," she said, settling herself on the cushioned seat as he eased the chair beneath her.

"You are most welcome," he said, leaning over her shoulder so his voice and breath brushed intimately against her ear. She sat facing the corner where Kenley stood, and she glanced at him. He had not missed this exchange between her and James, and though his expression seemed impassive, Charlotte was embarrassed nonetheless by James' possessive gesture. She shrugged her shoulder, frowning as she brushed James away.

"I suppose you shall need me to give you coins now," Reilly said, smirking.

"You know I will only win twice fold to repay them," she replied, and Reilly laughed.

"Do not tell me your sister is well-versed at cards," Lewis said, raising an impressed brow at Charlotte.

"She is well-versed at anything she considers unconventional," Reilly replied, shifting his weight to dip his fingertips into the fob pocket of his breeches. "Here. Six pennies," he said, dropping the silver coins in her palm.

"Will you not give her more, Engle?" Camden Iden laughed from across the table, as he dealt Charlotte into the hand in progress. "She will not last a full round with that."

"Oh, she will last," Reilly said. "She will see us all broke if she fancies to sit here long enough."

As the game resumed, Charlotte fell into her element. As much as she despised the conversations of women, she loved the discourse among men. Those at her table did not broach the subject of her robbery; they did not hound her for details or peer curiously at her. They did not care for such topics, finding them as trivial and inane as Charlotte did. Instead, they discussed politics and economics.

Charlotte listened avidly, chiming in with her own points of view as she wished. The men may not have granted her much heed, and they regarded her with more amusement than genuine consideration, but it did not trouble her. These were conversations about things she found interesting, if not fascinating, and she meant to be a part of them, whether welcomed or not.

"The aristocracy as we know it here in rural England is in its waning stages," she said. Several hands of cards had been played, and her meager allotment of coins had grown considerably. She fanned her cards before her face, considered the wager on the table, and took a sip of Reilly's brandy.

Julian laughed. "Waning?" he asked. He glanced about the table, his brow arched at his fellows. "I dare say that sounds a bit dire, does it not?"

"It is not dire," Charlotte said. "Our economy is shifting toward new ventures, even as we speak. Wealthy and poor alike will have to shift with it, and our money should be invested where it is most likely to grow—in industry."

Several of the men scoffed and scowled at this.

"Charlotte, darling," James said from across the table, drawing her gaze. "I certainly think most among us would agree that your interest in such matters is charming. However, we might be better served paying heed to the place where money is most likely to grow at this moment—the card table."

Other men chuckled at this, and Charlotte pressed her lips together as she glared at James, feeling hot patches of humiliated color rise in her cheeks.

"I should like to hear the lady's thoughts on the matter," Kenley Fairfax remarked from his corner. He stood in a comfortable pose with his shoulder leaning against the wall, his arms folded across his chest.

"Suppose I tendered my purse to your counsel, all of it in full, right now, this very moment," Kenley said to her, drawing away from the wall and stepping toward the table. He looked at Charlotte with interest. "Where would you tell me to invest? Which industries would you recommend?"

"You would be a fool to give all of your money to a woman," Camden Iden said. "I tell you where she will invest it—at the mercers and drapers of Cheapside!"

The other men laughed, but Charlotte and Kenley did not avert their gazes from one another. "I would recommend coal mining, Lord Theydon," she said. "Iron mining, steel production, and commerce."

Kenley raised his brow. "Why these?"

"Because they complement one another," Charlotte replied. "You are a landowner. You readily grow crops, and in the process feed more and more people. An increased populace means an increased work force, but one generally confined to where employment is abundant, while education and skill demands are low, such as mining and manufacturing. And increases in coal and iron mining allow for an increase in steel production.

"The colonies overseas are dependent markets for exported goods, and now England is opening charted trade routes with Asia. That means soon steel can be exported around the world into all sorts of new and profitable markets."

James sighed wearily. "Darling . . ." he began.

"Have peace, Lord Roding. I would hear her out,"

Kenley interjected, holding up his hand. James looked over his shoulder, shooting Kenley a scathing glance. Kenley ignored him completely and nodded at Charlotte. "Miss Engle?"

"The aristocracy has not invested in these developments, at least here, and in other rural counties, and that is why we are in our waning stages," Charlotte said to Kenley. "But these opportunities are being seized upon by noblemen in urban centers like London. They see what is happening—population growth, the promise of international trade—and they put their money down, just as any gambler at a card table. Only along with these, there are other investors with wagers to add—business owners, artisans, skilled laborers.

"Together, these investors are more willing to take chances because they understand a fundamental principle that we, as rural aristocrats, fail to consider—that wealth is not an entitlement. The noble investors will become the new aristocracy, rendering all but the most productive and competitive landowners obsolete. The lower class investors will become something new, a middle class, if you will, between wealthy and poor. We are all standing on the threshold of significant economic change, and we are blind if we do not recognize it."

Kenley's gaze was so intense she was nearly impaled by it. The rest of the room had faded around them, and to Charlotte it felt as if she sat alone before him engaged in conversation. "An industrial revolution," he said quietly.

"Exactly," she said, nodding.

"I do not know about the rest of you, but I have come to play cards," Camden Iden complained loudly. Charlotte once again became aware of the parlor filled with men and murmured conversations around them.

"Well said, Hallingbury," James said, his brows narrowed. "Is this a party or an impromptu meeting of the House of Lords?"

The men chuckled and guffawed, and the moment was gone. Kenley nodded once in concession and withdrew from the table, returning to his corner. "I say, Theydon, since you seem so insistent on interrupting our game, why do you not take a seat and join us?" James said, glancing over his shoulder.

Kenley smiled slightly, and shook his head. "Thank you, Lord Roding, but no. I have neither the heart nor mind for cards."

James turned away, his brow arched as he offered a soft, somewhat disdainful snort. He exchanged glances with Julian, who smirked with little humor and muttered, "Quite the pity your father did not feel the same."

Charlotte glanced to her left and saw Lewis stiffen visibly, his mouth opening to speak.

"No more so than yours not sharing your apparent tolerance for rancid beef, Stapleford," Kenley said before his cousin could offer a word. "Or was it lamb? I can never remember which."

Julian said nothing; he sputtered quietly, his face infused with sudden, bright color. Kenley nodded politely at the table. "If you will excuse me, gentlemen . . . and Miss Engle . . ." He nodded again for Charlotte's benefit. "I feel the sudden need for a spot of air, I think."

He walked away, leaving the table shrouded in momentary silence.

Lewis sniffed. "Hoah, well, I suppose he told you, did he not, Stapleford?" he said, and the men laughed.

"Bugger off, Woodside," Julian muttered, ablaze with embarrassment.

Charlotte watched Kenley make his way across the parlor. He paused at the threshold, apparently exchanging cordialities with the young ladies gathered there, and one of them momentarily turned her attention to Charlotte while whispering in Kenley's ear. When he left the threshold, all of the ladies turned to follow with their gazes, their faces soft with adulation.

"I believe some fresh air might suit me, as well," she said, rising to her feet. She pushed her coins toward Reilly. "There you go, doubled as promised and then some," she murmured, turning to leave.

James rose from the table. "I will accompany you, darling," he said. "Let me—"

"Do not worry for it, James," she said dryly. "I am certain I can make it on my own."

❋ ❋ ❋

She caught sight of Kenley standing in the foyer by the front doors. He was speaking with a servant, who nodded and turned, walking away to fetch his coat and tricorne. Charlotte shouldered her way through the party guests milling about. "Lord Theydon," she called.

He was admiring a large portrait framed against the wall, his hands clasped lightly behind his back, his chin lifted. He did not turn at her beckon, and she tried again as she drew near, reaching out and touching his arm. "Lord Theydon?"

He jumped, startled from his thoughts. When he saw Charlotte, he smiled, seeming surprised to see her, but pleased nonetheless. "Miss Engle," he said, lowering his face in courteous deference.

"I did not mean to startle you," she said, and he laughed quietly.

"Quite all right," he said. He tapped his fingertip against his brow. "Tending my own garden, that is all. Sometimes I can be rather oblivious."

The servant returned, presenting him with his coat and hat. Charlotte watched him shrug his way into the navy blue greatcoat, and press a penny against the boy's palm in thanks.

"I wanted to apologize, Lord Theydon," she said.

"Kenley," he said. "Social protocol is such stuff and nonsense. Lord Theydon was my father. I am Kenley."

"I . . . I wanted to apologize to you . . . Kenley," she said.

"For what?"

"For Lords Stapleford and Roding . . . Julian and James," she said. "They were untoward to you, and unkind besides, and I find their behavior offensive and reprehensible."

Kenley smiled as he settled his tricorne atop his head. "It is no terrible secret, what happened to my father," he told her. "I am surprised no one else has made such mention before now." He offered her a brief nod. "But thank you for your courtesy. Good afternoon, Miss Engle."

He turned and walked for the doors, obviously meaning to leave. "Charlotte," she said, and he paused. "I find social protocol absurd as well. My name is Charlotte."

He smiled again, his mouth curling slightly, and Charlotte could not explain why so simple and common an expression suddenly made her feel rather light-headed. She did not understand anything about this young man; why he might have such interest in her opinions, why he studied her so intently, or why his attentions left her so flustered. She only knew she wanted to speak with him again; she had enjoyed that fleeting measure of what had felt like mutual understanding, and she wanted it to continue. She did not want him to leave.

"Charlotte Engle," he said. "Your acquaintance at the

parlor doorway, Miss Tunstall, tells me you are betrothed to the man who has so offended you, Lord Roding."

Charlotte remembered the young lady who had glanced in her direction, and she frowned. "I am not betrothed to him," she said. "He is insufferable and I would rather see myself run through by some dulled and rusted implement."

Kenley laughed. "You are certain?"

"Positive," she replied.

"It is only gossip? I am not courting death by duel to stand here and speak in such close proximity to you?"

Charlotte laughed. "No," she said. "I mean yes. I mean, yes, it is only gossip, and no, you are not risking a duel to speak with me."

"Good," Kenley said. "I am a terrible shot."

She smiled. "Are you leaving?" she asked.

He brushed his fingertips against his hat, his eyes widening slightly as if he had forgotten he had donned it. "Oh, no. I would not get far. I arrived with Lewis. I have no coach of my own that does not look a disgrace. I was going to step outside for a moment, walk about, and breathe the damp English air a bit. I have missed it."

"That is right. My sister told me you have been in Italy," she said, recalling his Grand Tour.

"And Germany," he said. "Not France, given His Majesty's recent war, but it is just as well. I cannot speak French anyway."

She laughed, and then a peculiar silence settled between them. It was not precisely uncomfortable, and he looked at her all the while, as if giving some aspect of her a great deal of considerate thought. "May I ask something of you?" he said. "I have heard you are none other than the rather infamous Miss E., whose chapbooks have caused such a stir about London."

She could not tell if he was offering commendation or condemnation, and said nothing. His smile widened. "Not that I pay much mind to gossip," he added. "It is difficult to avoid in these sorts of circumstances." He flapped his hand to indicate the party they attended. "And I might not have been so inclined to lend it heed, had I not heard you speak so well and passionately in the parlor. Is it true?"

"It is," Charlotte said, bracing herself mentally for any ridicule that might follow. She had almost found him endearing at the card table, but he might have humored her without dismissal only to save her embarrassment in front of others. They were alone now, face to face, with no need for such courtesy. To her relief, he only smiled again.

"It is a delight to meet you, then," he said. "I have read your works, and found them quite thought-provoking."

"You . . . you have?" she asked, unable to keep her mouth in line. She smiled, genuinely pleased.

"I have, indeed," he said. "You demonstrate a great

deal of insight in your writing. I would not have placed you as so young. Your voice in your work lends itself to an older woman, a more matronly sort."

"I have never felt that youth is any preclusion to common sense," Charlotte said, and he chuckled.

"Certainly not," he agreed. He looked at her for a long moment. "If I may, I should mention that I have noticed a glaring discrepancy in your works," he said. "One that grossly undermines your ideas, and discredits your otherwise well-founded arguments."

Charlotte was caught off guard. "I beg your pardon?" she said. "What discrepancy is that?"

"Your sex," he told her. "You are a woman. It is contrary to what is socially acceptable for women to write about."

She was close to disappointment; had she truly harbored the fleeting, endearing hope he might be different than other men? She lifted her chin. "I suppose you expect a woman to write inane poetry, or editorials about shopping districts, wig makers, and fabric?"

"Flower arrangements, social engagements, that sort, yes," he said, and she fumed.

"You might be surprised to realize, then, that there are a goodly number of women with matters other than these to occupy our minds," she said. "Society may have relegated us to the unenviable position of watching purported gentlemen corrupt and ruin everything with their penchants for cards, brothels, wars, and dueling, but that does not mean all of us stand back idly and helpless. Some of us have long ago opened our eyes to the ailments you have brought upon this world we share, and simply because you dictate we should have no say in matters does not mean we are duly inclined to agree."

Kenley looked down at her, the smile she had only moments ago found engaging now rendering her incensed. "That would not surprise me at all," he said. "And you misunderstand my meaning. I did not say your being a woman was an offense. I said it discredited your writing.

"You write under a pen name," he continued. "You should choose one that is a man's. Most men cannot absorb the inferences of your work because they simply cannot get beyond the feminine byline. You are shouting logic to deaf ears. I think if you offered the pretense of being a man, you might find other men more inclined to at least consider your ideas, if not agree with them."

She said nothing. She had been so prepared for his dismissal, she had never even entertained a fleeting thought he might be suggesting something else.

"It is just a thought," he said.

"It . . . it is a good thought," she admitted, feeling color rise in her cheeks. She looked up at him, shamed by her anger. "It is a very good thought."

He studied her for a long, quiet moment. "Would

you like to go for a walk with me, Charlotte?" he asked at length.

She met his gaze, and when he smiled at her, she felt something deep within her flutter. "Yes," she said, nodding. "Yes, Kenley, I would like that very much."

CHAPTER 4

THUS BEGAN WHAT TURNED OUT TO BE AN afternoon spent in likely the most engaging conversation Charlotte had ever enjoyed with anyone. She and Kenley walked for hours, marking a leisurely pace as they followed the winding footpaths of Chapford Manor's garden and grounds. They walked abreast of one another, shoulder to shoulder, and when Charlotte spoke, Kenley would lower his face, canting his head to listen. He did not simply let her words pass in one ear and out the other, as James and the other men did. He listened to her, his brows lifted in interest, his gaze attentive as he granted her the same consideration he would have any of his fellows.

"When I was a little girl, my father used to let me sit in the gentlemen's parlor while he and his friends enjoyed brandies," she said. "I loved to listen to them talking about politics, economics, agriculture. And in the mornings, when he took to his library to read his gazette, he would hoist me up into his lap and let me read aloud with him, all of the news from Parliament." She laughed. "I used to tell him I wanted to be a barrister someday, and he would say what a fine one I would make. Mother says it is his fault, the way I am."

Kenley paused in his stride and regarded her intently. "What?" Charlotte asked, laughing slightly, momentarily flustered by the gentle but unwavering scrutiny.

"You really are remarkable," he said.

"Do not flatter me," she said, drawing her hand from her muff and slapping his arm. "I have enjoyed your company today. Do not dare prove you are no less a cad than any other man with witless attempts at charm."

He caught her hand before she could slip it back inside her muff. "Forgive me," he said. "You are right. That was a shameless and horrid attempt to endear myself to you."

He smiled, and she laughed. When he moved toward her, the margin of space between them closing beyond what was considered proper, she did not mind. When he continued to hold her hand, she offered no resistance. When he lifted his free hand and drew his fingers gently across her cheek, brushing aside a wayward strand of flaxen hair that had worked loose from her bundle, she felt her heart flutter, her breath tangle against the back of her throat.

"I should try again," Kenley said, his hand lingering on her face, the basin of his palm pressing against her cheek. "In earnest sincerity."

He leaned in, and Charlotte could not breathe. Her heart hammered out a frantic rhythm, caught between alarm and eager anticipation. Her eyes closed as the tip of his nose brushed hers, and she felt the soft, delicate intake of his breath against her lips.

"You are remarkable, Charlotte," Kenley whispered, his mouth dancing against hers before settling softly. They stood alongside the house, on their way back to the front entrance, but Charlotte forgot the fact that they were well within plain view of the westward facing windows. She forgot about propriety and the fact that this was anything but. The world around her faded completely, as if God Himself had drawn it all to an obliging standstill to mark the tender occasion of her first kiss, and her wits, breath, and voice abandoned her in a solitary, helpless whimper.

She opened her eyes and blinked dazedly when he drew away from her. Breathing seemed unnecessary and momentarily forgotten, and the cold, damp air had yielded to some incredible, comfortable warmth from deep within her.

"You . . . you kissed me," she whispered.

He smiled. "I did, yes."

"Why?"

He laughed. "Because I wanted to," he said. "I would be daft not to. Did you mind?"

Charlotte shook her head. "No," she said. "I mean . . . yes. I . . . I do not . . . I am not sure."

He chuckled, and she met his gaze. "I should slap you," she said.

"I would prefer if you did not," Kenley said.

A loud rattling, the sudden, heavy falling of hoof beats startled her, and Charlotte turned, her eyes wide as grooms drove a carriage toward them, heading for the front of the house. Two more followed almost immediately, and for the first time Charlotte took notice of the quality of daylight, and the hour it surely indicated.

"Oh!" she gasped, as the first carriage rolled past. She turned to Kenley, alarmed. "What time is it?"

He opened the front flap of his greatcoat and reached beneath, finding the fob pocket of his breeches and retrieving his watch. He snapped back the gold lid. "Nearly twenty past five."

Charlotte's alarm increased. She and Kenley had been wandering the grounds of Chapford Manor for three hours, surely, if not more. Lady Epping had undoubtedly taken notice of her absence—the entire bloody gathering likely had—and she groaned aloud.

"What?" Kenley asked.

"Nothing," she said, closing her eyes and shaking

her head. "My mother is going to throw a fit, that is all. I must . . . I have to get back inside."

"It is my fault," he said. "I lost track of time." He looked toward the house. "I will speak with her. Let me explain. I will tell her—"

"No," Charlotte said, shaking her head again with new horror. She remembered all too well Lady Epping's cold dismissal of Kenley the day before. She could only imagine her reception if Kenley was standing right in front of her, offering excuses for Charlotte. "No, no, that . . . truly, that is not necessary."

"I do not want to see you in trouble on my account," he said. "I did not mean for that, Charlotte. It was an honest oversight. Please, I insist. Let me—"

"No," Charlotte said firmly, shoving her hand into her muff. "No, thank you, Kenley, but you do not want to do that. Trust me."

She turned. "I have to go," she said, hurrying to the front corner of the house. "I am sorry. It was lovely, but I must!"

❀ ❀ ❀

"I should hardly think at your age, Charlotte, you need reminding that to disappear in an unfamiliar young man's company for the whole of an afternoon simply is not proper," Lady Epping scolded.

"He is not unfamiliar, Mother," Charlotte said, rolling her eyes. "Reilly has known him for years. It was more of a mutual sort of reacquaintance than anything."

They were in the carriage, on the road to Darton Hall once more. Lady Epping's diatribe had begun nearly ten minutes earlier, and continued full-force and unabated, with scarcely a pause for breath. Charlotte hunched her shoulders and wished she could simply shrivel.

"And we were touring the garden," she said. "Hardly a disappearance."

"For nearly four hours?" Lady Epping exclaimed, her voice ripping to shrill, outraged levels.

"You should have heard the whispering," Lady Chelmsford said. "I have not heard the sort since Lady Bickensworth took a steward around to the carriage house at Wentforth Folly Hall last season and was discovered by her lord!"

"We were talking," Charlotte said, her brows narrowing slightly. "That is all, Mother, no matter what rumors suggest to the contrary. We were enjoying friendly conversation and lost track of time. Surely you know me well enough to realize I would not consent to some tawdry midafternoon tryst."

Lady Epping glared at her. "Well, here is the end of your friendly conversations, then," she said. "At least with that man."

"He has a name, Mother," Charlotte said. "Not to

mention a proper title. I thought that appealed to you."

Lady Epping jabbed her forefinger at Charlotte. "Do not take that indignant tone with me," she said. "You do not dare, Charlotte, not after the humiliating afternoon you have subjected me to. You will not see him again. You will not even exchange passing greetings with him among a crowd of hundreds. He is a rotten cad from undesirable stock, title or not, and you will give him a broad berth."

"Mother . . ." Reilly began.

"And poor Lord Roding forced to politely bear it all," Lady Epping continued, ignoring Reilly completely. "You distressed him terribly, Charlotte, worrying him as to your whereabouts and any harm that might come upon you because of—"

"Audrey," Lord Epping said, bringing his wife to startled silence. Lord Epping seldom if ever addressed her by her given name. "I imagine that social occasions such as today's must be very difficult for Lord Theydon, given his father's repute. I am sure it required a great amount of courage for him to walk among his noble peers again. I doubt I could muster such mettle if I were in his position. I would think the lad surely appreciated Charlotte's efforts at courtesy and friendship."

Lady Epping stared at him for a moment. "Whatever the circumstances, it remains that it was highly improper to—"

"Charlotte has acknowledged it, and apologized besides," Lord Epping told her.

"But I—" Lady Epping began.

"No harm has come of anything," Lord Epping said, and frowned. "Let the girl be."

❊ ❊ ❊

"Well, you have certainly caused a fuss," Una remarked that evening as she helped Charlotte ready for bed. "And not even home two days in full. You have surpassed your own record, I do believe."

Charlotte winced as Una ran a brush through a tangled section of her hair, tugging on her scalp. "I do not want to talk about it, Una, please," she said. "Mother is still livid with me. I will likely never live this down."

Una met her gaze in the vanity mirror and smiled. "Why do you not tell me about the cause of it all, then?" she asked. "This young man, Kenley Fairfax, who so occupied your afternoon."

Charlotte smiled despite herself. "You would like him, Una," she said.

Una made a murmuring sound of piqued interest.

"He is very handsome," Charlotte said. "And intelligent, quick-witted, well-read, and well-spoken. He has this way about his face where he . . . it is like he does not even have to say anything. He just lifts a brow or cocks his head, or his mouth settles somewhat into a sort of crooked line, and you just realize what he is thinking, most plainly, you know it."

Una nodded once, her soft smile still lifting her lips. Charlotte's gaze had taken on a distant cast as she remembered; she looked wistful and ingenuous at the recall.

"He read my writings," she said to Una. "Not just skimmed them and scoffed, Una, but read them. We discussed them. We discussed all sorts of things, really. He listened to me. I could see it in his face; he took my point of view, my thoughts, opinions, all of it into consideration. He did not agree with me all of the time, but when he did not, he simply told me his own ideas. He did not insult or demean mine. He just . . . spoke to me, as he would have a man."

"It sounds as if he made a very good impression on you," Una said, holding Charlotte's sheaf of long hair against her palm and stroking the brush through it.

"He did," Charlotte murmured, her eyes still fathoms away, the corners of her mouth drawing upward slightly. "He kissed me," she said softly.

Una did not pause in her brushing. "Did he now?" she asked, sparing Charlotte's reflection a glance. "And it was . . . ?"

"Marvelous," Charlotte said, drawing her hand to her mouth and laughing as her cheeks flushed brightly.

Una laughed with her. "I have always rather enjoyed the experience myself." She smiled at Charlotte, the brush falling momentarily still. "Your first kiss," she said. "But not, I do not doubt, your last. I have never known anyone to stop with just the one."

❊ ❊ ❊

As Charlotte shrugged her robe from her shoulders to climb into bed, she saw Edmond Cheadle's knapsack on the floor by her wardrobe, where she had left it. Her curiosity roused, Charlotte carried it to her bed and sat cross-legged atop the coverlets, loosening the drawstrings that held the weathered pouch closed.

Una had left her alone for the night, and Darton Hall beyond her closed chamber door was silent. Charlotte had no worries of being interrupted in her investigation, or being scolded for her nosiness. She turned back the front flap of the knapsack, and began to pull the books and papers out.

She studied Cheadle's copy of *Improvement of the Mind*, finding it puzzling and somewhat surprising the man would keep such an assortment of literature with him. Cheadle had not struck her as the sort for intellectual thought; he was a big man with a squared, strapping form, stern gaze, and a quiet, somewhat brooding demeanor. Charlotte flipped absently through the pages of the book, and was surprised to discover a square of paper

folded and tucked about midway through the volume.
She set the book down on her bed and opened the page.

It was a clipping from a gazette; a small, brief article
highlighting one of the earlier Black Trio highway robberies. Written in the slim margin of empty space beside
the article: *Suitable for our needs?*

Charlotte frowned, perplexed. Edmond Cheadle
was a thief-taker by trade. She wondered if the note indicated he had come to Essex County for more than the
driving of James Houghton's coach. Maybe he had been
drawn north from London by the prospect of capturing
the Black Trio, and claiming the rewards.

She set the article aside and turned through the
book again. Toward the back, she found another scrap
of paper tucked inside, this one no more than a hasty jotting, as if written in reminder. *Oct. 26, 11 oc, W. Arms,
Epp. Prop.*

Something about the note struck Charlotte as familiar, and after a moment it occurred to her. She had
received numerous, unwanted correspondences from
James Houghton over the years, pathetic proclamations
of his unfailing adoration, long and rambling attempts at
poetry and even some brazen, not to mention repulsive,
descriptions of what he longed to do to certain parts of
her form with corresponding parts of his. She knew his
writing well enough to recognize it.

October twenty-sixth is tomorrow's date, she thought,

pressing her lips together thoughtfully. *W. Arms, Epp. Prop.* could have possibly been James' personal short-hand for the Wake Arms, a popular inn and pub in the village of Epping proper. The Wake Arms was situated at the crossroads from London to Newmarket, as well as Waltham Abbey and Loughton, and regular, daily coaches stopped there.

That makes a certain sort of sense, she thought. Cheadle was James' coachman. James' sister, Margaret was marrying in less than a week, and family and friends arrived daily for the ceremony's preceding festivities. The note must have been instructions from James to Cheadle to pick someone up in the morning upon their arrival by daily coach from London.

"Mystery solved," Charlotte murmured, somewhat disappointed. As with anything else pertaining to James, even this was relatively transparent and easily deciphered. She tucked both of the notes back inside of Cheadle's book and shoved everything back into the knapsack.

❅ ❅ ❅

The next morning, with the sun no more than a pale glow through the clouds and pre-dawn fog, Charlotte awoke from a sound and comfortable sleep when her sister, Caroline, plopped her bottom heavily against the mattress immediately in front of her.

"Charlotte, look!" she exclaimed, flapping a newspaper noisily in Charlotte's face.

Charlotte's eyes flew wide in bewildered surprise, and she gasped for breath. "What?" she said, her voice a groggy croak. She blinked at Caroline, pushing her disheveled hair back from her face. "Caroline? What . . . what time is it?"

"Half past six or there about," Caroline replied. "Look at this. Sit up."

"What are you doing here?" Charlotte groaned, shoving her face into her pillow.

"Randall dropped me off just now," Caroline said. "He is off for London again. Some sort of business too urgent to miss. He does not want me keeping at Heathcote with only the staff about and the baby soon due." She slapped the newspaper against Charlotte's shoulder. "Sit up. I have brought you something. Look."

"Caroline, leave me be," Charlotte said into her pillow. "You are all excited and you will drop that baby squarely on my mattress."

Caroline laughed. "I will not," she said. "It takes hours of conscientious pushing, shoving, and pain to birth a baby. You cannot just spread your legs and drop it. Sit up and look at this. It is positively thrilling. You will be delighted. Come on now."

Charlotte squirmed and scowled, scooting her hips

toward the headboard and sitting up. She tucked her hair behind her ears and took the paper in her hands, squinting in the dim light, her vision still sleepily blurred. It was yesterday's copy of the *London Evening Post*. Caroline had folded it back to one of the inside pages. It did not take Charlotte long to discover what so excited her sister. She read the words, *Thieves Deliver Funds to St. Bartholomew's*. She glanced at Caroline, and then sat up all the straighter, reading on.

"Is it not thrilling?" Caroline asked, grinning brightly.

"They gave their money to the church," Charlotte whispered, bewildered. "This says the Black Trio left money at St. Bartholomew's in London."

"Not they, Charlotte—*he*," Caroline said, her smile growing wider. "The highwayman who accosted you left it, and a note attached besides, written on a broadside proffering reward for their capture. Did you read?"

She leaned toward Charlotte, tapping her fingertip against the page. Charlotte read the description of the highwayman's charity, and the note he had left with the sums he tendered.

" 'As my lady asked of me,' " she read aloud. " 'And to which I gave my word.' "

She looked up at Caroline in absolute shock.

"Not just what was taken from you," Caroline said. "Did you read the amount? He left almost two guineas, eight shillings in full."

Charlotte simply stared. She had lost no more than two shillings and a fourpence in coins to the highwaymen. She doubted between Lady Chelmsford, Una, and Cheadle they would have netted such a sizable sum as was left at the church.

"All of his money?" she whispered. "He left all of the coins he has stolen? But that . . . that is preposterous. I . . . I never asked him to leave . . . I never asked him to do anything! What kind of thief gives away all that he has risked the gallows to take?"

Caroline arched her brow, smiling wryly at her sister. "A thief who is smitten," she said, tapping her finger against the gazette page once more, the words, *As my lady asked of me.*

❋ ❋ ❋

"Here are troubles I do not need," Charlotte muttered later that morning, as Una and Meghan wrestled her into her corset. "Kenley Fairfax be damned. Wait until Mother learns a bloody highwayman has taken a fancy to me."

"Maybe she will not learn of it," Meghan said.

"Oh, she will learn of it," Charlotte said. She gasped sharply, locking her fingertips around her bedpost while Una offered a mighty jerk on the stay ties. "Caroline knows about it, and what Caroline knows, the world does, too, in short measure."

She heard an unexpected sound from beyond her window, hoof beats approaching, and the rattle of a carriage. She glanced over her shoulder at Una. "I thought Caroline said Lord Harlow kept business in London."

"He does," Una replied. "He delivered her here this morrow along the way."

"He could not have made it yet, much less turned 'round and returned," Charlotte murmured, turning loose of the bedpost. She pulled away from Una and Meghan, crossing to her window. "Who else would pay such an early call?"

She peered through the glass, her breath frosting the pane. She watched a large gentleman's carriage pull up before the house, and the coachman, a tall, broad-shouldered man in a dark, sweeping greatcoat and tricorne, stepped down from his bench, striding briskly for the cab door.

She recognized the coachman when he drew open the door, and when the occupant stepped out, heralding his passage with the brass-tipped end of an ornamental cane, she recognized him, too. "It is James Houghton," she said, frowning. "What on earth is he doing here?"

James walked away from his coach, mounting the broad, tiered steps leading up to the threshold. Edmond Cheadle closed the carriage door and stood rooted, clasping his gloved hands together in front of him. He lifted his head; she could not see his face for the heavy shadows cast by his hat brim, but she seemed to feel his gaze settle upon her as he looked directly toward her window. It was a startling, disconcerting sensation and Charlotte drew back immediately.

"Help me dress," she said, turning to Una and Meghan. "Hurry now! Grab my crinolines."

"What are you going to do?" Una asked, raising a suspicious brow.

"James has no reason to be here," Charlotte said.

Una sighed wearily. "Charlotte . . ." she began.

"Cinch me up, Una, come now," Charlotte said. "I do not need a lecture. Reilly has told me often enough I am too nosy for anyone's good. Hurry up."

❋   ❋   ❋

Once dressed, Charlotte hurried downstairs to the main foyer. She saw the doors to her father's library had been drawn closed, and she stole to the threshold, pressing her ear to the polished oak. She could hear muted voices from within, her father's and James', but she could not discern what they said to one another.

Charlotte frowned, letting her knees fold beneath her as she squatted by the door handle. She peeped through the keyhole; she could see a brightly lit sliver of the library beyond, one of her father's bookshelves, and a corner of one of the intricate throw rugs that adorned the floor. She could see one of the room's large windows canting inward, partially ajar, firelight from the hearth reflected against the glass. She saw no more, and her frown deepened.

"Damn it," she muttered, rising to her feet. She gathered her skirts, lifting them as she hurried toward the kitchen. She made her way toward the back of the house, the rear exit. The library window was opened; all Charlotte needed to do was slip outside, steal around the east side of the house and crouch beneath it to eavesdrop upon her father's conversation with James. The fact that James met Lord Epping behind closed doors alarmed her; it could mean nothing good. Lord Epping knew Charlotte did not want to marry James, but that did not mean he would not consent to arrange it if James offered him sweet enough convincing.

It was cold outside, the air damp and frigid. Charlotte had not thought to shrug a redingote over her shoulders, and she shivered as she hurried around the back of the house for the east wall. She rounded the corner at nearly a running pace and plowed headlong and heedlessly into Edmond Cheadle.

Charlotte yelped, stumbling back from the man. "Oh!" she cried. She fell motionless and uncertain, trying to decide if she should whirl about and run away, or stand and face the weight of the coachman's aroused suspicions. She chose the latter almost at once, and forced a bright, wide smile onto her face. "Oh, Mr. Cheadle!" she exclaimed breathlessly, letting her hand flutter against her bosom. "You gave me a fright!"

"I beg your pardon, miss," Cheadle said, lowering his head in polite deference, drawing his thick finger-tips toward the front corner of his cap. Had she thought he was a large man in recall? Her memory of their introduction did him little justice; Edmond Cheadle was perhaps the most towering, broadly built man she had ever seen. She had to crane her head back on her neck to meet his gaze. He loomed over her as if she were a child.

Cheadle neither smiled nor frowned. His mouth kept a stern, unflinching vigil across the lower quadrant of his face. He had very large eyes and very low brows; the latter drooped over the former, lending the appearance of a perpetual scowl. He seemed to have no need to blink as he stared at Charlotte, studying her intently.

His attention left her decidedly uncomfortable. "Does James pay call?" she asked. "I heard a coach approach, but I could not tell from the window who had arrived."

"Yes, miss," Cheadle said, nodding once. "My lord would notify your father that he has sent word to his father, the Earl, in London regarding the offenses against you."

"Oh," Charlotte said. She could not hold Cheadle's gaze for too long; there was something heavy about it, as if it forced her to bear the weight of his hulking form. "Well, I . . . I hardly see need, but that was very kind of him."

"Lord Roding is pleased to help as he is able, if I may say, miss," Cheadle said. "His fondness for you is surely no secret. Lord Essex, his father, is well aware of this."

The cold air began to sink deeply through Charlotte's clothing and skin, a bone-shivering chill, and she trembled, drawing her arms about her torso. "Yes," she murmured, struggling to think of an escape from the encounter. "Yes, well . . ."

"My lord is also grateful for the opportunity to make amends for the occasion of your robbery," Cheadle told her. "He feels a certain amount of culpability for it, as do I."

Charlotte looked up at him. He did not look particularly remorseful to her, but he had offered words to this effect, and it would seem peculiar to him, rude even, if she did not at least acknowledge it. "Mr. Cheadle, it was three against one," she said. "Unfortunate circumstances, nothing more. James is not to blame for it, and neither are you."

"You are very kind, miss," Cheadle said.

It occurred to Charlotte that she should mention his knapsack; that she should go to her room and retrieve it for him. Just as she opened her mouth to speak, she remembered the note: *Oct 26, 11 oc, W. Arms, Epp.*

proper, and she paused. It was nearly ten o'clock in the morning. If Cheadle was to be in Epping to meet an eleven o'clock arrival, he would have to mark a brisk pace in order to be on time, and it would seem he would have to bring James with him.

This struck her as odd, and she realized why. "Mr. Cheadle, will James be attending the party at Rycroft House today?" she asked.

"It is part of the occasion for his sister's marriage," Cheadle replied. "Yes, he will be there. We will leave once his meeting with Lord Epping has concluded."

The midday social was slated to begin at eleven-thirty. There was no time for Cheadle to deliver James to Rycroft House and then travel to Epping to meet an eleven o'clock coach from London, even if they left at that very moment. Charlotte frowned thoughtfully, nearly forgetting about Cheadle until he made a soft har-rumphing sound to clear his throat and draw her gaze.

"Lord Roding is a good man, miss," Cheadle said. "You should bear that in mind, if I may say. There are plenty others who cannot be so commended. Your gentleman acquaintance, Lord Theydon, for example."

"I . . . I beg your pardon?" she said. "Lord Roding may be fond of me, Mr. Cheadle, but he has no claim to me. Surely he is not disapproving of an afternoon spent in perfectly polite company simply because it was not his own."

"Not disapproving, miss," Cheadle said. "Only concerned. Lord Theydon has a disreputable past. My lord would not see you discredited by association."

Charlotte met Cheadle's gaze evenly. "I am perfectly aware of what happened with Lord Theydon's father. My mother has made it well-known and plain to consider."

One of Cheadle's heavy brows lifted slightly. "Lord Theydon has transgressions of his own," he said. The corner of his broad mouth quivered slightly, as if he either entertained the thought of smiling, or this effort was as much as he could manage. "Jailed and pilloried, on more than one occasion," he said with a nod. "Has he not told you of this, miss, to see you perfectly aware?"

Charlotte could not speak at first, so great was her start. "No," she said softly. "No, he . . . he has not."

She did not know how Cheadle would have discovered such a thing, but she had a fairly good notion as to why he would have bothered. All at once, she did not know what angered her the most—that Kenley had not told her fully of his past, or that James had found some way to dredge it up and wield it to Kenley's discredit.

"Of course, Lord Roding will inform your father of these offenses, as well," Cheadle said. "And your mother. I am certain they will both share in Lord Roding's concerns. A man with such a past, even though of peerage birth, is certainly one whose company should be discouraged."

"As I am certain you, as a thief-taker, should fully

know, Mr. Cheadle," she said sharply. "Good day to you, sir." She snatched her skirts in hand and fled.

CHAPTER 5

"WHAT HAVE YOU DONE TO MY COUSIN?"
Lewis Fairfax asked Charlotte quietly, leaning over her
shoulder from behind and speaking directly into her ear.

She had arrived at Rycroft House for Margaret's social less than an hour earlier, and in the time since had
made a deliberate and concerted effort to ignore both
James and Kenley. While James kept trying to approach
her in the crowd, forcing her to purposely insert herself
into the most dreadful of circumstances—nearby gag-
gles of gossiping women—to avoid him, Kenley at least
observed a courteous distance. He continued to look
at her, however, and on those frequent occasions when
she stole glances in his direction, she met his gaze and
found his expression curious and somewhat amused, and
turned abruptly away.

She had still not decided with whom she was more aggravated at the moment, Kenley or James, but given the fluttering increase in her heart rate every time she caught Kenley watching her, and the infuriating tendency of her mouth to try and return his smile, she was swayed more toward James.

At the sound of Lewis' soft voice, delivered with intimate good humor, she turned, startled from her thoughts and the pretense of being absorbed in the rattling gossip around her. "I . . . I beg your pardon?" Charlotte said, managing to laugh lest he deduce she had been only just now thinking of Kenley. "I have done nothing to your cousin, Lewis. Whatever do you mean?"

Lewis inclined his chin to indicate the other side of the room, and she glanced over her shoulder discreetly. She saw Kenley again, standing near a window. He was surrounded by at least a dozen young women, eligible daughters, with their mothers hovering close at hand in proper chaperone. The girls jostled together, knocking panniers and elbows to simply be close to Kenley, all of them vying eagerly for his attention, and he seemed to be listening with courteous patience to their overlapping chatter. One girl in particular stood directly before him, so close that the swell of her skirts brushed his legs. Charlotte recognized her as the young woman Kenley had spoken with at the threshold of the card parlor yesterday, Miss Tunstall, who had shot Charlotte a glance as she undoubtedly told Kenley about Charlotte's mythical betrothal to James.

"Surely you have put a spell on him," Lewis said, just as Kenley seemed to somehow instinctively sense Charlotte's attention. He turned his head to meet her gaze, and he smiled again—damn him—rendering her almost senseless. Miss Tunstall noticed his distraction and followed his gaze, her pretty, painted and powdered face puckering with petulant disapproval.

"A spell?" Charlotte asked. She forced her eyes away from Kenley, reminding herself firmly he was a convicted criminal and had deliberately omitted this information, and turned to Lewis. "I assure you, Lord Woodside, I have done nothing of the sort."

"Well, you have done something, that is for certain," Lewis said. "I have never seen him in such a state as he has been since yesterday. I spent the night at Theydon Hall, eager for the chance to enjoy supper, brandies, and laughter to the wee hours of this morrow, as is my habitual indulgence when in my cousin's company. He would not sit still long enough to eat, much less down a snifter, however. He wandered about restlessly, his gaze all distracted . . ." Lewis flapped his fingers toward his face demonstratively. ". . . his face sort of softened and sappy."

Charlotte smiled despite her best attempts to the contrary. "Really?" she asked. "I am sure you exaggerate, Lord Woodside."

"Hand to God, and by my breath," Lewis said, laying one hand against the breast of his justicoat and raising the other skyward. "I have never seen him act like that."

Charlotte looked behind her again. Kenley still watched, despite Miss Tunstall's best and most insistent attempts to draw his attention.

"I . . . I have not the faintest idea why he would," Charlotte said to Lewis. "Perhaps he is ill."

Lewis made a thoughtful, rumbling sound in his throat. "Perhaps," he said. "I say, while you are on hand, where is your brother? I have looked all about, and cannot find him anywhere."

"Reilly did not come today," Charlotte said. "He looked rather dreadful this morning and begged off."

"Oh," Lewis said, still appearing pensive. He glanced toward Kenley and then at Charlotte again. "Perhaps this illness is making the rounds, then."

❋ ❋ ❋

Charlotte had not parted company with Lewis for more than ten minutes before Kenley managed to disengage from Miss Tunstall and the other daughters. She saw him shouldering his way through the crowd, and she turned about, meaning to dart into the throng. By now the social was well underway, however, and the parlor was crammed to capacity. Darting was not an option; people stood shoulder to shoulder and allowed precious little opportunity to shove heartily through them, much less move quickly.

"Good morning, Miss Engle," Kenley said over her shoulder, standing so close from the sound of his voice that she had no hope of feigning convincing obliviousness; she would have to be deaf to miss his greeting.

She did an about-face, forced into courtesy by their proximity. "It is afternoon, Lord Theydon," she said. "You should have your watch inspected. Given how often you seem to lose track of time, it might be due for repairs."

"Is it afternoon already?" he inquired. "Forgive me. I had not noticed time passing. I have been distracted trying to draw your gaze. I thought you mistook me for a stranger in the crowd, or perhaps you did not see me."

"I did not think you were a stranger," she said. "It was difficult to discern you among all of the ladies flocked about. I simply assumed I had used my allocation of time spent in your company yesterday, and would afford some other girl the chance today. Perhaps your acquaintance, Miss Tunstall. She seemed most determined to me."

"Were there ladies around me?" he asked, looking over his shoulder, feigning surprise. "I did not even pay mind. I saw only you."

He was trying to coax a smile from her. When the

attempt did not work, he cocked his head slightly, curious. "Are you sore with me?" he asked. "Have I offended you somehow? Nothing comes to mind I might have done, but whatever it was, it was purely unintentional, I assure you."

Charlotte met his gaze evenly. "You did not tell me you had been jailed before," she said, keeping her voice discreetly low.

A burst of laughter escaped Kenley. "I am sorry," he said, holding up his hands in concession. "Forgive me, I . . . I do not typically disclose that when I am trying to charm a lady. I have found it rather ineffectual."

"Is that what yesterday was?" Charlotte asked. "An attempt to charm me?"

"I thought we had established that already," he replied. "Yes, I was trying my damndest."

"So it is true, then?" she said. "You are some manner of scoundrel?"

"Most assuredly not," he said, laughing again. "I am merely a young man whose past saw him into mischief— a past I have tried diligently to put behind me in hopes of being a gentleman of some honor, in spite of it."

"What have you been in jail for?"

"Does it matter?" he asked. "I am a different man now. A better man, I would like to think."

"Of course it matters," she said. "I do not find associating myself with a common criminal to be the least bit amusing. You might have told me this yesterday, and afforded me some opportunity to preserve my reputation by avoiding you."

He looked genuinely wounded, and Charlotte regretted her sharp choice of words. He glanced about, uncomfortably, and then leaned toward her. "Would you come with me?" he asked.

"I should think not," she replied. "Your company has seen me in enough trouble."

"Please, Charlotte," he said softly. "I will explain to you. Everything. By my breath, I will, but not here. You would shame me."

She looked around at the guests nearby. Damn him, rot him, rot it all, he looked so sincere in his plea, so earnest in his effort to keep in her graces, she could not refuse him. She met his gaze and nodded once. "All right," she said. "But only for a moment. My mother will have a fit."

❀ ❀ ❀

Kenley found a small, vacant parlor beyond the foyer. She saw him poke his head inside; when he ducked through the doorway, she glanced about anxiously to make sure they were unobserved, and then followed. He closed the door swiftly behind her, and Charlotte had no reasonable accounting for the sudden, thrilled tremble of her heart to be alone with him in the shadow-draped chamber.

"I am sorry," Kenley said, turning to her. "You are right to be angry with me. I should have told you."

He closed what little space was left between them. He was so near she shied back, disconcerted.

"I have been jailed, yes," Kenley said. "And pilloried besides. My father died when I was twelve, and I came to live with Lewis and my uncle at Woodside. I . . . I was very angry and confused. I did not understand my grief and shame, and I was wild for it. I stood in the stocks when I was twelve and again at fourteen, twice for drunkenness, two more times besides for brawling. I also spent three days in jail for pickpocketing and another week for burglary when I was fifteen."

Charlotte met his gaze. "That is all?" she asked.

Kenley chuckled. "Yes, that would fairly well cover the gamut of my offenses," he said. "You are not impressed?"

"I just . . . from the telling, I had expected something a bit more nefarious," she said.

"I could go out and commit some grievous crime, if you would like," he offered. "If it would re-endear me to you, I will go right now."

She could not remain angry at him. He had offered her the truth with such vulnerability apparent in his eyes, his shame and remorse in the admittance were nearly tangible. Charlotte smiled, helpless to prevent herself any longer. "I do not think that will be necessary," she said.

He seemed visibly relieved.

"Thank you for telling me," she said, lowering her gaze. "I am not a gossip, and you do not have to worry that I will say anything. I will not."

"I know," he said. "I trust you."

She looked up at him, touched by his candor. "Why?"

"You have given me no reason not to," he said. He reached for her, brushing his fingers against her cheek, and her heart pounded. His proximity was dizzying; she did not understand the unfamiliar reaction any more than she wanted it to stop.

Despite the sudden warmth that suddenly spread through her, trembling through her form, a voice of reason within her cried in protest. She could not do this, she told herself. Not again. Lady Epping would bolt her in her room and forbid her to cross the threshold. "Lord Theydon . . ." she whispered as he cradled her cheek against his palm and leaned over her. She wanted to stay him; she wanted to seize his face between her hands and kiss him. She was torn between the two, hiccupping for breath, her mind spinning. "Lord Theydon, we . . . we cannot . . ."

"Kenley," he said softly, his mouth poised so near to hers she had to physically struggle not to lift her chin and let his lips touch hers.

"Do not," she said, ducking her head, drawing away from his touch, his proffered kiss. He lifted her chin, giving her no moment for reconsideration or recoil. He kissed her deeply; yesterday's fleeting brush had been only a whispered hint of this sudden, impulsive, impassioned advance. His mouth pressed against hers, and when she gasped for breath she felt his lips part, his tongue delve into her mouth.

She uttered a muffled whimper and he drew her closer, until her pannier buckled inward against his hips and her breasts pressed against the front of his jacket. His tongue moved against hers gently, exploring the intricacies of her palate with intimate, uncanny familiarity. Charlotte had never felt such wondrous friction before.

He canted his head; his mouth slipped momentarily from hers and then settled again, stealing her breath before she could even entertain dazed thought of reclaiming it. He tilted her head back gently with his hands, and she moved willingly. When his mouth left hers, his lips trailing along the line of her jaw before discovering her throat, she closed her eyes and gasped, laying her hands against his shoulders and pressing her fingertips fiercely against the wool of his justicoat. He followed the contours of her throat with his lips, the tip of his tongue drawing slow, concentric circles on her skin. The sensation of this—his breath and tongue—was new and exquisite to her; again, she whimpered, tightening her grasp on his shoulders.

He found her heart pounding out its frantic rhythm along the slope of her neck, and his mouth lingered there. Her voice escaped in a soft moan, and after a long, luxurious moment of his lips' tender attentions, he lifted his head.

"Do you want me to stop?" he asked, his voice little more than a rumbling murmur.

She opened her eyes, reeling, as if emerging from a dream. "No," she whispered, shaking her head. He smiled at her, and then that damnable voice of reason hissed in her head. Just as Kenley lowered his face to kiss her again, just as she felt her chin tilt of its own accord to let him, she ducked her head, shrugged her shoulders, and stepped back from him. "I . . . I mean . . . I mean yes. We should not do this."

In answer, he kissed her throat, his lips reacquainting themselves with the tremulous places only just abandoned, and then eased from there to the delicate curve of her earlobe.

"My . . . my mother will be looking for me," she whimpered, her head leaning back as she presented her neck to him. "I . . . I have to get back . . ."

His lips brushed against her ear; she gasped as he traced the lines and curves with his tongue. She felt his tongue touch the bottom of her earlobe, drawing it lightly between his upper teeth and bottom lip. Her breath hitched in helpless delight as he offered a gentle tug with his mouth. "Please . . . stop . . ."

She planted her hands on his shoulders. "Stop," she whispered. He looked up into her eyes, blessedly and cursedly pausing in his efforts. She forced herself to draw away from him,. "You will see me scolded," she said. "I just . . . I have to get back." She brushed past him, moving for the door, refusing to meet his gaze lest she be tempted to rush back to him.

"Forgive me," he said. "I should not have done that. It . . . it was untoward and impulsive . . . ungentlemanly, and I . . . totally out of line and character, I promise you. I . . . I forgot myself. It . . . by my breath, Charlotte, please, it will not happen again."

Charlotte smiled, her heart still trembling as the residual thrill of his touch and his kiss faded. "I did not say I minded," she told him. She caught a quick glimpse of his mouth lifting in a smile, opening as he began to laugh, and then she ducked out of the room and closed the door behind her.

❋ ❋ ❋

She waded back into the crowded parlor, still trembling and distracted. When her aunt caught her by the arm, staying her in midstride, she yelped aloud.

"Charlotte, darling, here you are," Lady Chelmsford exclaimed. "I have been looking all over for you!"

"I . . . uh, terribly sorry, Aunt Maude," Charlotte stammered. "I . . . I had to relieve myself. Dreadful inconvenience, but rather an urgent need that would not last until we returned home."

Lady Chelmsford hauled Charlotte in tow, using her broad bosom and the expanse of her pannier to cleave a path through the throng. "Your mother wants you," she said. "She thought you had run off once more, and on your own."

Charlotte laughed shrilly, nervously. "Dear God, no," she said. "I have yet to recover from yesterday's wrath."

Lady Chelmsford delivered her to the far end of the parlor, where Lord and Lady Epping stood together in amicable conversation with a small group. Charlotte recognized Margaret Houghton, the soon-to-be bride among them; she realized the tall man with the solemn, elongated face and powdered wig beside Margaret must surely be her betrothed, Frederick Cuthbert.

Another woman stood near Margaret, holding lightly to the arm of James Houghton. James spied Charlotte, and his smile widened with delight. "Darling," he called out. "At last—here you are!"

"Yes, splendid," Charlotte muttered while Lady Chelmsford yanked her forward, making her dance on her tiptoes as she was presented to Lady Epping. "Mother, hullo," she said, feigning nonchalant good cheer. "Sorry to have kept you waiting. A bit of a personal emergency arose—but all is tended to now. No need for any fuss."

"Charlotte, darling, you remember Lady Margaret Houghton, do you not?" Lady Epping asked, putting her hand on Charlotte's sleeve and steering her in a semicircle to face Margaret.

"Of course," Charlotte said, smiling like a witless idiot. She had not seen Margaret Houghton since she was thirteen years old; she could not have picked the young woman out of a crowd, but she accepted Margaret's embrace as if they were old and fond friends.

"Look how beautiful you are!" Margaret squealed against Charlotte's ear, nearly inflicting damage with her shrill tone. "James has told me so often, but I never would have dreamed he was not offering empty flattery! Oh, it is so delightful to see you again, Charlotte, darling!"

"Yes, well," Charlotte said, patting Margaret's back. "Simply marvelous. Congratulations on your upcoming marriage, Margaret. I am sure it will be splendid."

"And her mother, and Lord Roding's, besides," Lady Epping said by way of introduction, indicating the woman perched on James' sleeve. "Lady Essex."

"My lady, how do you fare?" Charlotte asked, lowering herself in a polite curtsy.

"Our father is yet in London," Margaret said. "He will be pleased to see you Saturday, though. Oh, I am sure he is just giddy with the news."

News? Charlotte thought, glancing out of the corner of her eye at her mother. *What news?*

At that precise moment, James held aloft a large brandy snifter. He tapped the edge of a small silver spoon against the side of the crystal, issuing a sweet, beckoning toll. Charlotte started, puzzled, when he repeated the gesture. He continued tapping until the tones drew the parlor to silence, and all attention turned in their direction.

"My good friends and fellows, I would like to propose a toast," James called out. "We are gathered together in formal anticipation of this upcoming Saturday, when my beloved sister and her dearly betrothed shall exchange vows to bind them together eternally."

He turned as he spoke so his voice rang out across the entire breadth of the chamber. "This has brought to my heart and mind my own marital status, or the lack thereof, as my mother so fondly reminds me," James said, and the crowd rippled with low, polite laughter.

"What is this?" Charlotte whispered to Lady Epping.

Lord Epping caught Charlotte's gaze from beyond his wife's shoulder. He gave Charlotte a somewhat sheepish and sorrowful glance, most often reserved for someone about to be drawn by open cart from Newgate prison to the gallows of Tyburn.

"While my father's county has never wanted for

an abundance of beautiful, charming, and magnificent women, I have only ever desired one, whom I have long considered Essex's greatest treasure," James said, and he turned in Charlotte's direction. "I wish I could express how even a fleeting glimpse of this exquisite lamb moves me. I have adored her from afar lo these many years, and at last, duly inspired by my sister's good fortune, I have made formal arrangement . . . and now announcement."

Charlotte stared at him with sudden, stricken realization. She felt the blood drain from her face. *No*, she thought. She wanted to scream it. *No, no, no!*

"I have made my intentions known to my gracious Lord and Lady Epping," James told the crowd. "And with their consent and blessing, my heart's joy is now utter and complete. I would like to introduce my bride to you . . ." James held out his hand to Charlotte. When she did not move, frozen with shock, Lady Epping gave her a shove. James caught her hand and drew her close.

". . . my bride, Miss Charlotte Engle," he announced, and the crowd erupted in joyous applause.

James put his arm around Charlotte's shoulders and embraced her. "Darling," he said against her ear, letting his lips press moistly against her cheek. Charlotte was stunned, her mind awhirl. This could not be happening, she told herself. She could not let it happen. She looked up at James and tried to shrug him loose. He smiled at her wolfishly, like a man who had just won a generous prize at the card tables, and Charlotte balled her hands into defiant fists and sucked in a sharp breath to berate him.

"I would like to extend my personal congratulations to you, Lord Roding," she heard someone call out from behind her. The voice was loud and resonant, drawing the throng to an uncertain and puzzled silence. Charlotte gasped in new shock when she saw Kenley step forward, shouldering his way through the crowd to approach them.

"I would like to, my lord," Kenley said to James. "But alas, I cannot. You offered sweet words regarding Miss Engle, and I am sure she thanks you for them. But she cannot be your bride."

The crowd muttered in startled bewilderment. Lady Chelmsford uttered a low, warbling moan, and swayed unsteadily on her feet, as if overcome by the vapors.

James' arm tightened possessively about Charlotte, jerking her against his lapel as he scowled at Kenley. "Truly, Lord Theydon?" he asked, his tone mocking although he offered the younger man courteous title. "And prithee tell, why can Miss Engle not be my bride?"

"Because she has already consented to be mine," Kenley replied.

At this, the parlor dissolved into absolute chaos, a sudden, sweeping, cacophonous din. Lady Chelmsford uttered another quavering yowl and then promptly keeled over in a swoon. She collapsed into four people standing close by, including Lord Epping, and brought them with her to the floor.

Charlotte felt James' arm loosen in reflexive surprise from her shoulders, and she took advantage of the moment, pulling away from him. She staggered forward, and reached out when Kenley offered his hand to her. She folded her fingers about his fiercely, and when he drew her to his shoulder, she huddled there. "What are you doing?" she gasped.

He lowered his face to hers, sheltering her from the noise of the crowd. "You told me you would prefer death to marrying James Houghton," he said. "I thought I might offer you another alternative."

"This is outrageous!" James yelled, his hands folding into fists. He jabbed his forefinger in the air at Kenley. "How dare you touch her! Remove your hands! You are a rot damn liar, Theydon! You only met Charlotte yesterday! You cannot expect one among us in this room to think she would marry you so quickly and heedlessly!"

"It is true that to your limited observation we were introduced yesterday," Kenley said. "But if the truth is to be told, I have known Charlotte these past six months."

"What?" Charlotte squeaked.

"We met in London," he told her brightly. "In London upon my return to England. Yes, we both . . . here in London, we . . ."

"We held season tickets to Vauxhall," Charlotte

whispered in suggestion.

". . . we both happened to hold season tickets to Vauxhall," Kenley said loudly. "And we . . . we then . . ."

"We met over discussions of Handel," Charlotte whispered.

"And we met over discussions of *Hamlet*," Kenley declared.

"Handel," Charlotte hissed, clapping her hand over her eyes.

"Over discussions of Handel," Kenley repeated. "Yes, Handel. My favorite."

He pressed his cheek against her brow and helped muffle her groan with his coat lapel. "As dear to your heart as you have described her, Lord Roding, Charlotte is a thousand-fold more so to me," he said. "She is the most captivating woman I have met in all of my days; if I should live millennia—if I scoured this earth from corner to corner and pole to pole, I could not hope for one to surpass her in my regard. She fills my thoughts; my every breath turns my mind again and again with sweet relentlessness to her. She fills my heart; with each beat, she courses through my form, infusing me with joy and sustaining me with the gracious gift of her most precious love."

Charlotte looked up at him, her mouth agape. Surely, these were the sweetest words she had ever heard uttered.

"She is my complement, my companion, my comfort," Kenley said. "Friend to me, and counsel besides.

Her wit and wisdom shame me for my own lacking. I wish that I could share her with you, Lord Roding, for I sympathize with your adoration. However, I more than adore and admire this magnificent woman. I love her plainly, truly, and with all of my being."

"This is an outrage!" James bellowed. He whirled toward Lady Epping. "My lady! Surely you cannot consent to such a daft arrangement as this! Surely you will not allow our darling Charlotte to wed under such ridiculous and outlandish pretense!"

Charlotte glanced at her mother. Lady Epping was as white as linen, shaking like a leaf caught in a gale's leading edge. She stared at Charlotte, her eyes filled with stunned disbelief. A peculiar, breathless cawing wheezed from her open mouth, and Charlotte realized it was likely as close as she had ever driven her mother to truly keeling over in a swoon.

"My Lord and Lady Epping, please accept my apologies, as I know this must seem sudden and reckless," Kenley said. "I promise you it is not, and that Charlotte and I had full intention of telling you of our arrangement after we were able to convince you our hearts and minds are bound fast and sincerely, and that we are not being impetuous or ill-advised." He glanced at James. "However, circumstances have not allowed for that, and I hope you understand my stepping forward as I have. I know the arrangements you have with Lord Roding were made with Charlotte's interests in mind, but surely you would agree that a marriage of her own choosing is one in which she is truly best served."

"Of course we do, lad," Lord Epping said. He had managed to wriggle out from beneath Lady Chelmsford and regain his footing. He looked between the young man and Charlotte, his face set in a broad, delighted grin. James staggered backward, sputtering. He looked as though he might collapse in his outraged shock.

Kenley extended his hand, and Lord Epping caught it in his own, pumping Kenley's arm with a hearty, eager shake. "Such a surprise!" he exclaimed. "Not an unwelcome one, but a surprise all the same! My darling Charlotte in love and never saying a word of it!"

He reached for Charlotte and drew her to him, hugging her warmly and kissing her cheek. "Where are the servants? May we not see another round of wine poured?"

Lord Epping drew back from Charlotte and waved his hand in the air. "Another round of wine," he called. "We are due another toast for my daughter and now for my son as well!"

CHAPTER 6

"ARE THEY STILL ARGUING?" CHARLOTTE asked, looking up from her pillows.

Caroline nodded, walking from the threshold of Charlotte's chamber to the bed. She moved slowly, her motions stiff, the hems of her gown and dressing robe swaying loosely about her ankles. She kept her hands pressed against the swell of her belly and groaned softly as she sat next to her sister. "Mother is in a state, that is for sure," she said.

Charlotte sat up, scooting back to her headboard. She looked at Caroline unhappily. "She will find some way to yet see me marry James," she said. "I just know it."

"I do not," Caroline replied, smiling as she patted Charlotte's foot. "You have found a fairly good ally for yourself in Father. He is not bending on this at all, and you know he has never been much to stand against Mother once she sets her mind to something."

Lady Epping had not said a word to Charlotte since they left Rycroft House that afternoon. Charlotte had spent the carriage ride home in a dazed sort of stupor, surrounded by a tension so heavy within the cab it had been nearly palpable. The only words offered at all the entire way had been Lady Chelmsford's, who kept rolling her eyes, leaning her head against the wall and moaning, "How could this have happened? Six months meeting in London! Where was I during it all?"

It was well past dusk. Lady Epping had hauled Charlotte's father into the library promptly upon their return to Darton Hall, and from there, behind closed doors, the arguing had commenced. Charlotte had no idea what might be happening behind the library doors; only occasional muted sounds of her parents' sharp, raised voices floated up from the first floor to offer hints and for once, her notorious curiosity seemed content to remain unpiqued.

"Here, do not look so glum," Caroline said. "It will all work itself through in the end. Turn around. Let me braid your hair. I cannot believe you do not wind up with a matted nest, sleeping with it unfettered as you do."

Charlotte did not have the heart to argue with her sister, and did as she was told. She presented her back to Caroline, crossing her legs before her. She hunched her shoulders and hung her head miserably while Caroline took up her brush from the bedside table and began to run it through her hair.

"I think it is rather sweet myself," Caroline remarked. "You marrying for love, and keeping it so secret."

"It was hardly a secret," Charlotte said. "We met in public places for public functions all the while in London—perfectly proper." She nearly clapped her hand over her face and groaned aloud, unable to believe she was going along with the preposterous ruse.

"I have only been reintroduced to Kenley on a couple of occasions these past months, but he is certainly handsome," Caroline said. "And his manners are quite dashing, I must say. You could do far worse for yourself."

"Tell that to Mother," Charlotte said, wincing when Caroline stroked the brush through tangles.

"Oh, piffle," Caroline said with a laugh. "Mother only wants what is best for you. She just happens to have decided James Houghton is what is best. She will come right 'round on things, you mark me. Do not worry about it."

"Is Father really standing up for me?" Charlotte asked, glancing over her shoulder.

"Oh, yes, and shouting quite a storm," Caroline said. "It is a good thing. She pushes him about something awful sometimes. I love Mother dearly, but she has grown dreadfully spoiled."

"She will not give up so easily on James," Charlotte said.

"Well, he is the son of the Earl," Caroline said. "To Mother's point of view, this makes him a far better choice of husband than a recently re-established young baron. You are the daughter of a viscount. Marrying a baron means marrying downward in status, and given the Theydon history of gambling away their money, it is a reasonable concern."

"Kenley does not gamble," Charlotte said. "He told me that. He saw what it did to his father. It had an effect on him, too. He is still answering for it."

Caroline set the brush aside. She gathered Charlotte's hair between her hands and separated it with her fingers into three long sections. "He was a very unhappy boy," she remarked as she twined the portions together in a plait. "You do not remember him well, do you, from when he used to visit Reilly? I remember. Mother thought he was one for mischief, but I always thought he was unhappy. Angry, I suppose, and that is why he found trouble for himself. With a father like Lord Theydon, I imagine the poor thing had plenty to feel angry and unhappy about."

"He is not like that now," Charlotte said. "He is trying to make amends for his past, to be better in spite of it."

"Yes, well, unfortunately every moment of his past is

perfectly available for Mother's scrutiny, thanks to James Houghton and that thief-taker coachman of his," Caroline said. "I am sure James has sent Mr. Cheadle out to find every whit and scrap of discredit that can be discovered."

"We all have pasts," Charlotte said, frowning. "And plenty of men have done things in their youths they regret upon maturity. Even Father. He agreed to that ridiculous duel when he was nineteen."

Caroline chuckled. "Oh, how he dearly loves to regale us with that story," she said. "And tell us over and over, as if we have never heard, 'Thank God I kept my snuff box tucked in my breast pocket, not my hip, else I might have been punched clean through.' "

" 'And I still drew first blood,' " Charlotte said, lowering her voice to mimic her father's.

" 'I yet have the snuff box, dented nearly in twain,' " Caroline said, dropping her pitch to match Charlotte's. " 'Here now, sit still, it will not take but a moment to fetch it from my highboy and show it to you . . .' "

Charlotte and Caroline giggled together. It was the first time since that afternoon Charlotte had smiled, and when Caroline paused in her braiding, touching her shoulder, Charlotte reached for her, squeezing her hand lightly. "I am glad you are here, Caroline," Charlotte whispered.

"I am glad to be here, Charlotte," Caroline said. "I would not have missed such a fuss for the world."

"What I need to do is have a thief-taker of my own,"

Charlotte said. "Someone to dredge up some awful, hidden part of James' past to prove he is a scoundrel and unfit to marry, Earl's heir or not." She glanced over her shoulder. "You are privy to all the Essex County gossip. Have you heard any about him?"

"No, nothing," Caroline said. "He is the Earl's son, and Lord Essex is a well-respected and wealthy man. No one would say anything against him or his kin." She paused for a moment, and then said, "But I could ask Randall of it, I suppose. He might know."

Charlotte creased her brow thoughtfully. "There must be something," she murmured. "I know James too well to think he has lived a totally guileless existence. The man keeps a bloody thief-taker in his service—by my breath, there is something peculiar, if not insidious."

Caroline secured Charlotte's hair in place with a small length of ribbon. "There you go," she said. "See how easily a brush runs through in the morning." She shoved her hands against the mattress and stood. "You should turn in to bed," she said. "Put this whole mess from your mind. Tomorrow shall be grand, I think."

"Why?" Charlotte asked, puzzled.

Caroline smiled. "Father did not tell you? He sent word to Theydon Hall, asking Kenley to come for proper introductions."

"He did what?"

Caroline nodded. "Eleven o'clock promptly. I think

you should wear your yellow dress with the cream-colored jupe and stomacher. That looks so lovely on you."

"Kenley is coming here?" Charlotte gasped. "Why did Father do that?"

"He likes Lord Theydon, if only because you do," Caroline said. "I keep hearing him holler at Mother that any man of worthwhile enough character to impress himself upon you is suitable for him." She dropped Charlotte a wink. "And I think Lord Roding's tidings of Kenley's sordid past have intrigued Father, given his own past penchant for such mischief."

"Oh, God," Charlotte moaned, flopping facedown on her bed and smothering herself in her pillows. "Mother is going to flay him alive!"

"No, she will not," Caroline replied. "If anything, Mother is at least a proper lady. He will make it out of here intact. I am fairly confident of that."

Charlotte groaned again. She did not even notice the soft creak of floorboards at her threshold as someone approached. "Reilly, darling, here you are! Are you feeling well now and recovered?" Caroline said brightly, and Charlotte lifted her head. She saw her brother in the doorway, his blond hair sleepily askew, his face twisted in a groggy scowl.

"I am better, thank you," Reilly grumbled. "What is all of that shouting from downstairs about?"

"No one has told you the news?" Caroline asked,

smiling broadly. Reilly's bewildered expression grew all the more confused, and she exclaimed, "Our lamb is getting married!"

"Married?" Reilly asked. "Lord Roding proposed?"

Caroline laughed. "So it was secret even from you," she said. "No, Reilly. She is marrying Lord Theydon. They announced it this afternoon at Rycroft."

"Lord Theydon?" Reilly asked. He stared at Charlotte, and she had no accounting for the sudden furrow that creased his brows. "You mean Kenley Fairfax, Lord Theydon?"

"Is it not delightful?" Caroline said. "For these past six months they have been meeting secretly in London and have fallen in love. I think it is quite charming."

Reilly leveled his gaze at his youngest sister. "These past six months?" he asked, and there was such doubt in his tone that Charlotte hunched her shoulders, ashamed. Reilly could not prove her a liar, but he still knew her well enough to smell rot when she offered it.

"You and Kenley Fairfax have fallen in love these past six months?"

"In London," Caroline said. "Is it not delightful, Reilly?"

"Bloody splendid," he growled, spinning on his heel. "My rot damn day is now complete."

He stomped off, his footsteps heavy, pounding in the corridor. Charlotte felt wounded, embarrassed, and somewhat puzzled by his reaction.

"My, he is in a mood," Caroline said, untroubled. She looked down at Charlotte, and her expression softened. "Did he hurt your feelings, lamb? Pay him no heed." She brushed her palm against the cap of Charlotte's head. "He has been in a state all day, ever since this morning. I do not know what has flown up his breeches, but it is not you."

❃ ❃ ❃

Charlotte tried to sleep, but could not. She was distracted by the sounds of her parents' arguments seeping through the floorboards, the closed door of her chamber. Finally, she heard footsteps in the corridor as Lord and Lady Epping retired, their conversation apparently not concluded.

"He is a common criminal," Lady Epping said, passing like a fleeting shadow across the glow of soft light beneath Charlotte's door.

"And the girl is in love with him," Lord Epping replied, sounding weary and aggravated. "She has set her mind to it and she is certainly old enough to be left to her own choices . . ."

There was more, but they walked past her room and it was lost to her. Charlotte waited a long moment, until silence descended upon the house, and then she sat up. She lit her bedside lamp and pushed her covers aside, swinging her legs around to the floor. She squinted against the glare of the lamp on her mantel; the clock read nine-thirty.

Since Caroline had left, Charlotte's mind had turned again and again to the idea of convincing her mother James would never make a proper husband for her, with or without the complication of her ruse engagement to Kenley. She also fretted about having had no occasion to draw Kenley alone and speak with him in the confused aftermath that had followed his bold announcement, and she still had no idea why he had done what he had. She was tremendously grateful to him, whatever his reasons, but in her heart she knew she could not see even that marriage through. No matter what they had offered in pretense, Kenley did not know her. He had obviously acted out of some sense of courtesy in rescuing her from James, but to hold him to the hasty declaration—one she felt certain he was likely pounding his head against the wall regretting—would be no less cruel than her mother's expectations that Charlotte marry James.

"There must be some way out of this," Charlotte whispered. If she did what she knew in her heart was right—release Kenley from his offer—then she would be left with a forced marriage to James. But if she married Kenley, it would still be something forced. True, she was drawn to him, charmed, captivated, and infatuated by him, but could one base a marriage on such curious fascination?

"Of course not," she told herself, shaking her head. "Do not be stupid. There is only one way out of this."

She had to prove James unfit in Lady Epping's regard.

Charlotte went to her writing table, where she had set Edmond Cheadle's knapsack. She opened the bag and pulled out his copy of *Improvement of the Mind*. Cheadle was decidedly creepy, and based on the newspaper clipping she had found, with the ambiguous note *Suitable for our needs?*, Charlotte had decided the thief-taker was in Epping parish with far more in mind than finding reputable employment as a coachman.

She flipped through the book and found the second note: *Oct 26, 11 oc, W. Arms, Epp. prop.* Both Cheadle and James had been at Rycroft House that morning; they had not picked up any wedding guests from London in Epping. Therefore, she surmised the note meant eleven o'clock at night.

Coaches might come from London at such a late hour. She did not know. No aristocrat in his right mind traveled so late in the night into an area reputed to be overrun with highwaymen—especially now, with the Black Trio preying at will.

"Who could they be meeting?" Charlotte mused to herself. Even as the words were out of her mouth, the realization dawned. *A woman,* she thought. Who else would a nobleman meet at such an hour and location?

James would no more meet even a fond acquaintance for pints at a pub than he would sprout wings and fly. The only reason he might consent to meet at the Wake Arms in the middle of the night was to meet someone in relative secret.

"A lover," she whispered, the corner of her mouth lifting in a smile. She nearly laughed aloud. *I will be damned,* she thought. *James Houghton has taken a lover!*

She could not have fallen onto her knees and begged God for better circumstances. If a lover did not convince Lady Epping of James' poor character, nothing would. And it would be so simple to discover him at it. All Charlotte had to do was ride to Epping, slip into the Wake Arms and come upon him in the act.

She flew to her wardrobe and drew on an old pair of Reilly's breeches she kept tucked away for horseback riding occasions. She pulled on a weathered pair of boots and shrugged her way into a blouse. She grabbed a greatcoat from her wardrobe, the one the highwayman had left with her, and drew it over her shoulders. She fished around in a traveling bag until she found her pocket pistol and loaded it quickly, tucking the handgun into the deep hip pocket of her coat. Last but not least, she found the tricorne that matched her riding habit in the back of her wardrobe. She plopped the hat on her head and made for the door.

Just as she reached for the handle, she heard soft

footsteps in the corridor and froze, her breath stilled. She heard a quiet rapping sound as someone knocked on Reilly's door down the hall, and then Meghan said softly, "Your tea, sir."

Charlotte opened the door a scant margin and peeped out. She watched Reilly's door open, and shied back reflexively. Reilly knew she was lying about having met Kenley in London; he knew her far too well. She could offer him no excuses he would believe if he caught her slipping out of the house.

"Thank you, Meghan," she heard him say. His voice sounded hoarse and weary. She risked another peek and watched Meghan step through the doorway and into his room. Reilly closed the door behind the maid, and Charlotte lingered, poised at her threshold, waiting for Meghan to leave.

The moment stretched. *What are they doing in there?* Charlotte thought. *How long can it bloody take to deposit a tea service, drop a curtsy and leave?*

Finally, she could bear it no longer. She eased her door open wide enough to slip into the hall, and closed it soundlessly behind her. Keeping a wary eye on Reilly's door, she scampered for the stairwell. She scurried down the stairs to the foyer, and ran into the kitchen. She used the back entrance of the house to leave, and crossed the yard, heading for the stables.

The coachman, grooms, and stable hands all lived

in quarters in the stable loft. As she crept into the barn, Charlotte could see the dim glow of lanterns filtering through the slim spaces between floor boards above her, dappling the straw-strewn ground. She could hear the men laughing together, playing cards, and sharing quiet conversations.

She paused long enough to collect a bridle from a wall peg and then tiptoed to one of the stalls. A roan gelding poked its head over the gate at Charlotte's quiet approach, its ears perked curiously. It knew her well enough to be unalarmed by her presence, and Charlotte reached for the gate latch to open the stall.

"What are you doing?"

Charlotte whirled, the tack dropping from her hand. She spied a small, silhouetted figure just beyond the threshold of the barn, and she sighed, the tension draining from her shoulders. "Una, you gave me a fright."

"Do you not think you have found enough trouble for yourself today without adding more to it?" Una asked, walking in Charlotte's direction. Una's hair was unbundled for bed, hanging to her waist in a thick plait. Charlotte could see the hem of her nightgown poking out in stark contrast to the edge of her dark, oversized coat. Una wore boots too big for her feet, and plodded clumsily across the floor.

"Where on earth did you get that coat and boots?" Charlotte asked.

"They are Mr. Pickernell's," Una replied primly, referring to Lord Epping's butler. "Where are you going?"

"Epping proper," Charlotte said, turning to the stall. She unlatched the gate and stepped inside. She slipped the bit between the gelding's teeth and drew the bridle into place. She took the reins in hand and led the horse from the stall to saddle it.

Una folded her arms across her bosom. "May I ask why?"

"No, you may not," Charlotte said, looping the end of the reins loosely about a vertical beam. She lifted a saddle in her arms, grunting at the weight.

"Then humor me, lamb, and tell me anyway," Una said, unamused.

Charlotte glanced at her as she plopped the saddle on the roan's back. "I found a note in that bag of Mr. Cheadle's," she said. "A peculiar note. Something about eleven o'clock tonight at the Wake Arms in Epping. I think James is meeting someone there, and I want to know who."

"I should think who James does or does not meet is no longer of any interest or consequence to you," Una said. "As you are betrothed to another."

Charlotte snorted as she tugged on the girth, tightening it about the gelding's middle. "If only it was that easy when it comes to my mother," she said. "She will never give up on the idea of me marrying James no matter who I am betrothed to. Unless, of course, it was bloody George the Second, and then she would consider him of higher rank, and a far better suitor. And since His Majesty and I shall likely never meet, much less marry, I figure I am on my own to discredit James and see Kenley freed from this pretense of marrying me."

"Oh, so it is pretense, then?" Una asked, arching her brow. "And here it was my understanding that the two of you were dearly in love, having been courting properly in London these past sixth months."

Charlotte paused in her work, ashamed at Una's admonishing tone. She glanced sheepishly at Una. "I am sorry," she whispered.

"As well you should be," Una said. "I had to stand before your mother as if I knew every last detail of this arrangement. I had to tell her that Lord Theydon was right and proper in his courtship, as I accompanied you in chaperone every time you met with him. It is damn near likely the only lie I have ever offered your mother and I have known her for twenty years. You might at least offer me the courtesy of forewarning before putting me in such circumstances again."

"I am sorry, Una," Charlotte said, touched Una had defended her. "You told Mother that? Thank you. I will make it up to you. Let me ride to Epping. I think James is meeting a woman there, a lover, and if I can catch him at it, if I can prove it, then I can fix everything. I know I can." She led the saddled horse to the stable doorway.

"And suppose you discover Lord Roding and his lover," Una said. "How will you prove it to your mother? Your word alone to the witness? You are not precisely high on her esteemed list at the moment, Charlotte."

"I have never lied to her," Charlotte said. She placed her foot in the stirrup and swung herself astride the saddle. "She will believe me."

"This entire day has been built around a lie," Una said, looking up at her sternly. "And Lady Epping is no fool. She has lost her wits to rage for the moment, but when she reclaims them, lamb, you had best believe she will figure you out. And then anything you offer as testimony against Lord Roding will be worthless."

Charlotte stared down at her, mute.

"I will go with you," Una said. "She will believe me. And with my help, we can make sure she never learns the truth about you and Lord Theydon."

"Do not be ridiculous, Una," Charlotte said. "You are not going with me."

"And how, precisely, would you discover Lord Roding with a lover otherwise? Would you simply march into the tavern, seek him out, and spy on him? He knows your face quite well, and fondly besides, or have you forgotten?"

This had not occurred to Charlotte.

"He only knows me in passing, and if you loan me

your hat for disguise, he will not know me at all," Una said.

She was right, and Charlotte knew it. "Damn it," she muttered.

"Watch your mouth," Una told her. "And give me a hand. I will ride behind you."

✳ ✳ ✳

"Be careful," she told Una, placing the tricorne hat onto Una's head and adjusting the broad brim to hide Una's face in shadows. The two stood outside of the Wake Arms inn. It was five minutes before eleven o'clock; they had arrived just in time. The tavern was in full humor, despite the late hour; the windows were aglow with bright, golden light, and the muted sounds of laughter, song, and fiddle music seeped through the thick stone walls. Plenty of men were coming and going from the pub, enough to allow for a comfortable crowd cover.

"It could be rowdy in there," Charlotte said, and Una laughed.

"I can handle myself," she said. "Who taught you to throw a proper punch?"

Charlotte smiled. "Do not tell Reilly," she said. "He thinks it was him."

Una patted Charlotte's cheek. "You keep out here and away from the stables," she instructed. "If Lord

Roding is here, Edmond Cheadle cannot be far."

Charlotte nodded. She watched Una walk purposefully up to the tavern door, as if she had every business
in the world to be there. The door opened wide, spilling out yellow light, a billowing cloud of pipe smoke,
and a deafening roar of music and voices, and then Una
ducked inside. The door closed behind her, and Charlotte was left alone, shivering in the shadows.

She paced about anxiously, eyes darting. She had
tucked her braid beneath the collar of her coat, and in
the darkness no one realized she was a woman. She
looked every bit a restless man, and shoved her hands
deep into her pockets, toying with her pistol.

"He will be leaving Eaton Square by dusk," she
heard a voice say. There was no mistaking Edmond
Cheadle's deep, resonant timbre and her heart raced in
sudden fright.

She did not turn; she forced herself to move noncha-
lantly forward, as if she had taken no notice. She heard
Cheadle's heavy footsteps behind her, moving toward the
threshold of the pub. She heard other boots falling in dis-
harmonic rhythm with his; he had companions with him.

"He will be on the road and northward bound,
at Beech Hill, by ten o'clock," Cheadle said. Charlotte turned, moving slowly, casually, and watched him
walk into the inn, the sudden swell of noise from within drowning out anything else he might have said. She

caught sight of two men on either side of him, and she gasped when she recognized them.

Julian Stockley and Camden Iden walked with Cheadle into the Wake Arms. The door closed behind them, and Charlotte stood rooted in place, trembling with confusion. What were Julian and Camden doing with Cheadle?

Charlotte tried vainly to peer through the tavern window, to catch a glimpse of the three men inside. The windows were smudged with dirt, soot, and smoke, and the pub patrons were crammed together nearly shoulder to shoulder inside; she could see nothing. She turned and began to pace again, anxiously. "What in the world is going on?" she whispered.

At last, after a painful eternity, Una came out of the inn. Charlotte rushed to her, catching her elbow and drawing her toward the stables. "Cheadle went inside," she said.

"I know," Una replied. "I saw him."

"Lords Stapleford and Hallingbury were with him," Charlotte said.

"I know," Una said. "I saw them, too. They joined Lord Roding at the back of the pub. There was no woman that I saw, only those three—Mr. Cheadle and the two barons who came to sit with Lord Roding. They fell together in conversation, but I do not know what they said. I did not want to risk drawing close enough to hear."

"I will go," Charlotte said, glancing at the tavern door. "Give me my hat back. I will slip inside and—"

"Do not be foolish, Charlotte," Una said, catching her firmly by the sleeve. "Lord Roding sits facing the full breadth of the room. He will see you."

"What could they be talking about?" Charlotte asked. "James has seen Julian and Camden all week at the parties. Why would he meet with them so late at night, and at such a place as this? Something is going on, Una. I do not know what, but I want to find out."

"Charlotte," Una said sternly, drawing her distracted gaze. "We should leave. You came here to discover Lord Roding's lover, and there is not one to be found."

"You do not think it is odd?" Charlotte asked. "The four of them meeting for no apparent purpose?"

"Their purpose does not matter," Una said. "It does not concern us. They are grown men who can meet socially as they please. Let us go. Come now, lamb. It is time to go home."

"Not yet," Charlotte said.

Una's lips pursed. "Charlotte . . ." she began.

"Not yet, Una," Charlotte insisted. "Something is going on. By my breath, I tell you there is. If they are all inside, then their horses must be in the stables. We will go there and wait for them. Maybe we will overhear something in the barn."

"Charlotte . . ." Una began again, but Charlotte

grabbed the older woman and pulled her toward the barn.

"Not yet," she said.

They waited in the stables for hours. They had ducked into a stall where Charlotte's roan was boarded, and squatted together in the fragrant hay, sheltered by the shadow of the gate. The more time that passed, the more aggravated Una grew.

"We should leave, Charlotte," she kept whispering, the furrow cleaving her brow growing deeper and deeper.

"Not yet," Charlotte kept whispering back.

At last, their patience paid off, and they heard the men's voices drawing near, entering the stable. "It is agreed then?" Charlotte heard James say. To her surprise, and Una's horror, the voices drew startlingly close to them; the four men stood directly beyond the stall gate to wait for grooms to fetch their horses.

"Beech Hill, nine-thirty?" James asked, and Charlotte heard the low rumbling sounds of Cheadle and Julian murmuring together in concurrence.

"I still say it is too risky," Camden Iden said, his tone fretful. "It is too soon, Roding. We should—"

Charlotte heard Camden yelp, and then a scuffling sound. The stall gate shuddered violently as something heavy slammed into it, cracking the wood. Charlotte and Una shrank into the shadows.

"Shut your mouth and muster some mettle," Cheadle said. Charlotte looked up, breathless with fright, and saw the back of Camden's tailed wig leaning precariously over the top of the gate. Cheadle had shoved him forcefully against it and held him pinned there with one large fist.

"Get your hands off me!" Camden gasped; apparently Cheadle had seized hold of his cravat and shirt collar, nearly throttling him.

"You will hold your peace and do your part, Hallingbury, do you hear?" James snapped. Charlotte pressed herself against the gate as she saw shadows move; James drew near to Camden, leaning close while he delivered a thinly veiled threat. "That is the plan, you simpering, witless bastard. We are all agreed to it."

Julian laughed. "Hoah, lads, do not rough him too badly," he crowed. "Hallingbury is a lover, not a fighter. Ask my sister! He plowed between her thighs often enough."

"If you muck this up for me, Hallingbury, by my breath, I will see you facedown in the Thames," James seethed, his voice floating with icy malice through the gate's wooden planks. Charlotte shivered at the sound of it; she had never heard such undisguised malevolence in all of her life.

"I . . . I will not muck it up," Camden bleated.

"You are damned right you will not," Cheadle told him. His voice was remarkably calm, nearly a purr, but tight with menace nonetheless. Charlotte had started to tremble; she shook uncontrollably.

She heard the shuffling of hooves in straw as stable hands delivered their horses. The four men exchanged mumbled farewells and took off into the night.

Charlotte and Una remained motionless for a long time after the sounds had faded, to be eclipsed again by dim fiddle melodies and drunken, boisterous song from within the pub. At last, Una closed her hand around Charlotte's. They locked gazes, and then both sighed deeply.

"I think you were right, lamb," Una whispered. Her face was as ashen with fright and her fingers were like ice against Charlotte's skin. "Something is going on."

CHAPTER 7

"CHARLOTTE, YOUR FATHER IS ASKING THAT you join him in the parlor," Meghan said from Charlotte's doorway.

It was shortly before ten o'clock in the morning. Charlotte had enjoyed precious little sleep upon her return from Epping, and had been dressed for nearly two hours. She had not left her room, taking a morning cup of coffee at her writing table, for fear of having to endure a barrage of consternation from Lady Epping.

"Is my mother with him?" she asked.

Meghan shook her head. "No," she said. "Lady Epping is still in her chamber. She has not even called for tea yet this morning."

"Oh," Charlotte said, visibly relieved. She started to rise, and then paused, her expression troubled again.

"What does he want, Meghan? Did he say?"

All at once, she worried that a night spent rethinking matters had left her out of her father's favor. Suppose Lord Epping had changed his mind, and meant for her to marry James? She must have looked overcome with trepidation, because Meghan smiled kindly at her in reassurance from the doorway.

"He did not say," she said. "But Mr. Linford, the sheriff, pays call from Epping, and they have taken coffee together in the parlor. I am sure Mr. Linford would like to discuss your robbery."

Howard Linford was a tall man with a form that would have probably been lean and fit in his youth. As age had set upon him, it had taken its toll, softening him, leaving his face and neck rounded around formerly etched angles and lines. He wore no wig; his shoulder-length grey hair was arranged wildly about his head, despite his efforts to draw it back in some semblance of a fashionable tail. His eyes were large, framed by weathered lines and swollen pockets of flesh. His justicoat was dun-colored and unadorned by embroidery; it was rumpled, in need of both mending and ironing. His boots were unpolished, scuffed, and mud-spattered from horseback riding. He struck Charlotte as somewhat bumbling upon their introduction when he offered a clumsy smile and an awkward bow.

"I was just telling your father that I am sorry it has taken me so long to pay call about the robbery," Linford said. He had jostled his cup when he rose upon her arrival. Coffee had sloshed on the rug, and he knelt, whipping a handkerchief from his jacket pocket to mop at it. When Lord Epping's butler moved to tend to the spill, Linford laughed. "I have it, sir. Do not trouble yourself. Dreadfully sorry, my lord, but it is coming right up."

"Quite all right, Mr. Linford," Lord Epping said. "Here now, let Pickernell see to it. I pay him well for such efforts."

Linford looked up, and he and Charlotte's father laughed together. "All right, then," Linford said. When he rose, he returned his attention to Charlotte, cramming the rumpled folds of his kerchief back into his pocket. "As I was saying, miss, I would have paid call sooner than this, but have had some matters in Epping to distract me. I own the local livery stables, and have hired a new hand, a nephew of sorts by way of my wife, though I would scarcely claim the boy. A sack of grain has more wits to its credit, and I have been loath to leave lest he sets fire to the barn, horses, and himself in the . . ."

His voice faded and he laughed. "But none of that matters. Pardon my digression. You have my assurances,

as I have offered them to your gracious father, that the rot
scoundrels who accosted you will be caught. I cannot
promise swiftly, because I am not God. If I was, none of
this would have happened in the first place, and I would be
living in the palace, sucking down brandy for breakfast."

Charlotte blinked at him, bewildered, and then
glanced at her father, who seemed to find Linford's
peculiarities delightfully entertaining. "Well, I . . . I
thank you kindly, sir," she said to the sheriff.

"I was just now explaining to your father that
I have printed up a mess of broadsides," Linford said.
He reached beneath the lapel of his coat for a pocket,
frowned, and reached for the other side. He patted his
hands against his jacket until he heard paper rustle, and
then found the right pocket. He produced a folded,
crumpled piece of paper and offered it to Charlotte.

NOTICE TO ALL TRAVELERS, the broadside
read in large, glaring black print. *Beware of the fiendish
highwaymen, THE BLACK TRIO, who prey upon the
unsuspecting in Epping parish. A REWARD OF FIVE
SHILLINGS is offered for information resulting in the
capture of these rogues who, while clad in black vestments
and bearing arms, have stalked the highways of our fair
parish, terrifying our citizens with their HEINOUS AND
FELONIOUS ENDEAVORS. These brazen scoundrels
assault at will, performing those most abhorrent crimes
of: HIGHWAY ROBBERY, BODILY ASSAULT and*

WANTON BATTERY.

"Five shillings?" Charlotte asked. "That is a very generous reward, Father."

"Yes, I thought as much myself," Linford said, before Lord Epping could reply. "The Earl must have taken a shine of sorts to you, miss, to front such a goodly sum on your behalf."

"The Earl?" Charlotte said, startled.

"Lord Essex has generously offered the reward, Charlotte," Lord Epping told her. "He had word delivered to Mr. Linford yesterday."

"Oh," Charlotte whispered. "He . . . you may wish to contact him before you post these, Mr. Linford," she said. "I . . . I do not know if his generosity would still be so inclined, given that yesterday, I . . . well, you see . . . his son . . ."

"It does not matter," Lord Epping said. "If Lord Essex will not see it posted, then I will tender it from my own purse."

"And I had the opportunity to speak with the Earl's son last night in Epping," Linford said, drawing Charlotte's gaze. "Lord Roding, a pleasant enough chap. He told me the reward would be met gladly. I heard his man's account of things, given he was your coachman that evening. What is his name? Cheadle. Big fellow. I cannot rightly see how he did not dispatch the bandits for you. Though three against one, no matter the one's girth, are poor odds."

There was something in Linford's eyes when he spoke. He seemed to study Charlotte intensely, in an almost inquisitive fashion. "I thought I might take your recollections of events, Miss Engle," he said.

Charlotte regarded him for a long moment. He did not believe Cheadle's account; she could see it in his eyes. "Very well, sir," she said, and Linford nodded, smiling.

She sat beside her father and described the robbery. She was somewhat surprised when Linford produced a small ledger and slate pencil from his coat pocket. While she spoke, he jotted in the ledger. He noticed her curious attention almost at once, and laughed sheepishly.

"I have a dreadful memory for details," he said, tapping his pencil against his brow. "My wife is fond to tell me I would waltz out-of-doors without my head most mornings, were it not attached by God's good foresight to my neck."

Charlotte smiled politely, and Lord Epping laughed. She continued her accounting of the robbery. Linford listened with an interested expression and little interjection or commentary. He held her gaze evenly except to glance at his notebook and scribble a line here and there. She tried to tell the story as Cheadle likely had; she had no idea why she should lie for Cheadle's benefit, but she had incurred enough of her mother's disapproving wrath for one week without adding to it with tales of punching and cursing at highwaymen.

"So they clapped Mr. Cheadle about, but they did not harm you," Linford said when she had finished.

"No, sir," she said.

"Because it is my understanding one of them groped you in rather untoward fashion," Linford said, a continuation of his previous comment that nearly overlapped her reply. "Lord Roding told me this and Mr. Cheadle recounted it as well. His hand down your stay, that is what they told me."

"Have you ever tried to put your hand down a lady's stay, Mr. Linford?" Charlotte asked. "I can scarcely draw breath in full when it is cinched. There is hardly room for me inside, much less the whole of a man's hand. The highwayman put his fingertips here, like this . . ." She demonstrated. "I was wearing a fichu fastened with a brooch. The brooch clasp is broken. I could not get it undone. He thought I was lying and tried for himself. That is all."

"Did he take the pin?" Linford asked.

"No, he did not."

Linford made a thoughtful, harrumphing sound. "That was kind of him," he remarked, scribbling a little note in his ledger. Charlotte had to resist the urge to lean forward, her curiosity stoked, to see what he was writing.

"Yes, I thought so as well," she said.

"It is peculiar they did no more than this," Linford

said. "A fetching young lady, if you will pardon the observation, traveling alone, her only capable chaperone beaten to semi-lucid helplessness. Most highwaymen would have treated you with far less courtesy, if you gather my inference."

She gathered indeed. "I think they rather pride themselves on being gentlemanly," she said. "That is what he told me, anyway."

Linford raised his brow. "You carried on quite a conversation with this lad, did you not?"

"I insulted him plainly, and he offered retort, if that constitutes a conversation, sir," Charlotte said. Her tone had grown defensive; her posture had stiffened, and she had no idea why. She was answering Linford's questions as if she drew offense on the highwaymen's behalf and felt ridiculously helpless to prevent herself.

She had given some thought only the night before as to why the highwaymen had not raped or molested her. She had told Una about the gazette clipping she had discovered among Cheadle's possessions with the note, *Suitable for our needs?*

"Perhaps Lords Roding, Hallingbury, and Stapleford are the highwaymen," Una had mused. "Mr. Cheadle drove your coach. Perhaps he delivered us deliberately to be robbed."

"They are not the Black Trio," Charlotte had replied. "Do you think if James had the opportunity to have his way with me—anonymously at that—he would have passed it up? He can scarcely tear his eyes from my breasts when we are face to face and in public surroundings. And by that measure, do you think he would let Julian or Camden touch me? No, there is no way they are the highwaymen. I think Cheadle is interested in claiming the reward for their capture. That is why he had the clipping."

"I have been sheriff of this county for twelve years, Miss Engle," Linford said. "And I have yet to meet a highway bandit who was a gentleman besides, no matter what the songs and chapbooks tell you." He rose to his feet, tucking his pencil and ledger into his coat pocket. "I have taken up your morning with such unpleasant recollections, and I apologize to you both."

"Not at all, sir," Lord Epping said, rising. "We are grateful to you for your efforts."

"Yes, sir, truly indeed," Charlotte said, standing beside her father.

Lord Epping reached into a pocket of his gilet, producing a small coin purse. He slipped out a penny and offered it to the sheriff.

"I will see these broadsides posted," Linford said, nodding at Lord Epping in thanks as he tucked the penny in his fob pocket. "We will find the lot, do not fret for it. No highwayman preying in Essex has avoided capture for too long. I even damn near laid my hands on

Dick Turpin's scruff once, did I mention?"

"Dick Turpin?" Lord Epping exclaimed, delighted. "I will be damned!"

"Hoah, yes, caught him galloping through the forest on that mare of his, Black Bess, in 1737, I do believe. Mid-summer. Anyway, he beat my horse's stride and was gone. I never had a clear shot at him for the trees, or another chance at his hide."

"They caught him in Yorkshire, did they not?" Lord Epping asked.

"Hoah, yes, strung him high and throttled him well," Linford said. Lord Epping offered his hand, and the sheriff clasped palms with him, exchanging a hearty shake. "Good day to you, my lord, and to you, miss."

❋ ❋ ❋

Kenley arrived promptly at eleven o'clock. He was handsomely dressed in an exquisite ensemble, a dark justicoat accentuated by broad panels of vertical embroidery running from the high-throated collar to the flaps of his coat tails. This same pattern of embroidery trimmed the cuffs of his breeches; his waistcoat was made of panels of silk dyed a complementary hue to his jacket, decorated with matching embroidered accents. Every portion of his form was meticulously settled, from his carefully coiffed campaign wig, to his impeccably arranged cravat and stock, to the starched, spotless lengths of his stockings. Simply to see him cutting such a striking and magnificent figure, Charlotte could scarcely catch her breath.

"Miss Engle," he said in greeting, slipping her hand into his own. He stooped in a deep, graceful bow, bussing her knuckles lightly with his lips. "You look radiant."

"Thank you, my lord," Charlotte said, struggling not to stammer or smile goofily at him when he lifted his gaze, straightening his spine. She dropped a curtsy for him.

His manners were as pristine as his appearance that morning. Not even Lady Epping's aloof reception seemed to dissuade him. He bowed for her as if she welcomed him graciously and with opened arms into her home. Where Lady Epping was unmoved, however, Lord Epping was absolutely charmed. As they retired to the parlor for tea, Charlotte distinctly heard her father tell Caroline, "A splendid boy, do you not think? Simply a delight!"

Reilly was noticeably absent from the gathering. He had left before dawn, setting out by horseback for unknown destinations, and despite being perfectly aware of the morning's appointment, he had not returned. This was yet another burr in Lady Epping's pannier, but one she wielded to some disparaging advantage when Kenley noticed, and inquired politely.

"He seemed a bit taken aback to learn of his sister's

engagement," Lady Epping said. She peered at Kenley as if he were a smudge of dirt she had only just discovered upon the rug. "Peculiar, really. I should think that among us all, Reilly would be the most in favor, considering he is the one who calls you a friend."

"Oh, Mother, Reilly had a poker up his ass before that," Caroline said. "He is delighted by the news, Lord Theydon, as are we all, and I am certain he will be with us shortly. He often loses track of things . . . the time, the world about him, his own obligations within it."

Pickernell, the butler, set about pouring tea and presenting a tray arranged with a variety of freshly baked scones. The food, though appetizing in its aroma, remained untouched, and they all sat in a broad circumference, sipping at their tea as an awkward silence settled upon the parlor. Charlotte glanced at Kenley and he met her gaze briefly, dropping her a quick wink, as if to reassure her in her mounting anxiety. Despite this, she did not feel any relief; her mother was sitting quietly again for the moment, but it was the sort of calm exhibited by a patient cat simply awaiting its moment to pounce at a hapless mouse.

"So you have taken up residence at Theydon Hall once more, I have heard," Lord Epping said to Kenley, breaking the silence so abruptly and brightly that Charlotte jumped, sloshing her tea into the shallow basin of her saucer.

"Yes, my lord, as of last month," Kenley replied. "My uncle, the former Lord Woodside, endeavored to maintain it in some manner of upkeep, but it was a difficult task given the number of years it stood empty. It needs some attention, but I have been tending to it as I am able. As for furnishings and décor, I am afraid it is rather lacking. It is my understanding such tasks are best left to the more capable eyes of a house's lady."

"Well, then, you have good fortune, indeed. Charlotte has marvelous tastes," Caroline said.

"I am sure they were instilled by her mother," Kenley observed, looking pointedly about the parlor. "As I dare say, this is the most resplendent home I have ever visited."

He happened to glance at Lady Epping when he made this remark, apparently hoping to endear himself somewhat in her regard. Charlotte wished she had been able to forewarn him of such effort's ultimate futility; she visibly winced when Lady Epping arched her brow and opened her mouth to speak.

"It is my understanding, Lord Theydon, that you have been jailed before," she said.

The silence that had only just waned returned in a rush. Caroline and Lord Epping both stared at Lady Epping, startled by her audacity, while Charlotte unsteadily set her tea on a table.

"Mother . . ." she began.

Kenley smiled, disarming and unoffended. "My lady speaks out of general honest thought, and common concern for her daughter's reputation and well-being," he said. "As is only proper and natural. Yes, Lady Epping, I have been jailed in my past, and pilloried as well. Momentary lapses in good judgment during my youth saw me in trouble for brawling, drinking, pickpocketing, and burglary. I wish I could offer more than heartfelt remorse for my ill-considered folly, and my solemn word that I will never know such occasion again. I would not see your daughter shamed, my lady, or you."

Lady Epping held his gaze, clearly unimpressed. Before she could snipe back some untoward response, however, Lord Epping harrumphed loudly. "Well, lad, of course not," he said. "While some noble sons never see the inside of a jail cell, it does not mean the lot of us have never deserved to. I do not know a man alive who has not enjoyed some manner of similar boyhood mischief. Why, as for myself, when I was nineteen, I drew offense at a raucous cad who called me a ninny. Challenged him outright to a proper duel, to which he agreed. I shot him clear through and with first blood drawn. His right arm is yet crippled. You might know him. Lord Childerditch of Brentwood?"

Caroline glanced at Charlotte, drawing a linen napkin toward her mouth to muffle a snicker of laughter.

"Truly, my lord?" Kenley asked, raising his brows,

dutifully impressed.

"It was folly, just as you say," Lord Epping said, flapping his hand, pleased by the younger man's interest. "He lobbed a shot at me, but providence proved in my favor, I suppose. The pellet struck my breast pocket, where I keep my snuff box by habit and nature. Dented the bloody hell out of it—nearly crimped it in two. I have it yet as a souvenir, given it saved my life and what-not."

"That is a remarkable turn of fortune, truly, my lord," Kenley said.

The two men leaned toward one another, both smiling, the tension Lady Epping had stoked forgotten in full. Charlotte glanced at Caroline and found her sister smiling at her as she lifted her tea cup. "I told you, lamb," she said softly.

"Returning to the matter of Theydon Hall," Lady Epping said loudly. "And your forthcoming and unexpected marriage to our daughter . . ."

"Yes, my lady," Kenley said. "Of course, my lady. I beg your pardon for my digression."

"Your home is unfurnished?" Lady Epping asked, raising a disdainful brow.

"For the moment," Kenley said carefully. "Yes, my lady. I have some personal possessions, a few pieces of furniture that belonged to my father my uncle was gracious enough to keep for me. But beyond this, as I said, I had hoped my lady might make proper arrangements."

"And the house is in disrepair?" Lady Epping said. "You described its state rather kindly, considering how I have heard tell of it—dilapidated and crumbling, mildewed and moldering."

"It does need some maintenance, yes, my lady," Kenley conceded.

"And yet you expect my daughter to call this her home?" Lady Epping asked. "You would make her the proper lady of a house that is in such a sorry state?"

"Mother, stop it," Charlotte said, drawing Lady Epping's gaze.

"I would like to know, darling," Lady Epping said. "Lord Theydon proclaimed yesterday that the two of you entered this arrangement with some aforethought and unhasty preparations. I would simply like to discover where the ruinous state of his home fits into your provisions."

"It is a reasonable concern, and one which I share in full, my lady," Kenley said to Charlotte, who was amazed. Nothing her mother threw at him seemed to fluster him in the slightest. She could not comprehend how he managed to maintain such an unoffended exterior, when it was all she could personally do at the moment not to reach out, clasp her hands about her mother's throat, and throttle her.

"You have my promise that I will see my house restored to comfortable quarters before I ever lead Charlotte as my wife across the threshold," Kenley said. "Already,

I have begun such endeavors. Many of them I have seen to through my own undertaking."

"Oh, are you handy about the house?" Caroline asked. "What a delight. My husband, Randall, is simply dreadful. The corner of a rug upturns and he stands there, blinking and bewildered, at a complete loss to correct it."

"I suppose you will be dependent upon a dowry to help in the rest of these repairs," Lady Epping said to Kenley.

"Not at all, my lady," he replied. "Upon his death, my uncle endowed me with gracious funds. Enough that I should never need or want for anything, and by my word, my lady, neither will my wife. I would see a dowry spent where it can only increase this security for us."

Lady Epping looked momentarily puzzled. "I do not understand your meaning," she said.

"I would invest it, my lady," Kenley said. "I have heard that the coal mining, steel, and commerce industries are all poised for substantial growth, and that many nobles within London are taking advantage of such blossoming profit potentials. I would do the same."

Kenley flashed Charlotte a fleeting glance, a crooked smile. She nearly laughed aloud, despite her fury with Lady Epping, and drew her hand toward her mouth to cover her sudden, delighted snort.

"I have a splendid idea," Caroline announced, leaping headlong into the fray before Lady Epping could challenge Kenley's proposal. "Lord Theydon, why do you not bring Charlotte to Theydon Hall today? My sister is of a capable eye and level head. Her opinion on the state of repairs, and ideas for décor would surely help expedite your own efforts."

Lady Epping started to speak, but she could not get a word out of her mouth before Lord Epping beat her to it. "Caroline, darling, that is a lovely thought," he declared. "Splendid indeed. Yes, lad, if it pleases you, I think that would be quite in order!"

"I . . . I would be delighted, my lord," he said. "If . . . that is, if Charlotte would consent upon such short notice?"

"She cannot go without proper chaperone," Lady Epping snapped, clearly meaning to impose herself on the outing.

"True enough," Lord Epping said. "Mrs. Renfred served her well in that capacity while in London. I think her company on this occasion would again wholly suffice."

Lady Epping sputtered ineffectually.

"Mrs. Renfred?" Kenley said, clearly puzzled.

"Yes, my maid, Una," Charlotte said, locking gazes with him and grinning broadly. "You remember Una, surely."

He returned her smile. "Oh, certainly, yes, Mrs.

Renfred. Such a delight. I have missed her acquaintance. It would be splendid to see her again."

"Then it is settled," Lord Epping said, clapping his hands once. He rose to his feet. "Caroline, why do you not help your sister find Mrs. Renfred, and summon her redingote and muff? I should like to borrow our young Lord Theydon before they depart. That snuff box of mine, of which I have made mention, is upstairs in a highboy drawer, if you would like to see it?"

Kenley stood, lowering his head in deference to Lord Epping. "My lord, I would be most pleased," he said.

CHAPTER 8

"MASTER WILLIAM! YOU ARE HOME!" exclaimed the withered, wiry old man who greeted them at the door of Theydon Hall. His face was long and lined with wrinkles, his skin the fragile texture of aged parchment. He smiled broadly, the creases in his cheeks and about his eyes crimping all the more deeply.

"It is Kenley, Albert," Kenley said with a gentle smile, letting the man embrace him, patting his shoulders with spindly, crooked hands. He turned his face to the man's and pressed his lips lightly on his cheek.

The man, Albert, blinked, seeming momentarily confused, and then his gaze settled upon Charlotte and Una, standing upon the threshold behind Kenley. His expression grew stricken, and he stared at Kenley, stammering helplessly. "Oh," he said. "Oh, I . . . of course, that is right. You have told me. I remember it plainly, and here I . . . I thought . . ."

"It is all right," Kenley said. "Do not fret for it, Albert. No harm." He turned to Una and Charlotte and smiled. "This is my butler, Albert Standage. Albert, may I introduce Miss Charlotte Engle, and her companion, Mrs. Una Renfred?"

Albert's smile restored at the mention of Charlotte's name. "Yes, splendid!" he exclaimed, shuffling in Charlotte's direction, his hands outstretched. "My lord has spoken often of you these past days, and with such fondness! I tell him it is a welcome distraction for him—he is a good boy and he should not keep cooped up in this moldering house with a moldering old man like me. He needs a lovely young lass to seize such hold of his heart as you have."

Charlotte laughed. "It is a pleasure to meet you, Albert," she said. She noted Kenley's focus was on his shoes, seeming somewhat embarrassed by Albert's admittance.

"Yes, well . . ." he said clumsily, making a show of peering across the threshold and into the foyer. She could have sworn he was blushing, and struggled not to laugh at him in his flustered state. "Hoah," Kenley said. "Where is Lewis?"

"I am up on your roof, you bloody bastard, trying to level out your half-rotted rafters and lay in some new peg tiles," called a voice from somewhere outside and above them. Kenley laughed, walking backward, and rather heedlessly, down the front steps of his house, craning his head back.

"Good! You are home again. Shuck that ninnyish jacket and get your bloody ass up here to help me!" Charlotte heard Lewis shout. She followed Kenley back down the steps, curious and amused. "How was your visit? Did Lady Epping leave any hide and sinew attached to your bones, or did she gnaw—oh, hullo, Charlotte."

Lewis looked down at them from the roof, three stories above them. His face was decidedly flushed, having caught sight of Charlotte, and she laughed at his mortification.

"My mother was as pleasant as she can muster on short notice, Lord Woodside," she called up to him. "But I will be pleased to offer her your fondest regards."

Lewis was in the process of patching one of the larger deteriorated sections of Theydon Hall's roof. Charlotte had taken notice of the ladder propped against the side of the house from their approach by carriage. Large quantities of peg tiles were stacked about the ladder on wide flaps of burlap. The two cousins had rigged a pulley system to the roof, and used lengths of heavy rope to draw the corners of the burlap closed and haul the tiles up the significant height.

To her observance, poor Theydon Hall needed to be

razed and built anew. It sat squarely in the center of a
broad meadow southeast of Darton, just beyond the pe-
rimeter of Epping Forest. It faced the long, winding,
rutted avenue leading up to it with a stern and solemn
façade, dark gray stone walls with large, expansive windows, and a roof marked by a half dozen chimneys and
three steeply pitched peaks on each side. Three stories in
height, it boasted twenty rooms or more within, to judge
by the breadth of its exterior. It was surrounded by trees:
tall, wayward firs, ivy-draped, crooked maples, and stoic,
piston-straight oaks.

The house's magnificent windows were all barren of
glass; the wink of muted sunlight through clouds against
broken panes bore mute witness to what had befallen
the others. The roof was littered with autumn's fallen
leaves—years' worth, from the looks of it—along with
broken limbs and fallen branches. In places, Charlotte
could see damage to the peg tiles; large sections had
crumbled inward, leaving gaping holes. The chimneys
were likewise in sorry states, with mortar visibly yielding
between the stones.

Lewis looked down at Kenley, seeming completely
untroubled by the rather abrupt and dramatic drop only
inches away from where he squatted. "You did not tell
me we were expecting company," he called.

"I did not know to expect it myself," Kenley called
back. "Are you going to come down, or shall we join you

up there?"

Lewis laughed. He reached out and grabbed the pulley line to the ground. Charlotte gasped when he stepped off the roof and into the open air. He swung away from the wall and dropped gracefully to the lawn. As he lowered himself, a heavy bundle of peg tiles rose skyward, counterbalancing his descent. He let his heels drop in the grass and then carefully eased the rope between his gloved hands, lowering the tiles to the yard again.

"Like swinging from the top yard," he told Charlotte, dropping her a wink.

"Do not dare tell me you and Reilly cavorted about the ship heights like that," she said.

"The heights, shrouds, ratlines, and rigging," Lewis declared proudly. "We are Royal Navy, not simpering ninnies. A little distance between your ass and the ground is no more than some wind and a change in perspective, I have always liked to think."

"Lewis, I will draw the carriage around and help with the horses," Kenley said. "Would you mind showing Charlotte and Mrs. Renfred to the parlor? Maybe put some tea on?"

"Not at all," Lewis said, waving his hand in beckon. "Come on, ladies."

Charlotte and Una followed Lewis "Is that man truly Kenley's butler?" she asked, puzzled. Albert looked seventy-five, if a day, far too old and frail to be tending to household duties.

"Who? Albert?" Lewis, stepped aside and allowed Una and Charlotte polite first entry into the foyer. "No, no. Albert is practically family. He was coachman to Kenley's father before Kenley was even born. Albert came to work for my father's stables when Lord Theydon passed. He has been at Woodside ever since, though in no real capacity. I am simply fond of him."

He closed the door behind them. "As is Kenley," he remarked. "More so, even, I should say. He invited Albert to come and live with him here at Theydon, but Albert is far too proud to undertake anything like charity. So Kenley made him his butler, at least in name."

Charlotte looked around the expansive foyer. The floors were of dark granite, matching the exterior of the house. She saw piles of windswept, forgotten leaves in the corners, and cobwebs shrouding the far edges of the ceiling. The dust was thick enough on the floor that footpaths were visible, marking commonly trod routes to a parlor, back corridor, and sweeping staircase.

"Has he no other staff?" she asked, craning her head back and studying a chandelier above them, its candles long since removed or fallen from cradles, its broad, gracefully extended arms draped in cobwebs and coated in dust.

"Not at the moment," Lewis replied, his footsteps echoing as he walked toward the parlor.

Charlotte and Una exchanged surprised glances. A house the size of Theydon must certainly command a full staff of no less than twenty, including the stable hands. Charlotte could not fathom two men, one of them frail and elderly at that, keeping up with all that was required.

"But Kenley makes do," Lewis said. "I have been staying with him and we have managed to work a few rooms into livable condition, I think. The other twenty-four or so we keep behind closed doors for now."

Charlotte and Una followed him into the parlor. A fire had been built in the broad fireplace, and a pair of dining chairs arranged before it. A small table stood between them. Judging by the half-filled decanter of brandy, a pair of empty snifters, and a littered pile of books surrounding the chairs, Charlotte judged this to be a place Kenley spent a good portion of his time.

"Why did Albert call Kenley 'William'?" she asked.

Lewis crossed the room to add some wood to the blaze. He paused, glancing over his shoulder.

"When he opened the door, he said, 'Master William, you are home,'" Charlotte said.

"Albert is old and slightly addled sometimes," Lewis said. "He gets confused. It happens quite a bit. William Sutton was a stable boy when he worked here at Theydon. Albert was fond of him and mistakes Kenley sometimes." He indicated the chairs. "Please," he said in invitation. "I will go hunt down some more seats and put the water on."

"Is William the stable boy who used to come with you and Kenley to Darton?" Charlotte asked, giving him pause again. "I remember one your father used to let you play with, and that my mother disapproved of it."

"You have a keen memory," Lewis said with a nod. "Yes, that was Will. He and Kenley were close in age and nearly as inseparable as kin."

"Where is he now?" Charlotte asked.

Lewis blinked, the smile fading from his face. "He died," he said, and Charlotte was immediately abashed that she had asked. "Shortly after my father. It broke Kenley's heart."

Charlotte did not know what to say.

"Please, make yourselves at ease," Lewis said, struggling to smile again. "I will be but a moment."

❉ ❉ ❉

"You have a lovely home, Lord Theydon," Una said when Kenley rejoined them. Lewis had accompanied Albert to the kitchen to finish preparing a tray of tea, and in his cousin's absence, Kenley seemed uncharacteristically shy.

He smiled at Una's remark. While they had taken seats in the chairs, he knelt near the fireplace, pretending to busy himself by poking an iron rod against the flame-lapped logs. "You are kind to say so, Mrs. Renfred," he said. "I know it must seem a mess. My uncle did his best to keep it from ruin, but it is a large house, as you can see. He had his own to oversee. I cannot blame him for letting this one deteriorate."

Charlotte watched intermingling shadows of melancholy and pride tussle for dominance in his eyes, the set of his brows. "It will be lovely again some day," he said, prodding at the coals with the poker.

"If it would please you, my lord, I would be glad to lend my services to you," Una said, and Kenley looked up at her, puzzled and surprised. "As a proper housekeeper, my lord, at least for a time. I tended to such a position at Darton until just last year, when my daughter, Meghan, took over in my stead. I grew up south of here in Loughton. I yet have family there, and many friends. I could easily arrange to hire a staff of local lasses for you, some boys for your stables. I think it would help you, my lord. It would ease the burden of your labors here if you had suitable servants to tend to these interior affairs."

Kenley rose to his feet. "That is very kind of you, Mrs. Renfred," he said. "But I . . . I could not dare to impose on your responsibilities to Lady Epping or Charlotte . . ."

Una waved her hand dismissively. "Charlotte is to be the lady of Theydon Hall shortly," she said. "I would be doing more service to her here than at Darton."

Kenley glanced at Charlotte, but she was as surprised by Una's offer as he was. "I . . . that would be lovely, Mrs. Renfred," Kenley said. "And I would be very grateful."

"Perhaps Lord Woodside and Albert could show me around the house," Una said. "I could level my head for what needs to be set upon first. You could escort Charlotte about your grounds. It is a fair enough day; the fog has faded, and the clouds drawn away awhile. Some fresh air might suit her."

"I would be pleased to," Kenley said.

"Pleased to what?" Lewis asked, walking in from the foyer, balancing a tray with tea pot and cups on his palm.

"I have hired a housekeeper, Lewis," Kenley said.

Lewis arched his brow and laughed. "Well, and by time," he said. "Welcome to the eighteenth century, cousin."

❀   ❀   ❀

"I would like to have a Palladian garden built here," Kenley said, as he and Charlotte walked together along the back side of the house. She kept one hand tucked in her muff, the other draped over the proffered crook of his elbow. The uncertain silence that had lingered between them ever since leaving Darton Hall remained, and they made idle conversation, like no more than casual acquaintances.

"Lord Theydon never had much of a mind for land-scaping," Kenley said. "I am afraid he did not have much of a mind for anything except brandy, cards, and dice. The house was in a sad state long before it ever stood empty."

"Is it strange for you?" she asked, thinking of what Caroline had told her. *He was a very unhappy boy. Angry, I suppose, and that is why he found trouble for himself. With a father like Lord Theydon, I imagine the poor thing had plenty to feel angry and unhappy about.* "Being here at Theydon Hall again, I mean?"

He smiled slightly, somewhat sadly. "Sometimes," he admitted. "I have a good number of fond memories here . . . and a fair number of poor ones besides. I try to dwell upon the former, rather than the latter."

Charlotte nodded. She drew in a deep breath and watched the hem of her redingote flap with each step. "Why are you doing this, Kenley?" she asked at length, her voice soft and tremulous.

"Showing you the hall? Your sister offered seeming escape," he replied. "I did not seem to be charming your mother to any effect, and thought it might be in order."

"No," Charlotte said, shaking her head. She stopped, forcing him to pause as well. "I mean, why are you doing any of this? Why did you step forward yesterday? Why did you say you would marry me?"

"Because I would marry you, Charlotte," he replied.

"That startles you?"

"You do not even know me," she said. "You have only known me three days. How could you possibly want to marry me?"

He turned to face her in full. "You kissed me despite having known me only days," he said pointedly.

"Well, that was different," she said. "People kiss all the time without the pretense of marriage, and . . ." Her voice faded and her eyes flashed. "And I beg your pardon. I did not kiss you. You are the one who kissed me."

"And I was the first you let do so, am I right?" he asked. Charlotte flushed brightly, her mouth opening as she stammered some unintelligible, sputtering reply. "There is no shame in it," he said. "I find it rather charming, as a matter of fact."

"How . . . how did you . . . ?"

"Know? It did not take a scholar. You stiffened against me like a plank of wood."

"I did not," Charlotte protested.

He chuckled. "You most certainly did. I could not tell at first if it pleased or horrified you."

"It took me aback," Charlotte said. "It was very impertinent and rude of you besides, and I was fairly well shocked, considering I had enjoyed our conversation, and had not anticipated you would conclude it in such a . . . a caddish, impulsive fashion."

"And yesterday at Rycroft?" he asked.

"At Rycroft, I could scarcely offer protest, as you kept stifling my mouth with your own. And by some sense of propriety and the faith you might be a proper gentleman, I simply . . ." Her voice faded and she hoisted her chin, meeting his gaze squarely. "How dare you turn this about and upon me? You kissed me on all occasions. I asked you repeatedly to stop and you were fairly well insistent in your efforts to the contrary."

Kenley laughed, and she fumed. "Why are you laughing?" she demanded.

"Because this is precisely why I would marry you, Charlotte," he told her, cupping her face between his hands. "You are wondrous, woman! By my breath, are you so blind to it? Any other daughter at that party I might have kissed and offered to wed, and they would be swooning upon themselves, and me besides. You, I kiss and offer to marry, and you puzzle over it, seeking some motive. You challenge it; you challenge me. You grow angry over it all because it defies any semblance of logic you deem proper."

"It defies logic anyone would deem proper, if they knew the truth of it," Charlotte said, shaking her head slightly to dislodge his hands.

"You fascinate me," he said. "I thought as much the first time I read your essays. 'Who is this woman?' I asked myself. It plagued me with wonder—what woman in her right mind would hold such ideas and notions so firmly and dearly to her heart and mind? What woman would set pen to paper to pronounce them publicly, without thought to hide her sex or status from those who would certainly turn upon her views with criticism and disdain?"

"No woman in her right mind, if you heed my aunt and mother," Charlotte said.

"And quite possibly the most perfect woman I might hope to imagine," Kenley told her. "You know the social circus, Charlotte. We spoke of it at Chapford Manor. You and I are helpless pennies tossed atop a tremendous card table, and all of our fellows are laying down their cards to have their chance to claim us. I am weary of lovely, powdered, primped ladies offering vacuous stares and bewildered looks should I dare make mention of a word exceeding two syllables in conversation. I have never lived my life like this, properly affected and displaying good breeding. I am accustomed to my habits and fairly settled in my ways, and while I play the game well, I am tired of it. Are you not? You cannot tell me you are not. I saw it on your face when Roding announced he would wed you."

Charlotte regarded him silently. Everything he said might have come straight and poignantly from her own heart, the desperate words she had longed to cry to her mother for years.

"You would never be someone cherished to James

Houghton," he said. "A partner and an equal whose opinions are valued, whose counsel is willingly, gratefully sought. You would be the silver coin he claimed after a long, hard-fought hand, and he would take the fire that is within you and he would see it more than waned, Charlotte. He would see it suffocated, extinguished. And that I cannot allow. Not after only just finding you. I had begun to believe I never would."

He brushed her cheek with his fingertips. "I could know you three days, three years—three minutes, Charlotte—and it would make no difference. I knew it from the start, from the moment I met you."

"You . . . you cannot love me," she whispered, tilting her face up to his, allowing him to brush his lips against hers.

She closed her eyes as his other hand touched her cheek, as the warmth of his palms enfolded her face. "I beg to differ," he breathed, and he kissed her.

Whatever hope she might have had to offer rebuttal or objection abandoned her, along with her wits and wind. His lips settled on hers, and she opened her mouth eagerly, whimpering when his tongue pressed against hers. She drew his breath as her own, and within her; it felt natural and right, as if they had been meant to come together like this, in an intermingling of breath and voice.

He held her face between his hands and canted

his head, moving, pressing himself fiercely against her. Charlotte drew her hands beneath his arms, her fingers splaying against his shoulders and felt his strength, the lean muscles bridging the graceful span between his spine and limbs beneath the heavy wool of his coat.

Kenley eased her gently backward until she felt her pannier bow against the wall of the house. He pinned her to the stones, his mouth abandoning hers for the slope of her throat. She gasped for breath as his mouth stoked sudden, urgent heat within her, a tremulous fluttering throughout her form. The tip of his tongue brushed lightly, deliberately beneath the angle of her jaw, and then moved toward her ear. Each breath against her skin—cool upon the draw, warm and slow upon the exhalation—sent her senses reeling, her mind fading to simple, exquisite pleasure. His left hand slipped from her face, sliding with delicious friction along the line of her neck to her bosom.

Charlotte's breath hitched in anticipation, her shoulders drawing back, her breasts seeming to swell and strain against the confines of her corset in anticipation of his touch. His hand moved slowly against her breast, his fingers curling to match her contours, his palm applying soft but insistent pressure. He moved his hand in deep, rhythmic circles that immediately ignited bright heat, and a myriad of dizzying sensations from her breast She could not think; she could not breathe. When he settled his mouth against hers, his hand yet moving, the pressure of his palm and fingers firm and deliberate, she clutched at his shoulders, her voice escaping in a soft, breathless moan.

His lips left hers, and his breath fluttered, hoarse with longing as his hand slipped slowly from her breast. She lifted her chin, letting her nose brush against his, their lips dancing together lightly, fleetingly. Her body trembled and ached from his abandoned touch, straining for his hands to find her again, to linger on her.

"Marry me, Charlotte," he whispered.

She nodded, letting her lips touch his, feeling his breath against her mouth. "Yes," she said softly, making him smile. "Yes, Kenley."

CHAPTER 9

"ARE YOU ANGRY WITH ME, REILLY?" CHAR-
lotte asked, standing hesitantly at her brother's doorway.
She had returned to Darton Hall in a giddy daze, only
to be reminded that the warm happiness she had enjoyed at Theydon Hall was not all-encompassing. Her
mother had fairly well barricaded herself in her chamber,
refusing to emerge even for supper, leaving Charlotte,
Caroline, Reilly, and Lord Epping to an uncomfortable
meal without her.

Charlotte had kept her gaze trained upon her plate
during supper, but when she glanced up occasionally,
it was to find Reilly's brows narrowed in visible, undisguised disapproval. She did not understand his reaction;
her mother had made the observation scornfully, but
the tone did not refute its accuracy. Kenley was Reilly's

friend. Charlotte would have thought her brother would
be pleased for them, if not happy.

Several hours had passed since supper, and it was
dark beyond the window panes. Reilly stood by his
fireplace, cradling a snifter of brandy in his palm as
he watched flames lick at the dry, crackling wood. He
turned his head at her anxious tone and met her gaze.

"Why would I be angry with you, Charlotte?" he
asked. He brought the rim of his glass to his mouth and
canted his head back, draining the brandy in a single
swallow. He turned and crossed the room for his writing table, where a decanter stood uncapped. She noticed
the tabletop, and the floor around it, were littered with
newspapers; it looked as though Reilly had sent his valet
out that day to collect every daily gazette printed in the
county.

"I . . . I do not know," Charlotte said, watching him
refill his snifter. Again, he drank it dry in a solitary swallow. Judging by the amount of brandy remaining in the
decanter, he had been drinking it quite rapidly. He poured
another glass and turned to her, arching his brow.

"Why indeed," he remarked. "So you do not want
to marry James Houghton. Why would I be angry about
that? I have already told you plainly. I understand your
point of view. I sympathize in full with your plight."

He walked back to the fireplace. Charlotte stepped
into the room. "Reilly," she said, concerned for him

when he stumbled.

"Why would I be angry that Kenley Fairfax is a self-absorbed, witless bastard?" Reilly remarked, gazing down at the fire. "An impetuous, reckless, incorrigible yob who acts without thinking, speaks without consideration, and does precisely what he sets his mind to—regardless of sensible counsel to the contrary?"

He glanced at Charlotte. "Why would this make me angry?" he asked.

"That is not true," she protested. "Kenley is your friend, Reilly. He adores you. What are you . . . why would you say such terrible things about him?"

"He adores me?" Reilly asked, pivoting to face her fully. "He apparently adores no one but himself, Charlotte. Obviously, he has no mind for anything except that which serves him. He has demonstrated he cannot think of others; he cannot lend one moment's coherent, rational thought to how the things he does, the words he says—the bloody foolhardy decisions he plows headlong and heedlessly into—affect others around him!" His voice rose sharply, making her flinch.

"He does not listen!" Reilly snapped. "And, I suppose, to stand here and tell you to call off this preposterous ruse of an engagement would be wasted breath, because you do not listen, either. Yes, I am angry at you, Charlotte. I am bloody rot furious with you, and with Kenley. Neither of you wield a whit of sense. You are both bloody damn idiots!"

"I am not an idiot," Charlotte said, her confusion fading to sudden anger

"You are an idiot if you marry him," Reilly said. "If you had any sense, you would let this go. You have triumphed over Mother. You have slapped her well and soundly into place, Charlotte. Congratulations all around! Do you not feel pleased? Does this not satisfy you? You have caused your stir, you have had your fuss, now let it bloody go!"

"I am not marrying Kenley to spite Mother," Charlotte cried. "I am marrying him because I love him!"

"Love him?" Reilly asked, incredulous. "You cannot love him, Charlotte. You do not know him! You met him three days ago!"

"I met him six months ago in London," she returned. "Six months ago, Reilly, and he courted me properly. He—"

Reilly strode toward her, his brows drawn, the force of his boot soles shivering through the floorboards beneath her feet. He clamped his hand on her arm, and Charlotte yelped.

"You did not meet him six months ago," he said. "Lie to Mother and Father all you wish, Charlotte. Shout it to the bloody damn moon. You no more met Kenley Fairfax in London than I have swapped spittle with the King."

"You are hurting me!" she whimpered, and Reilly startled as if snapping from a reverie. In that moment, as his expression shifted to something akin to horror, she realized he was not angry. No matter his vehement words, Reilly was not angry. He was frightened. Something had terrified him so badly it had driven him to this, to drinking himself to near oblivion to lessen its effect, to venting his frustration and alarm upon his sister and Kenley.

"Reilly, what has happened?"

His hand loosened, slipping away from her. "I am sorry," he whispered.

"Reilly, what has happened?" she asked again, reaching for him. He shied from her touch, her comfort, and turned around. He shoved the heel of his hand against his brow, forking his fingers through his hair.

"Please," Charlotte said. "Why are you being like this? What has happened?"

"It . . . it is nothing," he whispered, anguished. He walked away from her, his posture slumping, his shoulders hunched in shame. "I am sorry, Charlotte," he said. "I did not mean it. I did not mean any of it. I . . . I just . . . please, Charlotte. You do not understand."

"You are right, Reilly," Charlotte said. "I do not."

"Please just go," he whispered, standing over his writing table. He set his drink aside and brushed his hand against a haphazard pile of gazettes. "Please, Charlotte, I . . . I am sorry. I did not mean what I said. I was wrong, and I . . . please just go away."

❈   ❈   ❈

"It is my fault," Charlotte heard Reilly say.

She had left as he had asked, but she was worried for him, alarmed by the uncharacteristic fear she had seen in his eyes. She had never known Reilly to be afraid of anything before. She had returned to his threshold after hearing footsteps in the corridor beyond her own room, and Meghan's voice when she tapped on Reilly's door.

Meghan had been behind closed doors with Reilly for nearly half an hour. Charlotte had slipped into the hall, and padded over to his room, kneeling on the floor to try and peep through his keyhole. She could see them; Reilly sat in a chair by his dressing table in direct view of the keyhole. Meghan knelt on the floor in front of him, her hand on his knee, her expression etched with worry.

"It is my fault," Reilly said again, more sharply this time. He held one of the gazettes in his hand; as he spoke, he leaned back and let it fly, sending the pages fluttering across the room. He balled his hand into a fist and struck his tabletop with enough force to slosh the meager remnants of brandy in the decanter.

"Reilly . . ." Meghan whispered. Whatever secrets he harbored to torment him so, Reilly kept them as much from her as he had from Charlotte. He kept saying it was his fault, with no elaboration, and Charlotte could see his words left Meghan as disconcerted as she was.

"Maybe they do love one another," Reilly said, pressing the heels of his hands over his eyes and leaning his head back. His breath escaped him in a heavy, weary sigh. "I do not know, Meghan. Maybe they do. Who am I to say? It is not my place. Who am I to counsel anyone on the matter of love?"

"Reilly," Meghan said when he lowered his hands. She raised her hips and reached for him, cradling his face in her hands.

"Am I envious?" he asked. "Is that what this is, Meghan? I . . . maybe I am seized with regret because Charlotte has the strength I lack—to marry where her heart leads her, while I . . . I sit here . . . helpless to do the same."

"That is not true," Meghan said. He turned his cheek into her hand, his eyes closing, and Charlotte drew back from the keyhole. *My darling Reilly,* the letter had opened—one of many written to him by someone whose affections he held dear, and that also brought him sorrow.

"Meghan," she whispered, stunned. She looked through the keyhole again and watched her brother kiss Meghan, his mouth lingering on hers, his expression filled with tender emotion.

They had known Meghan all of their lives; she was

only a year older than Charlotte. By that reason, Meghan had always been more of a friend than a servant. It had never occurred to Charlotte she might have been more than this in Reilly's regard. He had fallen in love with her, and to judge by her letters to him, the kind and loving words, Meghan felt the same.

"It is my fault," Reilly breathed, pressing his forehead against Meghan's "He is young, and Charlotte is young, and they . . . who can blame them to abandon reason if they are fond of one another? I . . . I have not drawn a clear moment's thought since I came back here to Darton . . . and near to you . . ."

Meghan smiled, lifting her chin enough to kiss his mouth tenderly. "They are in love, Reilly," she said. "It is not a crime. No one is to blame."

He uttered a hurting sound and tucked his face into her shoulder. Meghan held him, drawing her arms about him, stroking his hair. "It is all right," she breathed, kissing his ear.

"It must be," Reilly said, trembling against her. "It must be all right. My God, we have no way to take it back now. It is beyond me."

CHAPTER 10

THE NEXT EVENING, CHARLOTTE AND HER family were slated to attend a formal ball for Lady Margaret and her fiancée at Roding Castle in Dunmow parish. Roding Castle was the Earl of Essex's home, and James' besides, and the place where Margaret would make her vows in three days' time on Sunday.

Caroline's husband, Randall Prescott, Viscount Harlow, had come to fetch her early that morning, en route from London to Roding Castle. Charlotte felt dismayed by her sister's departure. Caroline had proven to be an unexpected supporter, and Charlotte had appreciated her efforts. She was also extremely anxious at the prospect of entering James' home in light of her circumstances, and she had tried to draw comfort from Caroline as the sisters hugged their farewells.

"Do not worry for a thing," Caroline had whispered, pressing her lips against the corner of Charlotte's mouth. "Lord and Lady Essex are unoffended by the turn of events. Randall has assured me you will be welcome there. I will be with you, and more importantly, Kenley will be with you. You will not notice anything but this, and you will have a lovely time."

While Charlotte had spent the rest of her afternoon in preparations, aided only by Meghan with Una gone to Loughton for Kenley, Lady Epping had once more locked herself stubbornly in her chamber. When the time arrived in late afternoon for them to depart, Charlotte, Reilly, and Lady Chelmsford stood somberly in the foyer, listening to Lord and Lady Epping argue from the second floor.

"I am not going!" Lady Epping cried out, her voice shrill with indignation.

"You most certainly are," Lord Epping said, and Charlotte winced at the heavy clamor of his hand slapping his wife's chamber door. "We have tendered our replies, and there is no time for courteous regrets! The carriage is waiting. Come now, my lady!"

"I will not know such humiliation!" Lady Epping yelled. "How dare you ask me to lift my head and walk into my noble Earl's home as if all is well and unchanged in the world? If you had any sense of social propriety, you would lock the front doors to this house and bolt us all inside until the spring!"

Charlotte hunched her shoulders unhappily. Lady Chelmsford harrumphed. "I hope you are well satisfied, young lady," she said in a cold, admonishing tone. "To realize the indignities you have heaped upon your poor mother. Why, I should think to—"

"Oh, shut up, Aunt Maude," Reilly said. Lady Chelmsford let her eyelids flutter, and her balance wobble, as if near to swooning in outrage. "And do not keel over, either," Reilly said. "I will not catch you, and Father is in such a mood as to simply leave you prone on the floor until you gather your wits and raise yourself."

❅ ❅ ❅

Lady Epping did not accompany them. As their carriage rolled along the northern highway, Lord Epping did his best to reassure his family all was well, nothing amiss. "She is not feeling well, that is all," he said. "This damp chill that comes with autumn always affects her poorly. She will be right again in short measure, I am sure of it."

He made a point to lean over and pat Charlotte's hand, drawing her gaze. "She will recover, lamb," he told her gently, and she smiled at him, feeling some tender obligation to make him think his efforts worked.

She did not miss the whispers that greeted them upon

their arrival. She could feel the heavy weight of stares and sideways glances; with every step, as Reilly escorted her on his arm into the ballroom, she heard murmured comments, muffled sniffs and fluttering gasps.

"Can you believe she came?" she heard Payton Stockley say to another young woman as they moved past. "And into Lord Roding's own house, no less! Truly, how could she ever summon the nerve?"

"Pay them no mind, Charlotte," Reilly said.

"I am not," Charlotte replied. "Do not worry for that." She smiled, and he smiled back for her, an unspoken way of making amends.

The Earl of Essex's home, Roding Castle, was named for the ruins of a Norman fortress west of the house, along its broad, expansive grounds. Though unused, the solitary, crumbling tower stood as a looming sentry over the enormous, neighboring house; a venerable and dignified silhouette against a backdrop of vermilion and gold sky visible from every window in the ballroom as the sun settled beyond the horizon. Charlotte longed to simply steal away from the crowd, and the swirling gossip muttered at her expense, to slip outside onto one of the broad terraces overlooking the tiered gardens and enjoy the vibrant hues of dusk splashed against the ancient stones of the tower.

She did not have the chance, however. Caroline had overheard their arrival announced, and had waded through the crowd to reach them, dragging her husband behind her. "Here you are, darlings!" she exclaimed to Reilly and Charlotte, smiling broadly as she approached. "Oh, Charlotte, you wore the sacque dress! I knew it would suit you splendidly. Does she not look divine, Randall?"

"Indeed," Lord Harlow said, his heavy-lidded, somewhat bored gaze wandering briefly in Charlotte's direction.

"Lord Theydon is here," Caroline said. "He arrived only moments ago."

Charlotte smiled despite herself. "Where?" she asked as she struggled to peer over the crowded mass of heads and upswept coifs. "Where is he?"

"He is back in the corner," Caroline replied. "Lord Woodside is with him, and fairly well trapped for the moment by Lady Kelvinside and her loathsome daughter, Rebecca. She has tried for ages now to force that dreadful girl into Lord Woodside's company; she has the tenacity of a terrier set upon a gristly ham bone."

She took Randall and Charlotte by the hands, drawing them together. "Here, Randall, do be a love and see my sister entertained," she said. "I will go fetch Lord Theydon. Let the gossip hags wag their tongues to know your family approves so fondly." She grinned brightly, delighted at this prospect, and then whirled about and was off again before Charlotte could even draw breath to protest. She looked vainly to Reilly for rescue, but her brother was gone, having ducked into the crowd and disappeared, offering greetings of his own.

Charlotte gazed up at Randall and he returned her gaze with all of the interest of a man enduring a lengthy and droning sermon. They stood together for a long moment, an uncomfortable silence apparent between them.

"Caroline tells me you have been in London for business, Lord Harlow," Charlotte said at last.

"Yes," Randall replied with a nod. This seemed to be the extent of response he intended to offer, oblivious to her attempt to make idle conversation, and Charlotte struggled to smile.

"May I ask what manner of business, my lord?" she said.

"I am part of a collaborative effort with some of my more well-esteemed fellows," he said. "We should like to shortly establish a lending firm within the city."

Charlotte's interest piqued. "A lending firm?"

Randall nodded. "My associates and I shall each contribute initial capital to be made available by means of loan notes to finance endeavors, particularly potential new commerce ventures, importing and exporting. These loans would be remitted with generous interest accrued."

"That sounds like a lucrative opportunity," Charlotte said.

He rewarded her with a slight upturn of his lips, as

he might a curious child. "Yes, I should hope it will be," he said.

"It must require a great deal of upfront capital," she said.

"Yes, well, I am suitably endowed from my familial inheritance," Randall said. "And my constituents are in likewise financial circumstances. Our principle proponent and benefactor is Lord Essex himself. It was his idea, actually."

"The Earl?" Charlotte asked. She had known the Earl of Essex frequented London for business, but she had not imagined James' father would prove so unconventional and bold in his endeavors. She had to admit, at least to herself, she was impressed. "Is that what has kept Lord Essex all of this while? I have noticed his absence at the festivities this week, and have wondered, given it is his daughter's wedding, and all."

"Lady Essex is more than capable of handling social affairs, and my lord trusts her to it," Randall replied. "We have all been kept busy in London of late, but him more so than any other. He will wrest himself away for the nuptials. Do not fret for it."

He mistook her expression for bewilderment, and smiled condescendingly. "I am certain such things must seem confusing to you, my dear," he said. "I should not have troubled your fair head over the details."

Charlotte resisted the urge to scowl at him. She caught sight of Kenley in the crowd; Caroline had been true to her word, and found him. Charlotte's eyes met Kenley's and she smiled brightly.

"May I have this next dance?" asked a voice from her right, deliberately near to her ear. Charlotte felt a hand brush her sleeve in beckon, and she turned, startled to find James beside her.

"James . . ." she said falteringly.

James smiled thinly, his gaze crawling over her form. She could almost feel each lingering, creeping moment of his glance as he admired her bosom straining atop the confines of her stomacher, the cinched, tiny measure of her waist, the promising swell of her hips exaggerated by her pannier. "Lord Harlow, what a pleasure," he said, without averting his gaze from Charlotte's breasts. "How do you fare, sir?"

"Well indeed, Lord Roding," Randall said. "And yourself?"

"At the moment? Quite splendid," James said. A quartet had struck a melody from the dance floor, and he finally raised his eyes. "They have signaled a minuet," he told her. "May I have this dance?"

"I . . ." Charlotte said, glancing at Randall. It was obvious she could expect no escape through him, and her eyes darted to the crowd, desperate for Caroline and Kenley. "I . . . thank you, Lord Roding, but no," she stammered. "I . . . I have only just arrived, and I should like to offer greetings to familiar faces."

James' smile widened. "I might be inclined to accept your refusal were we later into the evening," he said. As he spoke, she caught a tangy whiff of brandy on his breath; it was strong enough to make her step back from him. "However, the night has only just begun, and proper etiquette says to turn me down prohibits you from accepting any other invitation to dance."

James was right. She was trapped by protocol.

"And considering your dashing young betrothed is present, and that he shall surely and dearly love his chance with you upon the floor . . ." James spoke with a particularly mean edge to his voice, shading his words with perfectly undisguised implication. "I hope you would reconsider before refusing my offer."

"I do not think it would be proper to accept, James, given the circumstances," she said tightly.

"But given the alternatives, I think you will agree it would be prudent to do so anyway," he replied.

Charlotte frowned. "Fine," she said. "It is only a dance. I imagine I can survive."

James offered his elbow genteelly. "Splendid, then," he said.

❄ ❄ ❄

"You look ravishing, darling," James said, bowing before her on the dance floor.

"James, do not," Charlotte said, holding his gaze as she lowered herself in a curtsy. She had spied Kenley when James led her to the floor. A mixture of bewilderment and alarm marked his features when he noted her company. When he drew away from Caroline and shouldered his way toward the dance floor, Charlotte brought him pause with a slight shake of her head.

It is all right, she wanted to tell him. James had been drinking; he did not move or slur his speech as a drunk man would, but the pungency of his overindulgence was apparent in his breath, and she did not want Kenley to risk a confrontation with him.

"Do not what?" James asked. "Do not offer the truth? You would make a liar of me?"

Charlotte ignored him, grateful for the reprieve the lead-in brought her. She fell in step with the other ladies in the dance row as they broke for their left, moving in file toward the back of the dance floor. She met James again at the center, presenting her hand to him.

"Am I not allowed to comment on your beauty anymore?" he asked, promenading her briefly before turning her about. They parted on a diagonal and stood at three-quarter turns to look at one another. "Does your fair young Theydon forbid that other men should admire his bride?"

"It is all that matters to you, is it not, James?" Charlotte said. "That I am beautiful. You have never noticed anything else."

They crossed corners and she held his gaze. "Of course I have, darling," he replied, and his eyes crawled across her breasts. "I took notice of the wondrous lines and curves of your form some time ago, and have admired them ever since. I have spent long moments deep in thought in their regard, as a matter of fact."

They crossed again, and he hooked her hand, sliding in a hissing breath through his teeth into her ear. "I have imagined tasting them," he whispered. "Your beautiful breasts. From the moment they were naught save nubs, I have given them pointed consideration."

She brushed past him and said nothing, the crease between her brows deepening. She let him slip his right hand into hers, turning her. "Far more than nubs now," he murmured, the corner of his mouth lifting. "Every part of you softened and curved, filled and swelled . . . I swell to consider it."

She recoiled from him, losing step in the dance as she backpedaled for her corner. "You are drunk, Lord Roding," she said.

"Drunk with need," he said.

They clasped hands again, turning to the left. "Have you need, James?" she asked. "Take it in hand, then, in some vacant parlor, you repulsive cad. How dare you speak to me so?"

"How dare you refuse my offers of marriage? Years

upon years, you rebuked me—only to turn about and agree to wed a man like Theydon, a man you have known for little more than the fluttering of eyelashes—that is to say, one you do not know at all?"

"I know him well," she said. "You may not have a concept for such matters, James, but it is possible for people to acquaint themselves fondly with more than just a fair face, pleasing form, and ample purse. You should consider it sometime. You might be the better for it."

They parted, and she tromped to the rear of the dance floor to meet him once more, fuming as she glared at the bobbing, plaited hairpiece affixed to the back of the woman's head before her.

"You know him?" James asked, taking her hand and leading her in promenade.

"Yes," she replied, glowering at him.

"So you know about his naval service, then?" James asked as they separated for their corners.

Charlotte's surprise was so evident James had to laugh. "He did not tell of it?" he asked.

"Kenley did not serve in the Navy," Charlotte said. "Who told you he had? Your faithful thief-taker-turned-coachman, Mr. Cheadle?"

"No," James replied as they crossed. "A Mr. Linford told me. Do you know him? He is the sheriff of Essex County. I met him by chance passing through Epping proper the other night. I asked him about Lord Theydon,

given he has held his post for so long, and that your betrothed had seen his fair share of troubles in the past."

They stepped together, presenting their hands and
turning. "Mr. Linford had vague recall of him, if only
by the benefit of the former Lord Woodside as his kin.
He told me the last he had heard tell of Kenley Fairfax,
he had enlisted in the Royal Navy."

"Lewis Fairfax enlisted in the Navy," Charlotte said.
"Kenley did not. Lord Woodside paid for his Grand
Tour abroad. Mr. Linford is confusing the two."

"I assure you he is not," James said.

She held his gaze. "I assure you that he is," she said.

The music concluded, and James let her turn from
him, keeping hold of her hand to present her to the au-
dience. The guests who had gathered about the dance
floor to admire the minuet clapped their hands in polite
approval, and Charlotte turned to James, dropping him
an obligatory and quick curtsy.

"Thank you for the dance, Lord Roding," she said.
"I bid you good evening."

She did not wait for his escort, but set out, abandoning the dance floor unaccompanied, and scanned
the crowd, looking vainly for her sister and Kenley. She
felt James catch the ruffled trim of her engageante, and
when she turned, his hand shifted, closing firmly about
her arm.

"Let go of me, James," she said firmly.

"I still love you truly," he told her. "No matter what has come to pass, or any dalliances with Theydon, you remain unsullied to me. I beg you to reconsider."

"You are hurting my arm," she said, and gave a mighty jerk to wrest herself free of his grasp. "Do not approach me again, or I will make a scene, James. By my breath, I will."

She whirled and left him, shoving her way into the crowd. She was immediately lost in a cramped sea of unfamiliar faces, shoved against panniers and shoulders, jostled into arms and ballooning skirts. She looked around, straining to find her family or Kenley, but she could not find them in the throng.

Someone caught her arm from behind, and she turned, stumbling, thinking at first James had followed her. She drew in a sharp breath to snap at him in rebuke, but her alarm waned abruptly. "Kenley!"

"Are you all right?" Kenley asked, taking her by the hands.

She looked up at him, the delight in her face faltering. Linford had told James Kenley had enlisted in the Royal Navy. It sounded preposterous, but then again, James had been the one to tell Charlotte's family of Kenley's criminal past. That had proven true enough. *Could it be true now?* she thought.

"What is it?" Kenley asked, concerned. "Did he offend you? Did he hurt you? Tell me, Charlotte."

If Kenley had been in the Navy, why would Reilly and Lewis have made no mention of it? Surely they would have known. Why would they have offered pretense of Kenley being abroad on a Grand Tour instead?

Kenley moved on, drawing her with him. She followed him, puzzled, as he led her through the crowd to the far side of the ballroom. They ducked through a door and out onto an expansive stone terrace. Night had fallen; the air was cold and damp, and their breath immediately floated in an iridescent haze about their heads. No one else was foolish enough to brave the weather, and they had the patio to themselves. The sounds of the party muted as Kenley closed the door and drew her away from the golden spill of interior light through the windows. She followed him to the balustrade, where the shadows were deep, engulfing them.

"You are upset," he said, touching her face. "What did he say? Tell me what he said. Please, did he—?"

Charlotte seized his face between her hands and kissed him, muffling his voice against her mouth. She felt the startled intake of his breath, and then he whimpered, pulling her near. "Nothing," Charlotte whispered to him when they parted. "He told me nothing, Kenley."

He touched her face in turn. She shivered; he kissed her lightly, sweetly, his lips coaxing passion from the hidden alcoves and quiet corners within her. Her breasts were swollen and filled with insistent heat; she brushed them purposefully against him in mute plea for his touch.

His hand slid from her face, following her neck, the friction and heat of his skin against hers making her close her eyes and gasp softly. His palm settled against her breast, his fingers closing gently, his hand moving, kneading rhythmically, finding the beat of her frantic heart and marking its pace.

The sound of muted laughter from the ballroom interrupted them, and he drew his hand away, leaving her aching for him beneath the constraints of her stomacher and stay; leaving her breath hitching, nearly hiccupping. Kenley glanced at the terrace doors and then reached for her hand, slipping it around hers.

"Will you come with me?" he whispered.

"Anywhere," Charlotte breathed.

He led her from the terrace to the gardens beyond. They hurried, stealing in the shadows along the side of the house until they came to the stables. They could hear the sounds of servants and coachmen enjoying revelry of their own as they gathered around fires, with pipes and pints in hand, laughing raucously. Charlotte and Kenley hunkered against the wall of the barn, and then ducked inside, scurrying through the loosely strewn straw covering the floor. The horses snuffled and whinnied softly as the unfamiliar figures darted past.

Charlotte followed Kenley to a ladder at the far end of the barn, and she climbed first, with him behind her. They ascended to the hay loft where there were accommodations for the household stable staff. The small cots, tables, and chairs were all vacant, the loft empty.

Charlotte turned and Kenley was there, pressed against her, kissing her. Her mouth opened reflexively to meet his, to greet his tongue with her own, to welcome him into her. They stumbled across the loft, and he closed his hand over her breast again, teasing her with the firm motions of his hand. He kissed her without allowing her a moment to reclaim her breath. She backed into a table, nearly knocking it over, and they stood tangled, kissing.

Kenley turned her around. "Put your hands on the table," he whispered into her ear. "Lean forward."

"What?" Charlotte wondered what he meant to do to her. Yet at the same time, she found herself seized with a tremulous excitement, an insistent and desperate need, and she felt it shuddering within her, a wondrous energy straining for release.

Kenley cradled her chin in his hand and tilted her head back to kiss her. "Put your hands on the table," he urged again, and she obeyed. "Good. Lean forward, Charlotte."

Charlotte folded herself over the table. He leaned

over, crumpling her pannier frame inward, and kissed the back of her neck, following the slope of her shoulder. She felt him gather her box pleats and skirts into in his fists and lift them, raising them over her pannier.

Charlotte stiffened reflexively. "I . . . I have . . . Kenley, I have never done this . . ."

"I know," he said, his lips dancing against the side of her ear. "And you will not tonight, either. Not here. Not yet. Trust me, Charlotte."

I do, she thought. No matter what James had said, she trusted him. She could not explain it anymore than she could explain the sudden, relentless eagerness overwhelming her. She relaxed, breath fluttering from her throat. *I trust you, Kenley.*

She felt his fingers delve between her legs and she tensed again, gasping in start. The gentle prodding lit something deep and primal within her, however; something she had never felt before, stirring within the very core of her form. She felt sudden, warm moisture flood between her thighs, and she trembled with fright, confusion, and anticipation. Again, his voice calmed her, mesmerized her, soft and deliberate in her ear. "I will not hurt you," he said and when his fingertips slipped against the warm, moist folds of her tender flesh, she gasped softly. "Trust me."

His hand moved slowly, exploring her, sliding against the velveteen warmth. His fingertips pressed against a place of particular tenderness, and when they settled, moving slowly at first, grinding deliberate, gentle circles, Charlotte moaned. When his fingers moved faster, marking a wondrous rhythm in her, she tensed, closing her eyes as he stroked her nearly to reeling.

All at once his fingers slid easily, deeply inside of her, driving her to crescendo. She had never felt anything like it in her life. Kenley stood so close to her, she could feel his arousal through his breeches, hard and warm, straining against the fabric, pressing with firm promise into her thighs. She moved against his hand, savoring it, needing it—wanting more.

"Not yet," she whimpered. She wanted him inside of her; more than his hand, she wanted all of him. She wanted him deep within her, where his fingers thrust. She was not frightened anymore; this was too wonderful to be frightening.

"Yes," he said, his hand stroking a dizzying, pounding rhythm into her. She trembled when she felt an enormous, shuddering pleasure. "Yes," he whispered again. "Yes, Charlotte, now."

She jerked against him, crying out in sudden, exquisite release as he moved her beyond anything she might have ever imagined, hoped, or dreamed possible.

When the feeling ebbed, her knees threatened to fail and her entire body shuddered uncontrollably. She crumpled back against him, and he held her in his arms, kissing her ear, her cheek, her throat.

He had brought her to pleasure—heretofore unknown pleasure—but when she had pleaded with him, begged him to take her, claim her, he refused. Had she done something wrong? she worried in dismay. Why did he not want her? She was virginal; the claiming of a young woman's virtues was something men boasted about, bragged about over and over, and yet Kenley had left her intact. Why? She did not understand; she closed her eyes and damned herself for her innocence and inexperience.

She had stiffened against him without realizing it, but Kenley noticed. "You do not know," he said, his voice breathless with need. "You do not know how much I want you, Charlotte, or how much of a struggle you just saw me through."

She was only more confused. *Why, then?* she wanted to ask him, but she could not summon her voice. *Why did you not?*

"I will make love to you," he promised. "If you want me . . . whenever you want me, Charlotte, as much as you need me, I will make love to you. But for the first . . . not here. Not yet—not like this."

She looked into his eyes. *I do want you,* she wanted to say. *I want you here, Kenley—now. I want you to make love to me. I do not care about your secrets. I want you, Kenley. I love you.*

❈   ❈   ❈

He led her from the hayloft. They walked back to the
house together, and he kept her arm tucked through the
angle of his elbow, her hand in his, his fingers twined
through hers. Though they said nothing along the way,
they did not need to. Even in the darkness, the fading
light from the coachmen's bonfires behind them, Charlotte could see Kenley smiling at her, his mouth lifted
gently, tenderly.

They reached the terrace, and stood by the balustrade for a long moment, neither of them wanting to
return to the party. "I love you," he breathed—the most
wondrous words she had ever heard.

"Charlotte, here you are!" someone cried from behind them.

Charlotte and Kenley whirled, jerking clumsily back
from one another, both of them wide-eyed with start.
Caroline stood in the doorway leading from the parlor
onto the terrace. She was smiling broadly and waving.
"Darling, do come inside!" she exclaimed. "You remember Lady Hinckford, do you not? Come and say hello."

Caroline waddled across the terrace, one palm
pressed to her belly. With the other, she caught Charlotte's hand. "Why, your fingers are like ice! You will
catch your death out here! Come in this very moment."

"Caroline . . ." Charlotte began in protest as Caroline pulled her toward the house. She looked over her shoulder at Kenley. "Caroline, wait, please . . . a moment, will you?"

Caroline laughed. "He can kiss you later at his leisure, though preferably before a hearth, where you might not turn so blue."

She dragged Charlotte across the threshold, guiding her into the ballroom. Charlotte frowned, trying to pull away, trying to call out to Kenley, but she was caught by her sister, and Caroline did not relent as she led her indoors.

CHAPTER 11

THE NEXT MORNING, AS CHARLOTTE STOOD at her wash basin to bathe her face, she heard hoof beats from the front yard of Darton Hall, and the whinnying of a horse. Curious, she walked to her window and looked down at the grounds. She saw a man on horseback; it was Reilly, wrapped in a heavy greatcoat, his tricorne pulled low on his brow. He had reined his horse to a stop plainly within Charlotte's line of sight. Reilly folded himself forward against the horse's neck, but she could not tell if he was doubled in pain or simply checking something on the horse's withers. Whichever the case, it seemed quickly resolved. Reilly sat back once more, his motions stiff and slow, and then drove his boot heels into the horse's flanks, spurring it forward.

"Reilly is about early this morning," Charlotte

remarked, watching her brother ride away from the house, vanishing from view into the fog.

He had disappeared in similar manner last night at Roding Castle. Charlotte had lost track of him upon meeting Caroline and Randall in the crowd, and had not seen him again until they were preparing to leave. He had spent the carriage ride home in silence, his eyes closed, his temple pressed against the wall. He had seemed exhausted, ill, or in pain, and their father had noticed as well. As Reilly had crossed the foyer, moving with a discernible limp, Lord Epping had called out to stay him.

"Are you unwell, son?" he had asked.

Reilly had smiled somewhat feebly. "I . . . I am fine, sir," he answered. "Merely weary, that is all. I made a bit too merry tonight, I think."

Charlotte frowned thoughtfully at her window. She had accepted his answer last night, having been too distracted with pleasant recollections of the evening with Kenley, but now, having seen him seem to buckle with pain astride his horse, she wondered.

"He did not sleep much last night, I think," Meghan said from behind her. She stood at Charlotte's opened wardrobe, surveying her clothes. "His light was still aglow beneath his door when I came down the corridor toward midnight. He has not slept well at all this past week."

Charlotte turned to her. "Has he ever said anything

to you of having served with Kenley in the Navy?"

"Lord Theydon? No. He served with Lord Theydon's kin, Baron Woodside, abroad."

"I know," Charlotte said. "It is just . . ." She looked thoughtfully out the window again. "Someone told me last night that Kenley had served, as well."

"What did Lord Theydon tell you of it?"

"I . . . I did not ask him," Charlotte replied. She had not wanted to ask him; she had not wanted to know. It troubled her he might be keeping secrets from her, despite what was growing between them.

"You have never been one to lend much credence to rumors," Meghan said, drawing Charlotte's gaze. "And you know what my mother always said of them—they begin with a glimmer of half-truth, and then swell into misnotion in the incessant retelling. Perhaps you should ask Lord Theydon and learn for certain."

"Yes," Charlotte murmured. "Perhaps I should."

"Would you care for the yellow dress today?" Meghan asked.

"No," Charlotte said. "No, if you please, Meghan, I would like my riding habit. I think Reilly had a splendid idea; it has been far too long since I enjoyed a morning ride."

And I have some matters weighing on my mind I hope a visit to Theydon Hall might dispel, she thought.

❋ ❋ ❋

By the time she reached Theydon Hall, the sun had risen in full, its warmth driving the heavy fog from the countryside. She had thought perhaps Lewis and Kenley would be at work on the roof that morning, but though the ladders remained propped against the side walls, and the broad panels of burlap stacked with peg tiles yet graced the lawn, Theydon Hall was silent, with no one seeming about as she approached.

She reined her horse and caught an unexpected whiff of a pungent odor as she rounded the corner of the house—smoke. Alarmed, Charlotte looked around and spied a thick, dark cloud rolling from the kitchen doorway.

Charlotte yelped, slipped her boot heel from her stirrup and dropped to the ground. She left her horse unfettered and rushed across the yard toward the house. "Kenley!" she shouted out. "Una! Are you there?"

She darted into the kitchen and was immediately enveloped in heavy smoke. She gasped, eyes smarting, and she flapped her hands in front of her face. "Kenley!" she called again, hoarse and nearly choking. "Una! Is anyone home?"

She heard a miserable little groan and turned. As she waved the smoke from her line of sight, she found Albert standing near the stove, his shoulders hunched, hands fluttering. "Oh!" he exclaimed. "Oh, I . . . I did not mean . . ."

Charlotte saw a kettle set atop the stove and realized where the smoke came from. She hurried to the stove, jerking her cravat from about her neck. She wrapped it about her hand, caught the kettle by the handle and whirled about, carrying it outside.

She coughed and sputtered as she dropped the smoldering kettle onto the stone stoop. She could not begin to tell what Albert had scorched. All she saw was something reduced to blackened cinders seared to the belly of the pot.

"Albert," she said, returning to the kitchen. With the kettle removed and the door standing wide open, the smoke dissipated. Charlotte saw the old man had lowered himself into a chair and covered his face with his hands.

"Albert, are you all right?" Charlotte asked. She knelt beside him and touched his wrist lightly, drawing his reluctant gaze. He was either weeping, or tears streamed down his cheeks from the smoke; no matter the cause, he looked ashen with fright, stricken with dismay.

"Master William usually sees to breakfast," Albert said woefully. "Oh, he . . . he usually tends to it so well, but I . . . he is gone. I do not know where he is, and my lord . . ." He hitched in a tremulous breath. "Oh, he will beat William again," he whispered, clutching at Charlotte's sleeve. "He . . . he will lay him open with his lash, he . . ."

"Who will beat William?" Charlotte asked gently, pressing her hand to Albert's cheek. He was distraught, and obviously mistook Kenley for the stable boy, William Sutton, in his confusion. "Hush, Albert. It is all right. No one will beat William."

"He hurts him so badly," Albert said, voice filled with anguish. "He . . . he is a good boy. He is a good boy, but my lord, he . . . he hurts him . . ."

"No one will hurt him," Charlotte reassured him. "I will not let anyone hurt William, Albert. I promise."

She said it over and over until it seemed to settle with Albert. He nodded, his expression softening, his thin mouth unfolding in a hesitant smile. "William is not here, Albert?" she asked.

"No, ma'am," Albert said. "He . . . he left a bit ago with Master Lewis. And Mrs. Colchester went at dawn for the market in Loughton."

It took Charlotte a moment to realize that "Mrs. Colchester" was likely Una. Like Kenley, Albert had seemingly assigned her a name from his more secure memories. "Would you like me to fix you some breakfast, Albert?" Charlotte asked, smiling gently. "What were you trying to make?"

"Porridge," he replied, looking momentarily forlorn again. "Master William usually tends to it for me."

"I will tend to it. I do not mind," Charlotte said. She stood and explored the kitchen, investigating the pantry. "Where did Masters William and Lewis go?" she asked Albert as she searched. She found it admittedly odd that both Kenley and Lewis would have left Albert alone. The cousins obviously understood Albert's addled state of mind, and ordinarily took doting care of him.

"I am not sure," Albert said. "Master William had an early morning visitor arrive little more than an hour ago, a rather severe looking gentleman with whom he had to meet." He smiled. "Master William kept late hours last night, you know. He had a splendid party to attend. He was still sleeping this morrow when his caller arrived. It seemed a rather urgent matter. I heard them speaking in the foyer, their voices sharp. It was Master Lewis who directed them outside."

Charlotte had set a fresh kettle to simmer on the stove. "What did the caller look like, Albert?"

"A fair-headed gentleman, tall, I suppose," Albert replied. "Limping somewhat, and seeming grave and ill-humored."

"Was he wearing a dark coat?"

Albert looked thoughtful. "I do believe so, yes, ma'am, and a tricorne cap besides."

Reilly had ridden to Theydon Hall; he had been the "severe looking gentleman" caller. Charlotte looked down into the basin of the kettle. "What are you playing at, Reilly?" she whispered.

She wondered if his visit had to do with Kenley's

supposed enlistment in the Navy. James might have made a point of mentioning it to Reilly at last night's ball, as well. Again, she could not imagine what difference it would make or why Reilly would have lied, had he known Kenley had enlisted.

An idea occurred to her. She was ashamed of herself at the very thought, but she could not resist. "I . . . I think the caller must have been a friend of William's," she said. "Known to him from the Royal Navy. Perhaps William must go out to sea."

"Oh, no," he said, chuckling. "Master William has promised he will not be at sea again. He is finished with the Navy, you know—he and Master Lewis both—all well and properly resigned."

"Then William has been to sea before," Charlotte said quietly.

"Yes, ma'am," Albert replied, nodding. "Two years, thereabouts, nearly three. To the colonies and all with Master Lewis. They sent me letters all the while." His expression faltered, growing momentarily solemn. "There was a war, you know," he said. "They were sent for the war."

Charlotte said nothing. Her throat had constricted all at once, and she doubted she could force air through, much less her voice. There had indeed been a war; King George's War. It had ended only the year before. The English Navy had dispatched a number of man-of-wars to the colonies across the Atlantic, to blockade the French port of Louisport. The 28-gun frigate, the *HMS Endurance*, to which Reilly and Lewis had been assigned, was among them.

"But they are home now," Albert said, brightened once more. "It was very hard for them at first, what with Lord Woodside falling so ill and taking to his grave. And then poor Kenley took on that terrible blight . . ."

"Kenley?" she whispered.

"What are you doing?"

Charlotte whirled, startled, and found Kenley at the back doorway, his expression caught somewhere between alarm and horror. He was dressed as if hastily roused from bed; his shirt tails were untucked from rumpled breeches, an unmatching justicoat drawn clumsily atop. He was barefooted, and without a wig, and for the first time, Charlotte saw his natural hair; thick, dark, disheveled waves that framed his face and fell to his shoulders in tousled disarray.

"Master William!" Albert exclaimed happily. "You are back so soon!"

Kenley glanced to his right, toward the stoop, taking into quick account the still-smoldering pot of ruined porridge. He looked frightened to Charlotte, just as Reilly had looked frightened two nights earlier upon their confrontation.

"It . . . it is Kenley, Albert," he said. He stepped across the threshold and hurried to the older man.

"What happened?" he asked. "Were you cooking? I told you I would not be long. I would be right back, I said. You were to wait for me, and I would fix you breakfast."

His tone had grown sharp with concern, and Albert blinked at him, his smile faltering, his eyes flooding with sudden, shamed tears. "I . . . I am sorry," he whimpered, trembling. "I . . . I forgot. I know you told me, but I . . . I could not remember, and I . . . I just . . ."

"It is all right," he said gently, and embraced Albert. He clutched at the older man, turning his cheek to kiss Albert's ear. "Please, Albert, I am sorry. I did not mean to speak harshly to you. Please do not weep. Please, Albert. You . . . you will break me . . ."

He leaned back. "Are you hurt?" he asked. "Did you burn yourself?"

Albert shook his head. "I am fine," he said. "Mrs. Colchester took the pot from the stove. She is home early from Loughton."

Kenley looked at Charlotte, or, in Albert's mind, Mrs. Colchester. "What are you doing here?" he asked. "You . . . Charlotte, you should not be here."

"I wanted to see you, Kenley," she said.

"Albert, I will be right outside," he said. "Just for a moment. Let me speak with Mrs. Colchester, and then I will finish your breakfast."

Charlotte let him lead her outside into the yard. "You have to leave," he said. He turned and walked away, forking his fingers in his dark tumble of hair, shoving it back from his face. "No," he said. "No, it is better you are here. I need to speak with you. It . . . it is important, and I . . . yes, it is better you are here."

What? Charlotte thought. *What are you so afraid I will suspect or discover, Kenley?* She was torn between wanting to comfort him in his obvious distress, and grasping him firmly by the lapels and shaking him until he told her the truth.

"I cannot marry you," he said.

Charlotte flinched as if he had just slapped her. "What?"

"This was a mistake," Kenley said. "I . . . it was impulsive and rash of me, and I . . . I did not think it through when I opened my mouth at Rycroft. It was a lie, a ruse, and it was never supposed to be more than that. A distraction for you, and it has gone too far."

"That is not true," Charlotte said, wounded.

He met her gaze evenly. "Yes, it is."

"I do not believe you," Charlotte said. "Maybe it was a ruse at first, but not anymore, Kenley. Not for me—or you. You told me you loved me. Last night, you . . . you told me . . ."

"And you told me no one falls in love in only days," he replied. "You were right. I was wrong. I . . . I was wrong, and I . . ." He shoved his fingers through his hair, his brows furrowing as if he struggled to find resolve. "Last night meant nothing to me, Charlotte. It was a dream. I was caught up in my own lie so much, I . . . I nearly fooled myself into believing it true, but I have come to my senses. A smattering of parties . . . an afternoon spent walking around these abandoned grounds . . . last night . . . it does not make us in love."

She struggled to compose herself, fighting against tears. She did not know why he was saying these things, but she tried to find some method—any means—to dissuade him. "If you break our engagement, my mother will make me marry James," she said.

"As well she should," Kenley said, nearly crying out. He raised his hands, as if exasperated. "He will be the Earl of Essex some day! It is a good match. You may not realize it now, Charlotte, but marrying me would be a mistake, and marrying Roding would . . . it would be best."

"I do not want to marry him," Charlotte said. "I . . . I want to marry you. I love you, Kenley."

"Do not say that," he breathed.

"At least give me some more time, then," she pleaded. "A week, even—just a week. Let me find a way so I do not have to marry him." He shook his head, opening his mouth to speak, and Charlotte's tears spilled. "Please, Kenley!" she cried. "Please, I love you!"

"Do not say that," he said again.

She drew no closer to him. She stood behind him,

whimpering and sniffling, trying to stay her tears, feeling foolish and anguished. "Did . . . did Reilly make you do this?" she asked. "He came to see you this morning. Albert told me. Did Reilly say something to make you do this? Does it have something to do with you both serving in the Royal Navy together?"

"I . . . I was not in the Royal Navy."

"Albert told me you were," she said. "He told me you were sent overseas to the colonies, to Louisport, and that is where Lewis and Reilly—"

"Albert also says my father is still alive," Kenley said. "And that I am his favorite stable hand. He . . . he is a confused old man who does not understand what he is saying!"

Charlotte felt fresh tears flood her eyes. "He also told me your father beat you," she cried, and he recoiled anew. "Or beat William, I should say. Did he . . . did he beat you, too?"

"He beat us both," Kenley admitted reluctantly. "He used to bloody my back with his belt and then he . . . he would take after Will and give it to him tenfold. Albert could not stop him. There was nothing he could do, but it shames him yet, and . . . and pains him all the more."

They stared at one another for a long moment. "Just go, Charlotte," he said hoarsely. "I will send Una back to Darton when she returns from Loughton, and I . . . I will give her a note for your father to settle it properly."

"Please do not do this," she begged. He did not want to do it; she could see it in his face, his helpless, agonized expression. He did not want to do it, but somehow felt he had no other recourse. "Please, Kenley, will you not talk to me? Tell me of it? Whatever it is, I will understand. I will accept it. By my breath, it will not change anything. Please do not do this."

"It is done, Charlotte," he said, and she fell silent, realizing his resolve. "I am not marrying you. Please, just leave."

He turned around and walked back to his house, ducking into the kitchen. He swung the door in a swift arc behind him, and Charlotte flinched at the sharp report as it slammed shut.

CHAPTER 12

LIKE A VULTURE WAITING FOR THE INEVITA-
ble moment of a dying animal's last, feeble exhalation,
James arrived at Darton Hall within hours of Charlotte's
return. She stood at her window, watching his carriage
approach and wondered who had been quicker—her
mother, writing to tell him the news, or James, scram-
bling into his coach and rushing to claim her.

Charlotte had known he would come. She steeled
herself for that moment when Lady Epping would rap
against her door to snatch Charlotte in hand, dragging
her off to the nearest parish chapel and forcing vows
upon her. She watched her mother hurry eagerly down
the front steps, her full skirts swirling about her as she
approached James' carriage.

Charlotte had barricaded herself in her room upon

her return from Theydon Hall. Reilly had not come home yet; he might have been the only one to coax her beyond her threshold—and only then so she could pummel the wits from him. She was seized with fury, dismay, and despair; torn between distraught tears and smashing her fists into the walls, windows, and furniture in her rage.

"Reilly did this," she said. She watched Cheadle disembark from the driver's perch of the coach. He walked around the side of the coach, pausing to tip the front corner of his tricorne politely at Lady Epping before opening the door for James.

"No, lamb," Una said from behind her. "Kenley did."

True to his word, Kenley had dispatched Una to Darton Hall, and though she had not said much about the reasons for her dismissal, she obviously understood what had happened.

"Kenley did not want to do this," Charlotte said, turning to Una. "Reilly made him somehow, said something to him, shamed him, forced him. I do not know what, but I know he did. Kenley did not want to do this."

"No, I do not believe he did," Una said. She sat in a chair before Charlotte's fireplace, holding a cup of tea. She turned, looking toward Charlotte. "He was very upset when I returned from Loughton, and when he told me what had come to pass, I could see plainly it pained him. But I could also see he had resigned himself to it.

No matter the reason, it is set fast in his heart."

Una stood and set her tea aside on the writing table. "Perhaps he did not want this, lamb, but he has done it all the same. His reasons are his own, as was the choice in the end. There is no one to blame for it."

Charlotte looked out the window in time to see Lady Epping take James' proffered elbow. "I will not marry James Houghton," she said.

Edmond Cheadle remained by the coach. He turned his face toward the house, and this time there was no early morning's poor light to hide his face in the shadow of his hat brim. He looked up at Charlotte's window; she saw the corners of his mouth hitch in a fleeting, crooked smile. Charlotte whirled away and fell across her bed in a billowing tangle of skirts and crinolines. She curled onto her side, drawing her hands to her face, her knees to her belly.

"I will not marry him," she repeated, tears spilling down her cheeks. "Mother cannot make me. She does not love me and she cannot make me."

"Of course your mother loves you," Una said, following her to sit on the side of the bed. "Do not behave like an overwrought child, Charlotte. Lady Epping loves you very much. If nothing else proves it, that she has let you go so long in the pursuit of your own chosen husband should without question."

"How can you say that?"

"Because it is true," she said gently. "And you know it, Charlotte."

A light tapping at Charlotte's door drew their gazes. "Do not answer it, Una," Charlotte whispered. "I do not want to see James. Please, Una. Not now, I just . . . cannot."

"Charlotte?" her father said through the door, brushing his knuckles against the wood. "Charlotte, kindly open the door."

Una rose, drawing loose of Charlotte's grasp. Charlotte sat up, dismayed, as Una walked across the room. "Una!" she cried in protest.

"Lamb, you cannot lock yourself in here forever in the hopes all of this will simply go away," Una told her. "And it is your father calling, not James."

Una unbolted the door. Lord Epping stood alone at the threshold, his head cocked as he peered at daughter. "Many thanks, Una," he said. "Frankly, I have had enough conversations passed through locked doors for the week. May I speak with my daughter in private for a moment?"

"Of course, my lord," Una said, nodding, and left the room.

"I am not marrying James Houghton, Father," Charlotte said, rising to her feet. She sniffled loudly and dragged the broad cuff of her jacket against her cheek, drying her tears. She affected the proper poise and chin-hoisting of a woman righteously indignant, and marched toward her hearth.

"Now, Charlotte . . ." Lord Epping began.

"I am not marrying him," she said, more sharply. "He is a despicable boor, and I would as soon pour scalding water down the length of my body as have that man touch me. I love Kenley. I know you and Mother do not give a rot whit for such things, but you cannot prevent them. I love Kenley, and I want to marry him."

"He does not want to marry you, lamb," Lord Epping said. He reached into his pocket and slipped out a folded sheet of paper. "He sent this to me and told me so himself, admitting he acted in haste, and demonstrated a decided lack of proper judgment."

"I do not know why he wrote that," Charlotte said. "I do not know why he has done any of this, but I know it is not what he wants. He told me he loved me, he told me last night, Father. How does one change their mind with such resignation in such order? It is not possible; it is not true. He does not want this."

"Charlotte, you are every bit as fiery-tempered and obstinate as your mother when you feel so inclined," he said at length. "But you have never suffered any lack of rationality in spite of it. I like to think you take this from me, as I pride myself on being a man of some logic. I had no qualms about standing against your mother's wishes when it made sense to do so. Your arrangement with Lord Theydon seemed consensual and not made in haste. He seemed a fine enough young man to me, most pleasant and endearing. There seemed to be genuine affection between you, and I was unopposed to your marriage. But now?"

He walked toward her, tucking Kenley's note back into his pocket. "Now, I have come to appeal to your reason, lamb. No matter what you think or insist, the lad has broken his engagement. I cannot force him to it. That is not the way it works."

"I love him," she said.

"I believe you think you do," Lord Epping said. "And I believe your heart has convinced you it is true. But now, in the light of these new circumstances, a great many of your mother's arguments that seemed baseless to me now make a certain sense, and I would have you hear me on them.

"This past week has been very traumatic for you. Your mother thinks the robbery frightened you more than you have admitted to anyone, likely even yourself, and I am inclined to agree with her. No one suffers such events without being shaken. And in the days that have followed, your heart and mind have been quite vulnerable. Your mother did not help matters any by arranging for Lord Roding's unexpected marriage announcement, I know, and whether you believe me or not, she realizes this, too, in retrospect.

"I think in the fragile and uncertain state brought upon by the robbery, you have seized upon something that seemed true and sure, but which was, in reality, only impulsive."

Charlotte closed her eyes. She tried to tell herself it was not true, it could not be true. But Lord Epping was right.

"You are a sensible girl," Lord Epping said. "And I think you know I am right. You may be too stubborn to admit it . . ." He offered this with a fond smile Charlotte did not see, and a tender caress Charlotte flinched against. ". . . but you are wise enough to realize it."

Charlotte kept her lips pressed together in a thin, defiant line.

"Lord Roding may indeed be precisely as you have described him," Lord Epping said. "For his sake, I hope that he is not. I have not walked into the woods with another man in many long years, but my dueling pistols are about here somewhere and I still carry a snuff box in my breast pocket for good measure . . ."

Charlotte smiled, even as she struggled not to

"I know this may not be as you would like," he said softly. "And you may not agree with the way noble society dictates our lives should be. You understand nonetheless, and I hope you understand, given the circumstances, I cannot change or prevent it."

Charlotte's eyes swam with tears, but she nodded.

Lord Epping had conceded, then, and it was over. She had no more hope. She would be made to marry James.

"Lord Roding has asked to see you," Lord Epping said, and before Charlotte could do more than draw a quick breath to object, he added, "But I have told him no. It was good of him in his concern to come as he has, but this is not the proper time, and you are not in the proper mood. He has asked to make the formal announcement this evening at Hudswell Hall. His mother's family hosts a ball for Lady Margaret, and they have extended an invitation, as of this morning, for us to join their kin and close friends in their celebration. I told him he could see you then, when he offered his announcement."

Charlotte nodded mutely.

"You will wed him Sunday," he said. She struggled not to weep as she nodded once more.

Her father turned and walked to the door. "We must leave for Hudswell by midafternoon," he said. "I will send Una to help you prepare."

Charlotte sank to her knees, face buried in her hands when she heard the click of the door latch.

CHAPTER 13

"CHARLOTTE, DARLING, LIFT YOUR HEAD. Let me look at you," Lady Epping said, her eyes aglow with delight. "Lovely," she murmured, brushing her hands against Charlotte's cheeks. "Simply lovely."

Charlotte could not have hoped that in this—likely her most broken and miserable hour—she might have at least had only Una's and Meghan's company to endure while she dressed. Instead, Lady Epping and Lady Chelmsford had fairly well insisted on loitering about Charlotte's chamber, fussing over her, cooing and squawking. To Charlotte, it was as if each of them poked her repeatedly and insistently with the sharpened tines of fish forks.

"That is such a fetching gown on her," Lady Chelmsford declared, walking in broad circles about Charlotte, inspecting her. "She is a beautiful girl, Audrey. By my breath, she is."

"Darling, here . . ." Lady Epping said, leaving Charlotte momentarily. She took a small box in hand and brought it back to her daughter, opening it and holding it up for Charlotte to admire. "Look what Lord Roding had delivered for you today."

Charlotte looked down at the matching diamond necklace and earrings with disinterest. "Are they not divine?" Lady Epping gushed breathlessly. She handed the box to Meghan, and pinched the necklace between her fingertips, lifting it and admiring the play of lamplight against the faceted stones. "Are they not exquisite?"

"Exquisite," Lady Chelmsford clucked in echo.

"They do not suit the dress," Charlotte said, and Lady Epping's smile faltered. "They are far too extravagant. I do not want to wear them."

"Well, you are going to wear them," Lady Epping declared. "Lord Roding had them custom-made for you, Charlotte. He meant them to be wedding gifts, but was so eager and pleased when he paid call today, he insisted I give them to you for tonight. Now lift your chin and let me fasten the clasp."

"I do not want to marry James," Charlotte said, feeling the cold press of the necklace against her throat. "I realize you think it is best for me, Mother, and that you have convinced Father, but I do not want this."

"I do not think it is best for you, Charlotte," Lady Epping said, finished with the clasp. "I know it is."

"I do not love him," she said. "I want to choose my husband for myself."

"You have already tried your hand at choosing for yourself, and look what has come of it," she said. "A worthless cad beneath your station in a dilapidated house with no servants, much less window panes. A man who, by his own admission, has overindulged in drink, engaged in brawling, been jailed and pilloried. You certainly chose well and wisely when afforded such opportunity."

"Kenley is a good man," Charlotte said. "I love him and he loves me. He told me he does."

"Of course he told you that," Lady Epping snapped. "He would tell you anything to see his way beneath your underpinnings and between your thighs. I know his sort, lamb."

"Obviously, you do not know his sort at all, Mother," Charlotte said retorted. "Kenley is far too well-mannered a gentleman to take advantage."

"A gentleman, she says," Lady Chelmsford muttered with a scornful snort.

"Yes, Aunt Maude, I do say," Charlotte said, angry now. "Go ahead, keel over," Charlotte said when Lady Chelsmford rolled her eyes. "You and your vapors! My God, why are you not airborne from them yet?"

Lady Epping slapped her across the face. "How dare you speak to your aunt with such disregard?" she said. "She has shown you great kindness, welcoming you into her home as no less than a daughter of her own. She loves you dearly. You apologize this moment, Charlotte."

Charlotte held her hand to her cheek. Lady Epping had never struck her in all of her days; more than pain, however, the shock of it left her stunned. "I . . . I am sorry, Aunt Maude," she stammered.

"Now you listen to me," Lady Epping said, grasping Charlotte by the arm and giving her a scolding shake. "You stop this ridiculous, childish petulance. You are marrying Lord Roding—a proper gentleman, an earl's heir and a suitable husband—whether you wish it, will it, want it or not! Do you understand me?"

Charlotte winced when Lady Epping gave her arm another firm shake.

"Yes . . ."

"Good," Lady Epping said. She drew in a deep breath to reclaim her composure and struggled to smile. "I am not sending you to the gallows, child. It is a wedding, not death! Can you not even offer pretense of some good cheer, Charlotte?"

Lady Epping turned to the doorway. "Reilly, darling," she said, startled. "At last! Where have you been all day?"

Charlotte saw her brother at the threshold. He had

obviously witnessed the entire exchange between mother and daughter. "I . . . I am sorry for my delay, Mother," he apologized. "I have been riding."

Charlotte wanted to launch herself at him. She wanted to pummel him with her fists and curse him. It was his fault this had happened; whatever he had done to make Kenley abandon her, she wanted to see Reilly answer for it.

"Well, no matter," Lady Epping said, managing a nonchalant little laugh, as if all were rightly well in the world. "Go now and change, darling. We have been invited to Hudswell Hall tonight. Do wear something appropriate, perhaps to match your sister's gown?"

"I . . . I am not feeling up to any engagements, Mother," Reilly said. "I thought I might take to my bed and—"

"Oh, no," Lady Epping said. "Not again, not tonight. If you are well enough to spend the day roaming about on horseback, you are well enough for a ball. Now go make yourself presentable. Put some powder on your face. You look ghastly."

He did look terrible, Charlotte realized. Reilly's face was ashen, his eyes ringed in heavy shadows that were more than just a play of the light and his position in the doorway. He seemed to be leaning heavily against the doorframe, as if mustering the strength to draw himself upright was beyond his capacity to bear. He looked miserable enough she nearly worried for him, until she reminded herself that he was to blame for her troubles.

Reilly straightened, his motions stiff and deliberately slow. "Yes, Mother," he said quietly.

"Reilly, darling, you have not even commented on your sister's good fortune," Lady Chelmsford said. "She is to wed Lord Roding now. It has been arranged properly and officially. And does she not look lovely for the occasion?"

Reilly met his sister's glowering gaze, and his brows lifted unhappily. "She is always lovely, Aunt Maude," he said. He turned and limped away.

✻ ✻ ✻

They arrived at Hudswell Hall that evening as they had to Roding Castle the day before—amidst a flurry of frenzied gossip. By now, the news of Charlotte's broken engagement and forthcoming marriage to James had reached the rumor mill—news made all the more shocking as most had yet to fully absorb the revelations of Charlotte and Kenley's arrangement.

James' friends and family swarmed upon Charlotte. Within moments of her arrival, she was surrounded by people smiling at her, bowing before her, offering a din of overlapping congratulations and fond wishes.

"Here is our bride-to-be," Camden Iden said,

affecting a slight bend at his waist. "And by far the most fair in this ballroom, I dare say."

"Hoah, now, Hallingbury, she is spoken for, and well at that," Julian Stockley exclaimed with a laugh, clapping Camden heavily on the shoulder. Julian bowed for Charlotte. "You have done our Roding a great service, or taken great pity on him," he said. "Either way, you have raised him a fair measure in our collective esteem. He should be eternally grateful for your tender mercies."

Margaret Houghton appeared out of nowhere, forcing herself against Charlotte in a crushing, unexpected embrace. "We shall soon be sisters! Is that not thrilling?" she squealed in Charlotte's ear. Charlotte murmured something in polite reply; the words did not matter, as they were lost beneath Margaret's gushing commentary on how beautiful she was, and what a divine bride she would be come Sunday.

"When is my darling not beautiful, Margaret?" James asked, stepping into Charlotte's view. He brushed his hand against his sister's shoulder, and she drew away from Charlotte. James took her place, drawing uncomfortably near; when he bowed, he let his gaze linger longer than was courteous on her breasts, as was his habit.

Charlotte dropped him an obligatory curtsy, but offered no greeting. James slipped her hand into his and bussed her knuckles. "You have made me more happy than any man has a right to expect," he said. He canted his head, eyeing the diamonds draping her throat, pinned to her ears. "I see you received my affectionate tokens. They suit you well, as I knew they would. Of course, they are only pale complements to your visage."

The crowd about them murmured and cooed appreciatively at his flattery. Charlotte said nothing. James did not release her hand; in fact, he turned, drawing her away from the party guests to a less crowded corner of the ballroom.

"I must apologize for my behavior last night," he said. "I admit, I was untoward, but when the matter comes to you, Charlotte, my reason and sense of propriety often abandon me."

He licked his upper lip, the tip of his tongue drawing slowly, thoughtfully. "I cannot express how eagerly I am anticipating our wedding," he said. "And our wedding night."

Charlotte shrugged, and he drew back, chuckling softly at her resistance. He hooked his fingertips beneath her chin to draw her gaze. "You do not know how much I want you," he whispered. "How long I have wanted you . . . how I have longed to explore and discover your every sweet and secret fold and crevice. Even now, I am hardening to imagine your supple flesh growing flushed with heat at my caress. I will leave you breathless and pleading at the anticipation of my next touch as I take you, fill you, pierce the barrier that marks a woman from a child so deeply nestled within you. You will writhe against me with pleasure, Charlotte. It will shudder through you as I pump my seed into the delicious warmth of your maiden's womb."

Charlotte swung her hand around, slapping his fingers away from her. "You will only see me shudder with revulsion," she said. "You disgust me, James. Do you think I would ever find pleasure in your vile touch? Go ahead and look forward to our wedding night. You might claim my body, but you will never hold my heart."

James held her defiant gaze for a long moment and then arched his brow, the corner of his mouth lifting wryly. "Very well, then," he said. He leaned toward her, nearly brushing his nose against hers. "It is only the former I have ever wanted anyway. I have never cared a whit about the latter."

Charlotte spat at him, spraying his cheek and mouth, then turned and shoved her way through the crowd. She could hear him behind her, chuckling as he brought his hand to his face, wiping at her spittle with his fingertips.

Her cheeks were ablaze with shame and rage; tears stung her eyes. She felt people reach for her, well-wishers trying to draw her attention, speaking to her, smiling and laughing, and she ignored them all. She forced her way to the foyer and darted for the front doors. She shouldered past the arriving guests, the valets and footmen arranged at the threshold to take coats, hats, and muffs, and rushed out into the cold night, down the stairs and into the yard.

She snatched her jupe in her fists, hiking her skirts to run. She raced clumsily across the grounds, her breath hitching, her tears spilling. She wanted to scream, to shriek her defiance until she was hoarse. She ran for the stables, her mind whirling frantically, desperately. She had no particular intentions; she was seized with the urge to simply snatch a horse from a groom, swing herself astride, kick it mightily and gallop away.

In the end, she ran through the barn to a ladder leading upstairs into the loft. She climbed it, ignoring the curious, bewildered glances she drew from the stable hands as they tended the horses. Charlotte climbed up to the loft, and then crumpled onto her knees. She clapped her hands over her face and wept, shuddering uncontrollably.

"I will not marry him," she sobbed. "I will not. They cannot make me. I . . . I will run away. Tonight—this very moment, I . . . I will run away. I will not marry James Houghton! I will not!"

"Yes, you will," she heard a deep, low voice rumble from behind her.

Charlotte whirled, hiccupping in breathless start as she scrambled to her feet. Edmond Cheadle had followed her up the ladder and into the loft.

"You seem to have an affinity for lofts," Cheadle

remarked. "Do you find fond reminders here? I know I surely do."

He . . . he knows, she thought, aghast as Cheadle's dark eyes, glittering with insidious and clever light, fixed upon hers, impaling her.

Cheadle's smile widened. "Did his touch please you?" he asked. "It certainly seemed to, the way your breath fluttered, the way you moaned and begged for him. I drew myself to my own conclusions just to watch, if you gather my inference."

Charlotte gathered it well, and felt her gut wrench with sudden nausea. The idea of Cheadle hiding among the hay bales and dim shadows, taking himself in hand and coaxing himself to climax left her shivering with revulsion.

"Theydon is a man of stronger merits than I would have given him credit for," Cheadle said. "Myself, if you were to plead with me so; if I was knuckle-deep and two-fingers wide inside of you; if I was faced with the sweet prospect of taking you deeply, shoving through that little maidenhead of yours like a spear through linen . . . myself, I could not resist or refuse."

"What do you want?" Charlotte asked.

Cheadle's eyes trailed along her bosom, and he chuckled as Charlotte instinctively drew her arms protectively about herself. "What I want is to let my hand visit those places only recently vacated by Kenley Fairfax's," he said, licking his lips slowly.

Charlotte looked about frantically. They were alone; the isolation that had seemed so ideal for her and Kenley at Roding Castle now proved ominous. If Cheadle meant to assault her, she had no avenue of flight; he was taller than her and broader besides. If he took such a mind, she had precious little hope of fending him off, no matter how furiously she tried.

"I will not," Cheadle said, holding up his hands in mocking concession. "My lord would be displeased if I enjoyed the first taste of his virginal bride. Do not worry for that."

Charlotte whirled, sprinting for the ladder. Cheadle followed; she felt the floor shudder with his swift, heavy footfalls, and she cried out as his broad fist closed on her arm. He jerked her backward, nearly flinging her off her feet. She slammed against the wall, rapping the back of her head soundly. Before she could reclaim her wits or wind to try again for the ladder, Cheadle crushed against her, pinning her fast, using his tremendous bulk to keep her still. Charlotte struggled, opening her mouth to scream, but her voice was reduced to a muffled mewl as Cheadle's large hand clamped firmly over her mouth.

"You will marry Lord Roding," he said, his hand crushing her face, mashing her lips painfully into her teeth. She glared at him and shook her head, screaming "no" with all of her might against his hand.

He rammed the cap of her head into the wall again,

hard enough to rattle her teeth, and she moaned, her
eyelids fluttering, momentarily dazed. "Yes, you will,"
he said. He lowered his face within centimeters of hers.
"You will be on time for the service and at your loveli-
est," Cheadle told her. "You will smile as you make your
vows, and you will wed him in proper fashion. You will
do as you are told—willingly, gladly—you will do it, or
by my breath, your beloved Lord Theydon will swing
from the gallows."

Charlotte fell immediately still, and Cheadle laughed
softly. "He will dance the Tyburn jig—and he will not
be alone," he purred. "His cousin will join him, with
your rot brother to mark the time."

Charlotte whimpered. *Reilly?* she thought wildly,
panicked. *Kenley and Lewis? What is he talking about?*

Cheadle cocked his brow. "This is a good look for
you," he murmured, smiling. "Frightened, complacent. It
suited your brother well, too, when we spoke last night."

What?

"He and I were able to come to a mutual understanding," Cheadle said. "As I am sure you and I will.
He has fulfilled his part of our bargain, and so I will
offer you the same barter that persuaded him. Do as I
tell you, precisely as I tell you, and no one stands beneath
the limbs of the Tyburn tree."

His hand clamped more tightly against her face,
forcing a pained mewl. "And if you cross me, if you con-

tinue this ridiculous refusal of my lord's proposal, then I promise you, all three of them will hang."

Charlotte trembled in terrified confusion.

"Have we come to an understanding?" Cheadle asked. "Will you marry my lord with no further complaint? Will you see them all spared? Answer me. Nod your head or shake it."

Charlotte did not understand at all, but she nodded her head, her eyes enormous. "Yes," she said, her reply muffled against his hand.

"Good," Cheadle said. His hand slipped away from her mouth, and he stepped back. Charlotte scuttled away from him and cowered against the wall. He made no more effort to approach her, turning instead for the ladder to take his leave.

"You should return to the party," he said, glancing at her over his shoulder. "I am sure your absence has been noted, and my lord has grown lonely for your company."

Charlotte watched him mount the ladder and climb down. She listened to the sounds of his boot heels on the ladder rungs; the rustle of straw as he stepped onto the ground below. She heard his footfalls, heavy and thudding as he walked to the threshold of the barn. She did not move all the while. She could not so much as breathe until the last sound of him had faded.

CHAPTER 14

ON THE COACH RIDE HOME TO DARTON Hall, Charlotte studied Reilly, who sat across from her. He seemed to do his best to try and sleep, oblivious to her attention; he rested his temple against the window frame and kept his eyes closed. Charlotte watched him intently, her lips drawn together pensively.

What does Cheadle hold over you? she thought. Cheadle was a thief-taker by trade and his turn as a domestic servant for James had always struck her as odd. Thief-takers were bounty hunters, usually thieves themselves, and were more concerned with fattening their own purses than with any sense of civic duty. They hunted down other criminals and turned them in for the reward money.

Reilly, however, was not a criminal. Even if he, Lewis, and Kenley had lied about Kenley's enlistment in the Navy, Charlotte could not believe they had conspired together to commit crimes. Reilly and Lewis were commissioned officers and both noblemen of good standing and some caliber. Despite his father's past, and his own youthful indiscretions, even Kenley was now considered a gentleman of proper status. All three of them were good men with good reputations that none would see compromised.

But Cheadle was an experienced thief-taker, which meant he had contacts in London and throughout England. His word was likely accepted without question on the matter of wanted criminals; when Cheadle turned someone in for a reward, the men he surrendered were surely assumed guilty.

Did Cheadle threaten you, Reilly? Charlotte thought. *Did he promise to frame you for some sort of crime—something heinous enough to see you hanged, and that you feel helpless to defend yourself against?*

Reilly's eyelids fluttered opened as the carriage jostled roughly along a deep rut in the roadway. He winced visibly, and blinked at his sister, noticing her attention. Charlotte held his gaze for a long moment until he closed his eyes again to escape her.

What did Cheadle do to you? she wondered.

At Darton Hall, Charlotte lay awake beneath her coverlets for a long time after the house grew quiet, the family and servants all taking to their beds. At last, when she felt certain it was safe, Charlotte shoved her blankets aside and left her bed. She drew her dressing robe about her shoulders and stole into the corridor.

She was not particularly surprised to find a light aglow beneath Reilly's door. She was surprised, however, to hear Meghan's voice cry out quietly from inside his room as she drew near.

"Reilly, what happened?" she exclaimed.

Charlotte knelt at Reilly's threshold, peeking through the keyhole. She could see nothing except for his writing table, the vacant chair beside it, but she could hear Reilly and Meghan clearly, as if they stood just beyond her view.

"Who did this to you?" Meghan gasped, her voice fluttering, near to tears.

"It is nothing," Reilly said, and then he uttered a soft, pained gasp that made Meghan whimper.

"Who did this to you?" she asked again. Charlotte frowned, trying to crane her head, to see them.

"I took a tumble from my horse this morning," Reilly said, and Charlotte drew back, startled when he walked into her line of sight. She saw the cause for Meghan's distress; Reilly wore only his breeches, and he had been brutally beaten. Charlotte could see distinctive bands of dark, vicious bruising wrapped from his belly to his back and kidneys where someone had taken to him purposefully and repeatedly with their fists.

"Reilly!" Charlotte breathed, feeling tears spring to her eyes. No tumble from a horse had inflicted such injuries; Cheadle had beaten him, and Charlotte knew it. Cheadle had pounded compliance into Reilly.

"I will have to rip the linens," Reilly said. "I think I have some cracked ribs, and binding them tightly will help."

At this, Meghan began to cry, and Charlotte heard her brother's voice, soft and anguished. "Please, Meghan," he whispered. "Please do not. It is all right. Just some broken ribs and some bruising. Help me with the linens. I know how to bind my chest. I made friends with the shipboard surgeon on the *Endurance*. Binding some splintered ribs is naught."

He was trying his best to make light of his pain, to reassure her, but Meghan would have none of it. "Who hurt you like this?" she cried. "Who did this to you?"

"It does not matter," he said, his voice tremulous, as if he, too hovered on the verge of tears. Charlotte had never known Reilly to weep before; the sound of his despair only drew more tears to her eyes.

"It is over, Meghan," Reilly said. "Please do not. I have seen to it . . . may . . . may God forgive me."

❀ ❀ ❀

Charlotte hurried back to her room. She closed the door behind her and leaned against it, trying to recover from the shock of seeing Reilly so battered. She would find no more answers than the grim, mute testimony of Cheadle's abuse apparent on Reilly's form, and Charlotte no longer had the heart to demand them of him.

"That bastard," Charlotte spat, Cheadle's face foremost in her mind—the wicked gleam in his eyes, and the triumphant smile twisting his mouth. Her hands curled into fists. "That bloody bastard."

She knew a place where she could yet find answers; where she might discover what power Cheadle wielded over Reilly. "Kenley," she breathed, and jerked open her wardrobe. She grabbed her old breeches and a rumpled shirt and hurriedly set about changing from her night clothes.

Whatever Cheadle had threatened to frame them with had been enough to send Reilly, despite his injuries, to Kenley that morning. It had been enough to frighten Kenley into doing as Reilly told him—breaking his engagement to Charlotte. Kenley knew what was going on, and he would tell her.

She drew her pocket pistol from her writing table drawer. "He will tell me, by my breath," she said. She returned to her wardrobe, reaching for her riding habit coat. Her hand came in contact with a heavy woolen sleeve, and to her momentary surprise, she inadvertently pulled out the black greatcoat given to her during her robbery.

She stared at the coat for a moment, and then gasped with realization. *The Black Trio!* she thought. She remembered the note she had found in Cheadle's book, the gazette clipping about the highwaymen. *Suitable for our needs?* someone had written in the margin, and all at once the words made stunning sense to her.

"Of course," she said. Cheadle meant to frame Reilly, Kenley, and Lewis for the Black Trio robberies. The three young men had only been back in Essex County for the last six months, the same timeframe as the robberies. James had probably been fully aware of Charlotte's homecoming to Epping, and her mother's intentions to see her married to him; knowing Lady Epping, Charlotte did not doubt the arrangement of their wedding had been discussed with James and set in motion months before her arrival.

James would have known Charlotte would consent to marry him with all of the eager willingness of a hog taking to the minuet. He would have made preparations to ensure her compliance.

She thought of the note again: *Suitable for our needs?* The bastard had set in his mind from the first to blame Reilly and his friends for the robberies. Kenley's attraction to Charlotte had been unanticipated, but countered by the same ploy. James knew well that Charlotte adored her brother and threatening Reilly must have seemed a secure way to assure her cooperation.

"Bloody bastard," she said, shrugging into the greatcoat. She shoved her pistol into the hip pocket. The

Black Trio. No wonder Reilly and Kenley had been so intimidated, so terrified. Cheadle had spoken truly; highway robbery was a hanging offense, and because the Trio's crimes had occurred on the King's highways, they would prove offenses punishable by execution at the most infamous of England's gallows—the Tyburn tree of London.

Charlotte had her suspicions; her inquisitive mind had set itself to the task and formulated a seemingly viable scenario. "Now all that remains is to prove it," she muttered, heading for her door.

There was only one place where she could hope to do so, and she knew it. She had to pay an unannounced call to Theydon Hall.

❄   ❄   ❄

Charlotte had expected to find Theydon Hall darkened and quiet upon her arrival, and was somewhat surprised to discover lights aglow when she approached. She dismounted while still a distance from the house, and tied her roan to a tree, lest the sound of hoof beats alert whoever was still awake and about inside the house. She did not want Kenley to suspect her presence. He would only avoid her or send her away without hearing her out. She had seen the alarm apparent on his face that morning. He was frightened, and Charlotte knew she needed to surprise him, to confront him before he had any opportunity to counter her.

She crossed the expansive front yard, shrouded in darkness and shadows. Crouching beneath the parlor windows, from which the glow of golden lamplight emanated, she heard the sound of voices.

"I cannot do this," Kenley said from within the parlor. "I cannot do this, Lewis. Please do not ask it of me. I cannot."

"You must," Charlotte heard Lewis say, his voice gentle, as if he meant to soothe his cousin. "There is no other way."

She heard Kenley utter a hoarse, sharp cry, and then the shattering of glass as he hurled a brandy snifter at the mantle. "It is my fault!" he cried. "All my bloody damn fault! Reilly told us if we just let it go, if we kept to ourselves, it would all go away with no one the wiser! And now?" His voice was anguished. "Now she is gone to me. She is gone, Lewis! I have lost her, and I . . . I cannot breathe for it! I cannot!"

He had told her they could not fall in love in only days, but they had She knew it, and he did, too, no matter how he tried to deny it.

"I have lost her," Kenley said, his voice muffled. Charlotte risked a peek into the parlor, peering over the bottom of the window sill. She saw Lewis embracing Kenley, his back to Charlotte. She saw Kenley's fingers clutch his cousin's shoulders in desperation. "It is all my fault," Kenley said.

"No, it is not," Lewis said.

Kenley jerked away and Charlotte shied back, crouching again lest he see her.

"It is my fault!" he shouted. "Reilly told us to let it lie, and I . . . I had to go to London! I had to go to St. Bartholomew's and now . . . !"

Charlotte's heart seemed to stop. *St. Bartholomew's?*

"I had to think with my bloody heart and not my head, just like Reilly said!" Kenley cried. "I am a fool, Lewis, a rot damn fool trying to impress her. Why? Why did it matter what she thought of it? We were not one and the same in her mind and regard—what was I thinking?"

"Oh . . ." Charlotte moaned in stunned realization. Cheadle had not threatened to frame the three friends for the Black Trio robberies—he threatened to expose them. Her mind snapped suddenly to the night of the robbery, to the young highwayman's quick wit, his sharp retorts and clever rebukes when she had argued with him. How could it have seemed unfamiliar to her when, only days later, Kenley had offered her the same reception? How could she not have realized?

"It is my fault," Kenley repeated. "You did not see Reilly's stomach, Lewis—the bruises where that rot bastard beat him. You did not see what they did to him—it is all on my account! I have brought this on us!"

"Do not say that, Will," Lewis said, and Charlotte rapped the back of her head firmly against the stone wall when she recoiled in new shock. *Will? He . . . he called him Will!*

Her hand reached for the left pocket of the great-coat. Her gloved fingertips brushed against the silver snuff box tucked inside, the one with the engraved initials: *W.S.*

"William Sutton," she whispered, her eyes enormous. "Oh . . . oh, my God . . ."

CHAPTER 15

CHARLOTTE REMAINED ON HER KNEES BE-
neath the parlor window as the spill of light from inside
dimmed, and Lewis and Kenley retired for the night.
She heard their voices fade along with their footsteps
when they abandoned the parlor. When silence settled
she stood again, wincing and shaking her feet to reac-
quaint blood flow with her calves. She followed the wall,
creeping around the corner toward the kitchen entrance,
then backed away from the house and looked up, keeping
carefully to the shadows. She watched a yellow glow ap-
pear in a second storey chamber overlooking the yard as
someone lit a lamp. After a moment, a silhouetted figure
appeared in one of the windows, forcing her to scuttle
for cover among deeper shadows. The figure paused only
briefly at the window before turning and walking away,

but she saw plainly he was too lean to be Lewis. She was looking up at Kenley's room.

She shivered in the cold, damp night air, waiting for him to snuff his lamp and go to bed. An excruciatingly long amount of time seemed to creep by, and then finally the glow from his windows was extinguished, plunging her immediately and thoroughly into darkness. She forced herself to wait a bit longer, knowing just because he had tucked himself to bed did not necessarily mean he was sleeping.

At last, she made her move for the kitchen door. She did not know if Theydon Hall was kept bolted by habit or not; with so many broken windows to choose from, even if the door was locked she would have no problem gaining entry. She found the kitchen door unlatched, however, and slipped inside, closing it silently behind her. She stood for a moment in the darkened room, gathering her bearings and trying to orient herself in the unfamiliar house.

She followed a corridor beyond the kitchen leading to her right and found herself in the foyer. She could see the dim, scarlet glow of waning coals from the parlor fireplace to her right. She turned and crept up the stairs, grimacing at every creak and groan her feet coaxed from the weathered wood of the risers.

When Charlotte reached the door to Kenley's room, she paused, slipping her hand into her pocket and curling her fingers around the butt of her pistol. Her heart was hammering and she trembled. She did not know exactly what she was doing, or what she hoped to accomplish any longer. All she understood was that she wanted the truth; she wanted to hear it from Kenley, or William Sutton, or whomever this young man might be.

She eased the door open and ducked inside the chamber. She looked around and found a large bed set against the far wall. There were few other furnishings; a wardrobe to her left, and another dining chair, like the pair in the parlor, to her right. Several large traveling trunks were arranged around the room, obviously utilized as makeshift tables, given the number of books, periodicals, and gazettes heaped atop each.

Kenley slept, lying on his back with one arm draped across the pillows and over his head. His face was tilted toward his shoulder; his dark, tousled hair swept across his brow and cheek. His chest was bare, the blankets swathed loosely about his hips. He kept his other hand pressed lightly against the flat plane of his belly, and his expression was softened with sleep. His bedside lamp was dimmed nearly to darkness, but it cast enough of a glow that once Charlotte became accustomed to it, she could admire its soft play against the lean, long muscles in Kenley's arms and chest.

She stood at the end of his bed, torn by such simple, poignant emotions she was momentarily immobilized.

She let her eyes trail along the length of his body, following the contours of his muscles. She watched the dim illumination from the lamp play across the waves of his dark hair. She looked at his hands, his long, graceful fingers relaxed on his belly, and curled loosely by his head on his pillow. Something within her trembled, a pang of helpless, distraught longing to think of his hands on her, to recall the sensation of his touch.

She loved him. Even now, faced with the overwhelming, staggering weight of what was surely the truth, she was gripped with love for him. At the same time, Charlotte shook with anger and frustration. Albert had not mistaken Kenley for a stable boy beloved by him. Albert was addled, all right—too addled to remember the ruse, as Will and Lewis must have instructed him. He had not called Kenley "William" in confusion; he had addressed him as such because it was his name. This man she loved, who had kissed her, touched her, coaxed such passion and pleasure from her was not Kenley Fairfax at all.

"William," she whispered, blinking against the sudden heat of tears. She walked around the side of the bed and looked down at him. She drew the pistol from her pocket and leveled it, her arm shaking, her aim unsteady. "William Sutton."

She pulled the hammer back, cocking it. At the soft, distinctive click, and the sound of her voice, William Sutton stirred. He groaned softly and his eyelids fluttered open.

"Who are you?" Charlotte asked, her voice hoarse with tears she struggled to hold in check.

His eyes flew wide and he sat back against the headboard. He caught the wink of lamplight on the brass-adorned, snub-nosed pistol and he froze.

"Who are you?" Charlotte demanded, the pistol shaking in her grasp.

"Charlotte . . ."

"That is my name," Charlotte snapped. "That is mine, you bastard—now tell me yours."

"Charlotte . . ." he repeated, reaching for her.

"Tell me your name!" she shouted. "You lying bastard! Tell me your name! I want to hear it from your lips!"

"Sutton," he said. "My name is Will Sutton."

Charlotte uttered a soft bark of pained laughter. "Well, then," she said, reaching with her free hand for her coat. "This is explained. You forgot it in your pocket."

She tossed the snuff box at him, and it slapped on his belly, falling to the coverlets. He clearly recognized it; he did not need to see the engraved *W.S.* to realize what it was, and he looked up at her. "Please," he said. "Please, Charlotte, let me—"

"What?" Charlotte said. "Let you explain? There is nothing left to explain, Will Sutton. I have it all figured out. You, Reilly, and Lewis—you served in the Navy together, fast as thieves, just like in childhood. Am I right? Fast as thieves for certain . . . you are the Black Trio! Edmond Cheadle did not threaten to frame you for the robberies . . . he said he would see you rightly hanged for them!"

Charlotte felt tears slip from her eyes, rolling down her cheeks. "That . . . that is why you broke our engagement," she said. "That is why you said you did not love me . . . why you have done all of this. Is it not?"

He did not answer her. She saw the glimmer of lamplight in his moist, dark eyes, and she shoved the gun at him, flexing her finger for emphasis on the trigger. "Is it not?" she cried.

"Yes." He nodded. "Yes, it is true."

She backed away from the bed keeping the pistol trained on his head. "Get up," she said. "Get on your feet, you bastard."

Will rose slowly from his bed to stand in front of her. His shoulders hunched and his hair drooped into his face as he lowered his gaze, hanging his head in shame.

"Look up at me," Charlotte said. "You lift your eyes and face me, you coward rot."

He raised his gaze, his eyes round and forlorn. She steeled her heart against him; against the pain and sorrow in his eyes. "Where is Kenley Fairfax?" she asked. "The real Kenley Fairfax. What happened to him?"

"He is dead," Will said. "He died six months ago, shortly after my uncle passed. A blight came upon him

. . . a lung infection and terrible fever."

"And you assumed his name," Charlotte said. "You took his identity for your own. You, Lewis, and my brother conspired to take what was rightly his—this house, the Theydon title and lands—and put you in his place. You stole his life."

"No" Will shook his head. "No, Charlotte, that is not—"

"Do not move!" Charlotte shook the pistol at him. He halted and lifted his hands slowly, his gaze fixed upon the gun. "How dare you stand there and lie to me even now!" she cried. "You took what you had no entitlement to—no bloody right—and you made it your own!"

"They were Kenley's by right," Will said. "But they . . . they were mine, too. Kenley wanted me to have them. He told us on his death bed that he . . . he wanted . . ."

His voice faded, and he ran his fingers through his hair. He looked at her, his eyes swimming and glossy with tears. "Kenley was my brother."

The gun barrel wavered.

"My mother was a kitchen maid here at Theydon," Will said. "My father—Kenley's father—turned to her after Kenley's mother died in childbirth. Kenley always knew. Lewis, my uncle . . . they knew it, too, and they loved me for it, even though my father would not admit or accept it. He used to punish me for it, as if it were something I could be held accountable for.

"He used to beat me." Will lowered his gaze to the floor. "With all of his might, he would take his lash to my back. Kenley tried to protect me . . . spare me from it. He would provoke his father to see himself beaten, not me. And when we were older . . . right before Lord Theydon died, he . . . Kenley took one of his dueling pistols and drew it on him. Kenley told our father if he ever raised his hand or strap to me again, that he would shoot him dead."

Charlotte lowered the pistol slightly.

"When our father died, they took care of me," Will told her. "Kenley and I lived at Woodside, and they treated me as though I was no different than any of them. They were my friends, my family. Kenley and I found trouble together sometimes, but he . . . I loved him with my whole heart. I would do anything for him. When we joined the Navy to be with Lewis and Reilly, Kenley gave them a false name, one without peerage, so he would not receive an officer's commission. He wanted to be with me . . . an able seaman like me.

"He asked this of us, all of this," he said. "He asked Lewis to give me Theydon. It was as much mine by right and blood as it had ever been his, he said. He told me to take his name, make it my own, and he swore me to it. I could not convince him otherwise. I tried. Please, Charlotte, I tried with all that was within me, but he told me he wanted this for me.

"He swore us to secrecy on it—me, Lewis, and Reilly. We agreed to say Kenley Fairfax had been away on a Grand Tour. There was no other accounting for his absence all of this time. We agreed to it all because he was dying and we loved him. We would do what he wanted of us."

"And the Black Trio?" Charlotte asked, summoning her anger again, refusing to succumb to his pleading gaze, his piteous story. She hefted the pistol, aiming at him. "Was that Kenley Fairfax's idea, too? Another deathbed wish? The three of you undertook it because you loved him and he wanted you to?"

"No," Will said. "No, that was Reilly's idea."

Charlotte felt as if she had been punched in the gut. "Reilly's?"

"It was a joke," Will said. "A joking idea he came up with on the ship, something we tossed about to pass the time, and a way he said he and Lewis could shrug aside all of the responsibility and duty that had been forced upon them by their families, the Navy. He had always done what was expected of him, what was proper and right, and he . . . I thought he meant it all in jest. And when we returned from the colonies after the war, he became restless with the thought of it. He told us he was in love, but because of his noble birth, he could never acknowledge it . . . never marry her . . ."

"Meghan," Charlotte whispered. "My mother's housekeeper."

Will nodded. "He felt trapped, suffocated he told us, and he wanted to see it through. All of the plans we had only laughed over aboard the ship he wanted to put into motion."

He stared at her, pleading. "We did not do it because we loved Kenley," he said. "We did it because we love Reilly, because Reilly asked us to.

"Please," he said. "Please, we did not know it was your carriage. That was what ended it—what was supposed to have ended it. Reilly was devastated. He said he would never forgive himself. It was to have ended there. We all agreed. Reilly said if we let it go, it would fall behind us and be forgotten.

"It is my fault it has come to this," he said. "I did not recognize you at first, but you . . . you were so beautiful, Charlotte, I nearly lost my breath to draw near you. And when you challenged me, stood your ground against me, even with a pistol in my hand, I . . . I was astonished. I had read your works—that was not a lie. Reilly shared them with me aboard the *Endurance*. I had wondered about you. That was no lie, either. I could not wrest you from my mind after the robbery, no matter how I tried. I gave my share of our money as you asked of me. I wanted so badly for you to think kindly of me . . . to think of me at all."

He looked at her forlornly. "It is my fault," he said

again. "I meant no harm, but it brought more interest to our robberies. It made us all the more notorious, and Reilly . . . I thought he would beat me himself, he was so furious with me. And then when I announced we would wed . . ."

His voice faded momentarily. "To see you, speak with you, I lost my reason," he said. "And when Roding said he meant to marry you, I spoke without thinking. I said the first thing that came to my heart, my mind. I could not let Roding have you—I told you that. I had no idea his coachman was a thief-taker, that he would so quickly figure us out, or that my words would bring as much trouble on us as they have.

"Cheadle beat Reilly. He told Reilly he had evidence to prove us guilty, and when Reilly challenged him, Cheadle beat him nearly witless. He forced Reilly to agree to see us apart and when Reilly came to me—battered and bruised, all on my account—I could not refuse him."

"What proof does Cheadle have?" Charlotte asked.

"I do not know," Will said. "He did not say. I told Reilly he was bluffing, but Reilly told me the circumstances alone of our arrival in Essex and the beginning of the robberies could prove enough to see us hanged with a reputable thief-taker to bring us in for bounty.

"Please," he begged. "I never wanted to lie to you, or hurt you. By my breath, I never meant for any of this. Last night with you . . . the terrace . . . the stables . . .

those were the most wondrous moments of my life."

"I thought last night was a dream," Charlotte said. "I thought you had come around to your senses again, that it meant nothing."

He looked at her, ashamed. "It meant everything," he said.

Charlotte let the tension in her arm drain, the pistol lower slowly to her side. She could not muster anger any longer; she could not convince herself to hate him. He had lied to her, hurt her, abandoned and betrayed her, and yet she did not harbor a moment's doubt or reservation about his sincerity. She had trusted him from the first, and somehow, even now, she trusted him; it felt instinctive to her, as it had from the moment of their introduction.

"Please," Will said. "Please forgive me. I beg of you, Charlotte."

Her fingers uncurled; the pistol dropped to the floor. When he approached her, she did not step away from him. When he touched her face, she looked up at him, her eyes tearful.

"I love you. By my breath, Charlotte, there has never been anything more true in my heart than this. I love you."

He took her face in his hands and pressed his mouth to hers. She opened her lips at his kiss, and whimpered softly when his tongue delved inside. She moved against him, and she felt him stir, a swell of heat and sudden pressure as he hardened.

She tilted her head back as his hands guided her gently, and then he traced the line of her throat with his mouth, finding the sensitive, exquisite place where the quickening of her heart could be felt. He eased the coat from her shoulders and she let it fall to the floor. He cupped her breasts in his palms and caressed them, drawing a whimper of pleasure from her.

She felt his fingers draw gentle, concentric circles against her nipples, and the wondrous sensation of the intense friction left her stomach muscles fluttering. She felt moistness between her thighs as one of his hands slid against her shirt, his fingers fumbling with the buttons.

He unfastened all of the buttons on her blouse, and drew it from the waistband of her breeches with gentle but insistent tugs. She shrugged her shoulders and the shirt fell in a heap behind them as they stumbled together toward the bed.

He tangled his fingers in her long hair, kissing her, drawing her so near the heat of his body felt as her own. She felt the back of her knees meet the edge of the mattress and she sat, lying back as his lips left hers, following the contours and curves of her body toward her breasts. Charlotte arched her back at the unanticipated, magnificent sensation of his tongue traveling against her sensitive, nearly electrified flesh. He suckled lightly, his tongue fluttering, and she gasped, touching his head, splaying her fingers in his hair.

His mouth and tongue teased her for a long, dizzying moment, and when his hand moved between her legs she reeled, her eyelids fluttering closed. He slid his hand beneath her breeches and she raised her hips as he drew them off.

She wanted to kiss him; she was desperate to kiss him. She tried to sit up, to draw his face to hers, and he raised his head as if reading her mind, knowing without her uttering a word what she wanted. He kissed her, laying her back, pressing himself atop her. Their bodies molded together in a perfect complement of forms, as though they had been made for no other purpose but this—to be together.

He kissed her, his hand moving between her thighs, his fingertips brushing against the silken, sensitive folds of flesh, lighting against the wispy tufts of golden curls marking the apex of her body.

"Please," Charlotte whimpered, and then his fingertips prodded against someplace hidden deep within her hot, moist flesh; at his touch she cried out breathlessly, the muscles in her thighs tightening reflexively. His hand lingered, his pace quickening, and Charlotte moved with him, wanting him. She gasped against his mouth, over and over drawing his breath as her own, and when his fingers slipped away she was left shuddering with the anticipation that came from having approached the brink of ultimate pleasure.

She reached for him, trying to push his breeches down. She looked up at him, trembling and breathless, frightened and eager all at once as he shifted his weight to help in her efforts, letting the hard, hot length of him press against her, poised and ready. Charlotte whimpered, clutching at Will's shoulders, pressing her thighs against his hips, wanting him.

"Charlotte," he said, stroking her disheveled hair back from her face. "I do not want to hurt you."

She touched his hips. He was lean and strong, and she wanted him as she had never wanted anything else in her days. "It is all right." She used her palms to guide his hips, pulling him down to her.

She felt him press against her threshold, and she lifted her hips to welcome him catching his soft, breathless cry when he slipped into her. He moved against her, the motion gentle. It was her first time, and there was pain, but he was slow, deliberate, and careful with every movement, as if she she were fragile, something he feared to break.

"Charlotte . . ." he breathed. He moved deeper still, easing his body into hers, and she closed her eyes until she felt his hesitation, his uncertainty.

"We do not have to do this," he whispered, stroking his palm against her cheek, his hips motionless. "I do not want to hurt you."

"It is what I want," she said. "You are what I want. I love you, Will."

Their lips touched, and he moved in her once more. She found his rhythm and matched it. They moved together for a wondrous eternity and Charlotte lost all concept of time as he moved between her thighs. He moaned and she kissed him, taking his voice, his need into her mouth. He moved faster against her, and faster still. He clutched her hands, folding his fingers through hers, as his rhythm quickened and grew more powerful, delivering him into her with sharp, pounding strokes.

She met his every advance with her own, drawing him in deep, and deeper still. She closed her eyes, tilting her head back; like the roar of the sea as an enormous wave bore toward the shore, she felt something immense rushing within her, tensing her entire body. When the wave broke within her, it was shattering in its intensity.

Her release drew his own; he cried out as he offered one last mighty thrust. He tightened in her, every muscle seizing with sudden, shuddering pleasure.

They lay still for a long moment, both of them reclaiming their breath. He looked down at her, and touched her face, brushing sweat-dampened tendrils of flaxen hair back from her flushed cheek, her brow. He smiled for her, and it was as if daylight had spilled into the room, she was filled with such joyous and radiant warmth.

"I love you, Will Sutton," she whispered. He leaned over her, kissing her gently, sweetly, his lips lingering against hers as if it was something he savored; something he never wished to end.

"I love you, Charlotte," he breathed.

She fell asleep with him spooned against her, his body marvelously warm and contoured against her own, his breath soft upon her shoulder. He kept his arm about her waist, his fingers drawn through hers, holding her gently as her exhausted mind faded. She had never known anything that felt more natural and right to her than this; to lie in his arms and share in his warmth, feeling safe and sheltered and beloved by him. She could not stay the night through; she knew it, and yet she could not bear to leave him. Her mind drifted, but after a time she felt his lips light on her shoulder; he had been lying awake all the while, listening to her breathe, watching her sleep, and he had kissed her.

"What are we going to do?" She was to marry James on Sunday and they both knew it. The brutal truth invaded their quiet, tender moment, and they were both silent with the realization.

"Run away with me," he offered, kissing her shoulder again.

"We cannot," she said as his lips traveled along the slope of her shoulder to her throat. She smiled when he kissed the delta of her jaw, as the tip of his tongue brushed against the outer curve of her ear. "We cannot leave Reilly and Lewis. I do not know what James will do."

His mouth drew away from her ear, his playful passion immediately subdued. She turned toward him, rolling onto her back into the shelter of his shoulder and chest. He placed his hand on her bosom, letting his fingers drape gently over her breast.

"It is not hopeless," he told her, although his eyes were filled with sorrow. She brushed her fingertips against his lips to draw a reluctant smile from him.

"No," she agreed. "It is not. We still have a day. We will find something, some way."

His hand moved slowly on her breast, a light but welcome pressure, and she felt fresh heat stir within her belly. She murmured softly, a quiet sound of pleasure, and his smile widened as the movement of his hand grew more insistent. She felt him stiffening against her thigh; like hers, his interest had been rekindled .

"We will find a way," she insisted as he leaned over, kissing her. He shifted his weight, rolling atop her, and she spread her thighs to enfold his hips. He had already hardened in full, and slid easily into her, filling her suddenly, unexpectedly. She gasped against his mouth, and he began to move again, slowly at first, a teasing, deliberate pace that in short measure left her breathless with urgent desire. *I will find a way,* she thought, as his motions, the friction of him clouded her mind, making her think of nothing else but this, but him.

CHAPTER 16

"CHARLOTTE?" UNA SAID, PLACING HER HAND on Charlotte's sleeve, turning her mind groggily from sleep. "Charlotte, wake now, lamb."

Will had ridden back to Darton Hall with Charlotte to see her safely home. They had reined their horses alongside one another, stopping a distance from the house and remained there in silence for a long while, fog curling about them, enfolding them in shadows.

He had kissed her farewell, leaning precariously in his saddle. The kiss had lingered for long, precious moments, their breath intermingling, until Charlotte's horse had snuffled and stomped its feet, impatient at their delay. Will had laughed softly against her mouth, and she had smiled, even though to leave him filled her with profound sorrow.

"I love you," she had said when they drew apart, and he righted himself astride his horse.

"I will always love you, Charlotte," he had told her. He had caught her hand in his, hooking fingertips with hers as she had pressed her heels to her gelding's flank to coax it forward. They had held their fingers locked together until the margin of space between them widened beyond their arms' full reach, and then, as she felt his hand slip away, as she watched Will disappear into the fog, dissolving into silhouette, the ache in her heart grew unbearable.

She had returned to the house and slipped upstairs to her chamber, promptly crumpling into her bed. She had not imagined sleep would be possible, not with her heart so wounded, her breath so tangled with tears she stubbornly refused to acknowledge. She had been unable to accept that this marked the end, that she would not be with Will. She knew there had to be a way to set things right, and if she only thought long and hard enough, she would discover it.

She had steeled herself with this firm resolve and then her eyes had drooped closed, and she had fallen into an unintended, exhausted sleep.

"Charlotte," Una said again, and Charlotte became aware of dim, golden light seeping through her eyelids; a lamp aglow. Una shook her and Charlotte felt her dazed mind jostle from murky unconsciousness. She opened her eyes, groaning aloud.

"What?" she croaked, blinking at Una. The maid was little more than a blurry figure draped in shadows and light. Another solid shaking corrected this; Una snapped into view as the cobwebs were swept from her mind, and she realized it was not yet dawn. The room was still dark and the only light came from the bedside lamp Una had lit. It was too early for Una to rouse her for dressing and breakfast, and Charlotte sat up in alarm.

"What is it?" she, terrified that she had been discovered, that her mother had learned somehow of her clandestine trip to Theydon Hall.

"You must get up, lamb," Una said. "Hurry now. You must dress. Lord Harlow has sent word. The midwife has been summoned and consulted. Your sister's baby is coming."

Charlotte shoved her blankets aside. She swung her legs to the floor and stood, stumbling sleepily. "Caroline, is she . . . ?"

"Come now," Una said, taking Charlotte's elbow and steering her toward the wardrobe. "Babies seldom come quickly or easily, but you have no time to dawdle. Your mother is nearly ready. She will be waiting for you. Come on."

❊ ❊ ❊

Charlotte rode by carriage to Caroline's home, Heathcote
House, with Lady Epping, Lady Chelmsford, Una, and
Meghan. Their driver whipped the horses to a frantic
pace; the coach bounced and swayed as they raced north.
An anxious silence held sway over the women; not even
Lady Chelmsford moaned, chattered, or offered pretense
of swooning to disturb it. Childbearing was a precarious
circumstance. Much could go awry, no matter a woman's
health or the quality of her pregnancy. They all knew
well the horror stories of hemorrhaging, breech-births,
and other complications—events which could not only
leave the infant dead, but the mother as well.

Charlotte spent much of the day, well into the afternoon, in Caroline's room at Heathcote. No men were
allowed into this inner sanctum, and the heavy draperies
had all been drawn and fastened to keep the room filled
with shadows per the midwife's instruction.

Charlotte had never before observed a birthing.
Upon entering the chamber, she had spent a few uncertain moments loitering by the threshold as her mother
and aunt hurried forward into the fray—a swarming
mass of housemaids, the midwife and her assistants, and
Caroline, who sat propped in a large birthing chair, huff-
ing and crying out. Finally, Lady Epping took notice of
Charlotte's hesitation, and beckoned her with a wave.

"Charlotte, do not just stand there, darling. Come
and hold your sister's hand," she had called.

Charlotte spent hours perched at the left of the birthing chair. She clasped hands with Caroline, wincing every time a spasm wracked her sister's form, and Caroline's fingers would crush against hers with surprising and brutal force. Caroline's face was glossed with a sheen of sweat; her long, dark blond hair had worked loose of its plait and clung to her face in wispy, dampened strands. Her brows furrowed so deeply when she leaned forward, gritting her teeth, she was nearly unrecognizable. For each new swell of labor, Charlotte and the other women slid their arms behind her back and helped prop her upright in the chair; Caroline would hold her breath, uttering a hoarse, gritty squeal with each contraction, and when it waned, she *whoofed* the air from her lungs.

Charlotte helped to lean her comfortably back against the chair in between the contractions. She and Lady Epping took turns rinsing linens in basins of cool water and dabbing Caroline's face, smoothing her disheveled hair back and wiping at her perspiration.

"Here, darling," Lady Epping murmured, offering a cup of tea to Caroline. "Drink, love. Just a sip. Drink, drink . . ."

At some point, hours into the ordeal, Caroline looked up at Charlotte, her eyes glassy. "Oh," she whispered. "Hullo. I did not hear you arrive, darling."

Charlotte leaned over and kissed Caroline's cheek.

"Are you hurting?" she whispered, an ignorant question considering Caroline was flushed from enduring the pain, and her breath was still fluttering from the severity of her last contraction.

Caroline laughed softly. "I shall survive," she breathed. "I . . . I told you one could not simply drop a baby. There . . . there is some effort to it . . ."

Charlotte smiled, helping to support her as Lady Epping offered another sip of tea.

"I am glad you are here, Charlotte," Caroline said. "I must speak with you at . . . at once. Someplace private. Perhaps . . . perhaps the parlor? Randall . . . he told me . . ."

"You never mind the parlor," Lady Epping said, stroking Caroline's hair. "You can speak with your sister later, darling. For now, you set your mind on seeing this little lamb of yours out among us for proper introductions."

Caroline tried to smile again, but grimaced instead. "Here comes another!" she gasped. "Hoist me up . . . hold fast to me!"

There was no time for Charlotte to consider any more of her impending wedding, much less a means to avoid or prevent it. There was no time for anything but Caroline; her birthing was excruciating, exhausting, and relentless. When the child finally came by late afternoon, it was a son, a squirming, sopping little thing. Charlotte examined the tiny, flushed creature with wonder as the midwife leaned back, cradling it when the babe emerged at last from between Caroline's thighs.

She watched the midwife poke two pudgy forefingers into the infant's mouth and offer a swift swipe, drawing out a globule of thick, pink-stained mucous. The child hiccupped and Charlotte stared, mesmerized to watch him draw the first, whooping breath of life into his tiny lungs. This was followed promptly by a wide-mouthed, scrunched-face yowl of righteous indignation, his little hands swatting the air, his tiny feet drumming furiously. The midwife and her assistants swaddled him in blankets, nearly hiding him from view beneath the soft folds. His umbilicus was cut, and the damp, caterwauling boy was presented to his mother.

Caroline held him and burst into tears, smiling with a joy Charlotte knew she could not fully understand or appreciate. Charlotte wept with this joy nonetheless, her hands to her mouth, trembling. She felt her mother's arm about her shoulders, and she leaned against Lady Epping, both of them weeping and laughing.

The baby was whisked off to be bathed and introduced to the teat of his wet nurse, while Caroline struggled to expel the remains of afterbirth from her womb. This process, seeming no less painful than the birthing itself, lasted another hour, and when it was finally over, Caroline was semi-lucid, reeling with exhaustion. She was brought to her bed, and collapsed there. As the chamber slowly cleared, Charlotte and Lady Epping sat together at Caroline's bedside, keeping vigil while she slept.

"We should wake her," Charlotte said quietly, after a time. They were alone in the chamber, just the three of them. "The midwife said we should see her take sips of this now and again."

She nodded to indicate a small mug of caudle on the bedside table. Lady Epping shook her head, not averting her gaze from Caroline, whom she watched with a soft smile fixed to the corners of her mouth. "No, lamb," she murmured. "Let her rest awhile. She is spent."

Lady Epping reached for her daughter's hand, and Charlotte spread her fingers, letting her mother's twine through.

"Was it like this for you?" she asked in a quiet voice. "When you had us, I mean?"

Lady Epping smiled. "I think every birth is different," she said. "Just as every woman is. God makes no two the same. Reilly was my first, and my longest. He took nearly two days to come into this world."

Charlotte tried to imagine enduring that sort of pain for so long.

Lady Epping chuckled softly. "I suppose by about midway through the ordeal, I started grunting at him. 'You come out of there,' I remember saying. 'I cannot keep you in me until you are grown, and besides, the world is not nearly so horrid as you would make it seem by your refusal to enter it'." Lady Epping, a distant look in her eye. "Your sister came more quickly, but I bled for her," she continued. "It gave everyone a fright, myself included. Such a fuss, and I could scarcely catch my breath. The midwife whispered to my mother that I would never have another for it. She did not think I could hear, but I could, and then I cried. I just burst into tears right there upon the birthing chair, wracked with pangs and gasping for air."

She smiled again. "But then you came and proved her wrong, and you, lamb, were the sweetest, easiest effort I had known. My water doused me at breakfast. I remember soaking my skirt and the chair and blinking at your father as if he had sopped me with it. Four hours later, and scarcely a pant, and there you were in my arms, wriggling and yowling."

There was unfamiliar softness in her mother's face. "Every time, the process was different," Lady Epping said. "But in the end, when I held you each in turn, the feeling was always the same. From Reilly to you, it never changed. I looked down upon your little faces; you each wiggled and squealed, and I was overwhelmed. I understood."

"Understood?" Charlotte asked.

Lady Epping nodded. "I had never found much purpose in the world as a girl," she said. "It always seemed rather foolish and tawdry to me, I suppose. This custom of primping and powdering, of parties and protocol. It never made much reasonable sense to me. I went along with it, of course, but it seemed such a . . . such a waste of time. But I understood my place in the order of things when I held you each upon your births."

Charlotte looked at her mother. She had never imagined Lady Epping might have found society's functioning foolish, given the degree of fervency she had always demonstrated in forcing Charlotte into it.

Lady Epping offered Charlotte's hand a gentle squeeze. "I am sorry for last night," she said softly. "For speaking so harshly to you . . . striking you. I know you do not want to marry Lord Roding, and that he has his flaws. I am not blind to his character. I know the impetuousness and impropriety of pampered youth when presented plainly with it. But with his hand, you will be the wife of an Earl some day, Charlotte, and you will never know want or need. Your children will never know want or need. That may not mean much to you at this moment, because you are confused and hurting, I know, but it will one day."

Lady Epping gazed down at Caroline again and smiled. "One day, you will understand, and that will be all that matters to you, too."

Charlotte felt a gloss of tears swimming in her eyes.

"I love you so very much, lamb," Lady Epping said.

"I love you, too, Mother," she said.

"Do not be frightened tomorrow night alone with James," Lady Epping said. "He will lay with you. Do you know what that means?"

"Yes, I . . . I have . . . heard of such things," Charlotte said, feeling the color drain in momentary mortification from her face.

"It will be clumsy," her mother said. "Painful at the first, and you will bleed for it. It is sticky and sweaty and disheveling, but it is over soon enough. Close your eyes, purse your lips and moan as if it pleases you. You will offend his sensibilities otherwise."

"You do not enjoy it, Mother?" There had been pain for Charlotte last night, but it had waned to pleasure repeatedly, increasingly.

"It . . . it is not so bad . . . and it seldom takes long," Caroline murmured from the bed. "I think . . . anything else is only gossip."

"Caroline, you are awake!" Charlotte exclaimed.

"Darling, you should be resting," Lady Epping said, and gently caressed Caroline's face.

Caroline batted her eyes sleepily. "Where . . . where is my baby?"

"With his nurse," Lady Epping soothed. "You are exhausted. Close your eyes and try to sleep."

Caroline shook her head. "Will they let me hold him again? Even for a moment, I . . . I should dearly enjoy to. Would you ask them, Mother?"

"Of course, darling," Lady Epping said, rising from her chair. She pressed her lips to Caroline's brow. "I will be right back."

Charlotte watched her mother leave the chamber, and turned to her sister. Caroline gazed up at her blearily, and seemed to struggle to keep her eyes open. "How are you feeling?" Charlotte asked, slipping her hand into Caroline's.

"As though . . . as though I have been hurled from horseback gut-first onto a fencepost," she said. She closed her fingers around Charlotte's. "Mother is right."

"About what?" Charlotte asked, trying to offer Caroline a sip of caudle.

"About you never wanting for anything if you marry James Houghton," Caroline said, shaking her head at the proffered mug. "He . . . he might be a . . . a boorish hound, but his father is a good man, and he will never see you know debt or disgrace. I have been speaking to Randall of it, and he told me about his business in London . . . with Lord Essex and others . . ."

"The lending group," Charlotte said. "Yes, he told me of it at Roding Castle. I had no idea Lord Essex was of such unconventional mind."

Caroline nodded, her eyelids drooping. "Randall is very confident in their endeavors," she murmured.

"Is James involved in it?" Charlotte asked. "He spent a lot of time in London these past months, but I always thought it was to pester me. He never mentioned anything about helping his father . . ."

"He is not helping his father," Caroline said, opening her eyes and closing her hand more firmly around Charlotte's. "James Houghton has been in London as he has been here, to enjoy the card tables and dice games."

"What?"

Caroline nodded. "That . . . that is what I wanted to tell you," she said. "Randall told me James' gambling has grown well out of hand. He is the Earl's son and Lord Essex loves him dearly, but he . . . he has cut his purse strings."

"What do you mean?"

"He was remitting James' debts," Caroline said. "And he grew tired of it, as James only accrued more. He has refused to provide James any more funds than his customary allowance. He had hoped it might teach James some responsibility, but it . . . Randall told me it has not."

"How badly is he in arrears?" Charlotte asked.

Caroline looked at her solemnly. "He will be lucky if he does not see the inside of debtors' prison," she said. Her face softened and she smiled at Charlotte. "But you do not need to worry for that. It would only mean you endure his company briefly as his bride. Lord Essex promised Randall he would take care of you, as the future mother of his son's heir. He would not consent to see you suffer for James' failings. Lord Essex is a good man. You will see. Randall told me he is coming from London tonight. He will be here for the weddings."

Caroline reached up, brushing the cuff of her hand clumsily against Charlotte's cheek. "Marry him," she whispered. "No harm will come of it. When he is gone to prison, take Kenley for your lover. I know you love him yet, and I suspect he loves you, too, no matter his reasons for not marrying you. A lover is perfectly prudent as long as it remains discreet." She closed her eyes and smiled mysteriously. "Not that I would know," she said. "But I have heard tell."

The chamber door opened, and Lady Epping returned, holding the swaddling-bound baby in her arms. "Look, little lamb," she purred sweetly to the child. "Look, here is your mama. Here is your pretty mama."

"Has Randall seen him yet?" Caroline asked while Charlotte helped her sit up, arranging pillows behind her back and shoulders to support her

"Yes, he said he thought it was a rather puny thing," Lady Epping said, frowning slightly.

Caroline kissed the baby's brow. "He might try forcing one from his gut and out his bloody ass some time, then," she remarked, cooing at her son. "How do you do, my little sweetling? Yes, indeed. How do you do?"

CHAPTER 17

BY THE TIME THEY RETURNED TO DARTON Hall, dusk had settled. The collective mood on their coach ride home was considerably lighter than during the journey to Heathcote as the women chatted together discussing Caroline's infant son. This fond cheer continued upon their arrival at Darton, and Charlotte even managed to graciously endure her mother and aunt's company in her chamber as she tried on Caroline's wedding dress.

Caroline had insisted her sister wear the gown; a simple but elegant dress of heavy white satin overlaid with ivory embroidered flowers. The skirt was buoyant but not too broad. Its modest design and shape suited Charlotte's tastes, while the well-tailored dress fit her as if it had been made to her form.

She had not come up with a plan to avoid marrying James. Charlotte found that over the course of that day she no longer possessed the desire to fight her mother. Not because she had changed her mind, or her feelings for Will had lessened any within her heart, but simply because she felt like she and Lady Epping had come to some manner of mutual understanding. They had not declared a truce by any means, but the tension that had been drawn so painfully taut between them since her return from London had at least slackened. As if a thick veil had been lifted from Charlotte's face, she could plainly see Lady Epping was not trying to hurt her. As she had insisted all the while, Lady Epping only acted as she thought best for Charlotte. It was no one's fault mother and daughter shared diametrically opposing viewpoints on what constituted "best" for Charlotte.

Lady Epping regarded Charlotte approvingly as she stood in Caroline's gown. Charlotte watched lamplight flicker off of tears in Lady Epping's eyes, and she could not summon the heart to protest. "You look so beautiful," Lady Epping whispered, her hands fluttering against Charlotte's cheeks. "Would you wear the diamonds Lord Roding gave you? They would look so lovely with the dress."

This was Lady Epping's concession as much as Charlotte's lack of objection was hers; she had not demanded one thing from Charlotte since they returned from Heathcote. She had asked her daughter's opinions on things; did she like the gown? Did she want a broader pannier beneath? Would another petticoat suit her? There may not have been surrender on either woman's side, but there was a subtle peace nonetheless.

"Yes, Mother," Charlotte said, knowing it would please Lady Epping. "I think you are right. They would suit it well."

She tried not to look miserable. The day had been so joyous otherwise, and she did not want to impose her own unhappiness. She kept thinking of what Caroline had told her about James being doomed for debtors' prison. She tried to find some measure of comfort in the thought that perhaps her sister was right, and she could satisfy her mother, and see to her own happiness in the end by marrying James and taking Will as her lover.

She knew what Will would think. It would hurt him beyond measure, just as it would pain her to ask it of him. However, Will was the type to resign himself readily to circumstances, as he had so aptly demonstrated. Charlotte tried to tell herself Will was logical and reasonable. He would understand and be forgiving, conceding to her pleas. He might not like his place in the ultimate end result of matters, as Charlotte did not, but he would likely admit there was no other alternative.

Lady Epping took her by the hands and kissed her cheek. "My darling girl," she murmured. "You must be exhausted. I will leave you to Una. Sleep well, Charlotte."

"And you, Mother," Charlotte said, returning her mother's buss.

Lady Epping and Lady Chelmsford took their leaves, and Una helped Charlotte loose from the gown and underpinnings, offering her nightdress to her. "You are certainly being agreeable," Una observed, as she undid Charlotte's stay.

"I am too tired to argue anymore," Charlotte replied, shrugging herself out of the confines of the corset. She took her nightgown and slipped it over her head.

"There is a first," Una said in surprise.

"What is the purpose in arguing anyway?" Charlotte asked glumly. "There is nothing I can do or say to prove James so ill in Mother's regard to change her mind. Caroline told me he is in debt—damn near in prison for it—but his father is so fixed on seeing me saved from even this, it would be no argument against Mother."

She walked to her bed and sat wearily on the side of the mattress. "Caroline said I should marry James and keep Kenley for a lover."

Una made a thoughtful murmuring sound as she hung Charlotte's wedding dress. "Such things are not unheard of, I have been told. I suppose it depends on your point of view."

"What do you mean?"

"I mean, there is a decided difference between a lover

and a love," Una replied. "Though it is not always indistinguishable, it remains. You should ask yourself which you want more: a lover? Or a love?"

Charlotte felt the stinging warmth of tears in her eyes. A lover had been nice enough, wonderful, even, but that was not why she wanted to be with Will. "How do I get out of this, Una?" she whispered, feeling a teardrop trickle slowly from the corner of her eye, sliding along the side of her nose.

"I do not know, lamb," Una said. She walked over to the bedside and stroked Charlotte's hair. "But you are not wed yet, and God sometimes takes after such matters in His own fashion."

Charlotte looked up at her, and Una smiled, brushing her fingertips beneath the shelf of Charlotte's chin. "And no matter what, I am with you," she said. "We will make do together, whatever comes to pass."

A soft tap against Charlotte's doorframe drew their attention. The door stood open, and Reilly was at the threshold. "Pardon my intrusion," he said, dropping a polite nod to Una.

"Of course, my lord," Una said.

"May I . . . may I speak with you a moment, Charlotte?" Reilly asked. "I know you are tired, but I . . . it will not take long."

"Of course, Reilly," Charlotte said. She watched him walk into the room as Una took her leave, closing the door behind her. Reilly moved slowly, his footsteps shuffling, and Charlotte was moved with pity for him, remembering the vicious damage Cheadle's fists had delivered.

He approached her, slipping his hand into an inner pocket of his justicoat. He pulled out a small sack, bulging with its contents. He tossed it to Charlotte, and she blinked in surprise, her hands darting upward reflexively, fingers closing about the sack. She heard a loud jangling at the impact; the pouch was filled with coins.

"Take it," Reilly said.

"What?"

"Take it," Reilly repeated. "Take my horse and go to Theydon Hall. Leave here, Charlotte. Take Kenley, and the two of you go."

Charlotte simply stared.

"There are at least twenty pounds there," Reilly said. "More than enough to buy whatever you might need—a home, lands, a new life. Ship fare if you choose. Whatever you will need."

"Where did you get this?" she whispered, although she knew. It was his portion from the Black Trio robberies. Charlotte did not doubt for one moment Reilly had likely harbored an idea such as he had just described for him and Meghan, to use the money to buy them a new life where they could be together. He was giving away the life he wanted with Meghan so Charlotte could have one with Will.

"It does not matter," Reilly said. "James Houghton is a rotted bastard, and I will not stand by any longer while you are forced against your will to marry him. You told me you love Kenley. Do you?"

"Yes," Charlotte breathed.

Reilly nodded once. "Take it then," he said. "Take it and go."

"I . . . I cannot do that," she said.

"Of course you can."

"You know I cannot."

"Do not be stubborn about this, Charlotte," he said. "Not now, not with me. I want you to have the bloody coins. Take them and go."

"You know I cannot do that, Reilly," she repeated, rising. "You know what will happen if I do not marry James."

The mild aggravation on Reilly's face turned abruptly to stunned realization.

"It is all right," Charlotte said gently. "Please, Reilly. It is all right."

"I . . . I do not know what you are talking about," he said, but it was a miserable attempt at a lie.

"I will not let James or Cheadle hurt you again," she said. "And I will not let them hang you, Lewis, or Will."

Reilly recoiled as if she had just kneed him in the groin. "Will? How . . . how do you . . . ?"

"Cheadle found me at Hudswell Hall," she said. "I ran from the party to the stables and he was there. He told me he had struck a deal with you to ensure I married James. I did not understand it at the time, but then I heard you talking to Meghan, and I saw the bruises on you . . ."

"Cheadle spoke to you?" Reilly asked, and anger flashed in his face. "That bastard! Did he hurt you? Did he touch you? By my breath, if he lay his hands on you—"

"He did not hurt me," Charlotte replied quickly. "He only frightened me. He told me James would see you hang—you, Lewis, and Kenley if I did not marry him. I did not understand, but I do now, Reilly. Last night, I went to Theydon Hall, and Will told me. He told me everything. I know who you are. I know why Cheadle said you would hang. I know where this money came from, what you did—and why you did it, Reilly. I know you did it for Meghan."

She felt him tremble when she put her arms around him, and then his arms crept slowly about her waist. "I never meant for it to be like this," he said. "It is my fault—all of this is because of me. I have brought this on you—on us all—and I . . . I am so sorry, lamb!"

"It is all right, Reilly. It's all right . . ."

They sat together on the side of her bed. "They cannot get away with this," Reilly said, his hands closed into fists. His sorrow and shock had waned to frustration and anger. He stood, sucking in a sharp, pained breath, and paced restlessly. "There must be something we can do, some way out of this. There must be."

"If you can think of something, let me know," Charlotte said. "I have wracked my mind witless and cannot come up with anything."

"You said he is in debt," Reilly said, turning to her, wincing when the movement pained him. "Caroline told you he is facing debtors' prison, his owings are so out of hand. Mother must not know about this. If she did, she would never consent to see you marry—"

"Caroline also told me Lord Essex would not see me know disgrace or debt for James," Charlotte said. "He will take care of me as James' wife, if only to protect his own familial interests. Telling Mother of James' debts might delay the wedding, but only until she speaks to the Earl and he tells her himself. He will be here tomorrow. Caroline said he is traveling from London tonight."

"Still, a delay is better than naught," Reilly said, pacing again. "It would gain us some time, at least, even if only a few hours, to figure out something better. If debt will not discredit Roding enough in Mother's regard, then we will simply need to find something else, something worse, that will. The man has employed that bastard Cheadle to his service. Given Cheadle's reputation, it has to mean there is more between them than this—something rotted. I know it. I can fairly well smell it."

Charlotte watched her brother stride briskly back and forth. "Reilly . . ." she said.

"Cheadle is a thief-taker," Reilly said. "He makes a living turning bandits in for reward money. Perhaps James hoped to learn the trade, to split reward monies with Cheadle. Cheadle's purse is padded while James tenders back his debts."

"Reilly," Charlotte said, but again, Reilly was lost in his own thoughts and paid her no heed.

"That cannot be it," Reilly said, shaking his head. "If that was what James had in mind with Cheadle's service, they would have seized upon it by now, from the moment they suspected me, Lewis, and Will were the Black Trio. There is a big enough bounty offered for us they should have at least been fairly tempted."

"Reilly . . ."

"If they were not," Reilly mused, pausing in mid-step, "it means there must be something better, tempting them the more."

"There is," Charlotte said, and Reilly turned to her, his brows lifted in surprise. "There is something better to tempt them. There is James' inheritance."

Charlotte stood. "After we were robbed, one of

Cheadle's bags was delivered here by mistake," she said. She went to her writing table and rifled through Cheadle's knapsack, finding the copy of *Improvement of the Mind*. "I found this," she said, flipping among the pages until she found the gazette clipping. She carried it to her brother and held it out to him.

Reilly read the note jotted in the margin. " 'Suitable for our needs'?" he murmured.

"And there was this besides," she said, turning pages swiftly until she found the second note. Reilly looked at this one, too, with undisguised interest. "I thought it implied a meeting of some sort, that perhaps James was seeing a lover in Epping. I had hoped so anyway, to prove to Mother he is a cad. Una and I went to the Wake Arms together to see. He did not meet a woman there. He met Julian Stockley and Camden Iden."

"Stapleford and Hallingbury?"

"I had not given it much thought until just now, because I had convinced myself this note . . ." she tapped her fingertip against the gazette clipping. ". . . meant that threatening to frame or expose you as the Black Trio would be suitable to make me marry James. But now . . ."

Charlotte sighed heavily, frustrated with herself for her own rather conceited misreckoning. "It has nothing to do with me," she said to Reilly. "It has to do with Lord Essex. I heard the four of them talking in Epping—James, Cheadle, Julian, and Camden—and they mentioned someone traveling the north highway from London by dusk on Saturday, and reaching Beech Hill by ten o'clock. They spoke of meeting there at nine-thirty."

Reilly met her gaze, his expression grim. "They are going to murder Lord Essex," he said.

"And make it look as though the Black Trio is to blame," Charlotte said. "Camden Iden is in debt himself. James must have offered him a generous sum to help. And you know what people say about Julian Stockley."

"He poisoned his father," Reilly said, and she nodded.

"Who better to help James murder his own?" she asked.

Reilly frowned. "Those bastards. Roding and Cheadle would keep their peace as long as you marry Roding, until the vows are made, that is."

Reilly had just broached something that had yet to occur to Charlotte, and she stared up at her brother in horror. "They will see you hang anyway," she whispered.

"No matter what," Reilly said. "They mean to turn us over anyway in the end—this time with the murder of Lord Essex to our credits."

He brushed the flap of his justicoat aside and reached into his fob pocket, withdrawing his watch.

"What time is it?" Charlotte asked.

"Nearly forty past eight," he replied, tucking the watch back into his breeches. "How swiftly can you ride to Theydon Hall?"

"At a full gallop and not keeping to the highway?" she said. "Forty minutes, maybe less."

"Go," Reilly told her, nodding. "Get Lewis and Will. Have them ride hard for Beech Hill and meet me there. I will be waiting for them."

"What are you going to do?"

"I do not know," he said. "Not yet, at least. But I will think of something." He nodded again, motioning her toward her door. "Go," he said. "As fast as you can, Charlotte. We are running out of time."

298

CHAPTER 18

"THOSE BLOODY ROT BASTARDS!" LEWIS EXclaimed. "I figure they have us dead to rights on the robbery charges, but framing us for murder? Now, that I draw offense at!"

Charlotte, Lewis, and Will stood in the parlor at Theydon Hall. She had arrived less than ten minutes earlier, nearly frantic, and the two cousins had listened in stunned surprise to her revelations.

"We have to leave," Will said, looking at Lewis grimly. "It is already twenty past nine. If we bypass the highways and ride straight through the forest, we can at least reach Reilly before Lord Sussex passes north at ten."

Lewis nodded. The two of them had been preparing even as they spoke; as soon as Charlotte relayed to them all that had come to pass, they set about shrugging on their greatcoats and shoving their feet into boots. Now they each loaded a brace of pistols.

"I am going with you," Charlotte said to Will.

"No, you are not."

"I most certainly am," she retorted. "If James and Cheadle have conspired with Camden and Julian, that makes four of them to contend with, and all of them likely armed. You need me. I know how to handle a pistol."

"She did damn near shoot my head off during the robbery," Lewis said pointedly.

"Absolutely not," he said. "James Houghton is a coward. He hired Cheadle to tend to the messy details. He is probably tucked safely away at Roding Castle, keeping company with his mother and sister and securing an alibi for himself should suspicions ever swing his way. That means there will only be three of them—Cheadle, Stockley, and Iden—and three of us to stop them."

Charlotte closed her hands into fists. "I am going with you, Will," she said stubbornly, and the corner of Will's mouth lifted wryly.

"No," he whispered, kissing her swiftly. "You are not."

"You cannot keep me from it. I am as much a part of this as any of you. I am the one who bloody figured it out. I will be damned if I am just going to stand quietly and idly aside because I am a woman, and you think I have no—"

"I have no problem with you being a woman," he

said. "I rather fancy that about you, in fact."

"Then do not dare presume to dictate to me what I can and cannot do on the arbitrary basis that you consider it in my best interests," she snapped. "I am fully aware of my best interests. I—"

"Please, Charlotte," he pleaded, and she fell silent. "Please."

"Are we agreed, then?" Lewis asked, clapping them both on the shoulders.

"Damn it," she muttered.

"Splendid!" Lewis declared. "Let us ride, Will. Reilly is likely to get himself shot if we wait much longer."

✷ ✷ ✷

Charlotte could not remain sore with Will, but she could not return to Darton Hall either. She mustered her resolve and decided she would not be relegated to the role of the fretful female, pacing anxiously about her chamber, helpless to do anything but wait for news. When the three of them rode from the grounds of Theydon, Charlotte at first steered her horse northward, as if to make for Darton Hall. She rode a distance until she felt she had granted Lewis and Will a safe enough lead, and then she reined the roan southwest again, making for Beech Hill.

This path, well off of the established highways, led her

deep into the bowels of Epping Forest. The woods were shrouded in the shadows of nightfall, draped in heavy folds of fog. Trees twisted and twined their way across the surreal landscape, their autumn-barren limbs splayed in the shadows like the desperate hands of those buried alive groping and clawing their way outward from graves.

She heard no evidence of Lewis and Will ahead of her, and began to grow fearful that in her haste, and in the dark, she had lost her way, turned too far south. The longer she rode without any sign or sound of them from ahead of her, the more dismayed and alarmed she became, the more lost she grew, and the more frantic she became at the prospect of wandering the ancient, creepy acres of Epping Forest in the dark.

She was nearly panicked by the time her horse stumbled headlong and at a full gallop out onto a rutted stretch of muddy road, the northward highway from London. Realizing where she was, Charlotte drew back on her reins, bringing the roan to a halt.

She stood in the middle of the deserted highway, and looked about in all directions, straining her ears to hear above her own ragged breath, the heaving of her weary, winded horse. There was nothing. Moonlight seeped through the fog, offering pale, muted illumination. She was in the wrong spot; either she had come too far south and had yet to reach Beech Hill, or she was somehow too far north, and ahead of the hill. She could not hear any hint of hoof beats or a carriage along either direction of the highway.

"Damn it," she muttered. Here was all she bloody needed: to miss the fray entirely, spend the night lost in Epping Forest, and then be teased about it, and her own stubborn insistence on following, when it was all over and ended. She looked down at the horse; its velveteen ears had pricked at the sound of her voice.

"Any suggestions?" she asked, but the horse apparently had none. It snorted, shuffling its heavy hooves in the dirt, but offered no other counsel. Charlotte looked around again, struggling desperately to get her bearings. In Epping Forest, this proved a difficult enough task in the full light of day; at night, it seemed hopeless.

The sharp report of gunfire made her flinch, and she jerked her head toward the sound. It came from a distance, resounding against the overhanging ceiling of moon-infused fog, echoing along the channel carved through the trees by the highway. She froze in her saddle, her eyes wide as the din rolled through the forest; the roan pranced anxiously in place.

"Whoa, now," she soothed, patting the gelding's neck. She caught the sound of distant voices, unintelligible but loud enough to carry, and tilted her head, trying to pinpoint the noise. She jumped at another report of gunfire, and then another and another.

"Bugger me," Charlotte said, jerking on the reins,

kicking her horse to a gallop as she charged toward the sound. As the horse galloped, as Charlotte clasped the reins in one hand, and reached with the other for her pocket. She slipped her pistol in hand, sliding her finger against the trigger and drawing the doghead back with her thumb.

She caught sight of something coming toward her, moving fast—a man on horseback. She had less than a second to register his approach before he burst out of the fog and upon her, rushing past at a gallop. She whirled, looking over her shoulder, unwilling to risk a shot at someone she did not recognize, and who might well be Reilly, Lewis, or Will. Instead, she pulled on the reins, turning her horse around in midstride, and spurred it forward in pursuit.

She saw him ahead of her, weaving in and out of the mist, but she still could not see enough to chance shooting friend rather than foe. "Damn it," she muttered, kicking the horse. The roan was tired, but fleet-footed yet; the margin of space between Charlotte and the faceless rider closed. As she came alongside of him, she had no time to lift her arm and shoot. She saw his profile clearly.

Cheadle!

Charlotte acted without thinking. She swung herself around from the saddle with her horse still spurred to a frenzied gallop. Keeping her boot heel loosely in the stirrup for leverage, she launched herself at Cheadle. She plowed into him, wrapping her arms around him, and heard him utter a startled cry as they tumbled in a tangle of arms and legs from the saddle.

They hit the ground hard, with Charlotte atop. The impact *whoofed* the breath from them both, and they fell apart, tumbling and sprawling against the unforgiving dirt and rock of the road.

Charlotte came to a halt lying facedown, stunned, her mouth filled with dirt and grit. Her pistol was lost, rattled from her hand, and her head swam from having rapped repeatedly and hard against the ground. She struggled to sit up, spitting and coughing.

A large hand seized her tightly by the hair—Cheadle. Charlotte yelped as he dragged her to her feet.

"You!" he exclaimed, and Charlotte rammed her knee into his crotch.

He cried out hoarsely, doubling over, his hands falling away from her. He staggered backward, and Charlotte whirled, bolting. She saw a misshapen shadow and a wink of moonlight off of brass against the ground ahead of her—her pistol—and darted for it. Just as she stooped, reaching for it, Cheadle ran into her from behind. He had recovered from her blow and tackled her; Charlotte hit the ground, grunting with his heavy weight collapsing on top of her

Cheadle uttered a gravelly, furious cry, like a snarling animal, and shifted his weight, grabbing her shoulders and flipping her over onto her back. "Rotted bitch!" he screamed. Charlotte struggled beneath him, kicking her feet futilely, balling her hands into fists and swinging wildly.

"You rotted bitch," he said, seizing her by the wrists. "This is your doing, is it not? Do you think you have stopped anything? Do you think you have saved anyone?"

His hands moved, releasing her arms, but before she could strike him, his palms mashed against her throat, crushing the wind from her. Charlotte gagged, her mouth open wide as she struggled vainly to whoop in air. She fought wildly beneath him, planting her heels against the dirt and bucking her hips, trying to throw him off.

"Do you think you have saved your love?" Cheadle said, putting his full weight behind his hands, throttling her. Charlotte drove her fists against him; it was like pounding her hands against a mountainside for all of the effect the effort had.

"Do you think you have saved your brother?" he said. "You have only hanged them the more, you bitch. They will hang for the Earl's murder, and for yours."

Charlotte strained to suck air past his hands; there was none to be had, and she could see tiny pinpoints of dazzling light dancing before her eyes. She could hear the sounds of the life strangling from her, a desperate, sodden cawing. Shadows seemed to be swooping in from every side, engulfing her, drowning her vision. She abandoned the attempt to beat Cheadle away, and reached out, moving her hand desperately over the ground, fumbling in the dirt, groping for her pistol. She felt her fingertips brush against the polished brass cap of the butt, and she clawed at it.

"Lord Roding will grieve deeply for your loss," Cheadle said as her eyes rolled back, her eyelids fluttering, her mind abandoning her. "He will scream until his throat is raw from the strain to see them all hang from Tyburn. You have prevented nothing. You have only killed yourself."

Charlotte curled her fingers around the pistol, and with the last waning, feeble ounce of mettle and strength she could summon, she swung the barrel around, her finger closing around the trigger. The report of gunfire was loud and sharp; the air between her face and Cheadle's suddenly filled with a blinding flash of sparks and a thick, stinking cloud of smoke. She felt his hands wrench away from her as he slipped sideways. She forced the sole of her boot against his gut and heaved mightily, shoving him off of her.

Charlotte gasped for breath, nearly gagging, as she rolled over. She clutched at her throat, dragging in lungful after lungful of blessed air. Her arms and legs felt tremulous and weak. She struggled to draw her knees beneath her, to rise, but she stumbled, unable to manage. She looked over her shoulder, her vision blurred and swimming with tears.

Cheadle lay sprawled in the dirt behind her, his legs spread wide, his hands flung out to either side.

Charlotte still held the pistol clutched in her hand. She turned it, grasping the hot barrel in her palm and leveling the butt like a club. She crawled toward Cheadle, her voice whimpering helplessly, hoarsely from her throat. She expected him to suddenly leap up and attack her again.

She stopped beside him kneeling, her pistol raised and at the ready in her hand. The gunshot had caught Cheadle nearly square in the brow; she could see the entry wound where the lead pellet had punched through his skull. Blood oozed down the side of his head, glistening and black in the pale, dim moonlight. She realized what she had mistaken for shadows at first glance was really more blood. It pooled beneath his head in a dark, broadening circumference.

Her fingers loosened about the pistol, and it dropped to the ground as she began to shake. It began as a slight twitch, no more than a shiver in her shoulders, and then it ran through her, a deep, uncontrollable shuddering.

She heard approaching hoof beats marking a furious pace, and she jerked about, her hand darting for her pistol. She saw a horse rein to an abrupt a skittering halt ahead of her on the road, its hooves kicking up a swirl of dirt about its legs. She saw the silhouetted outline of a man astride the horse, his arm outstretched to her, and caught the flash of moonlight off of the brass-adorned barrel of his pistol.

"Charlotte?" someone called out, and she nearly swooned in relief, the strength in her arm fading. Her gun fell to the ground.

"Will!" she wanted to scream, but her throat was damaged, her voice no more than a warbling croak. "Will!"

He swung down from his horse, the broad tails of his greatcoat billowing gracefully about him. He ran to her, crying out her name, his voice shrill with panic. "Charlotte! Oh, God, Charlotte!"

His boot heels skittered in the dirt and loose gravel, and he fell to his knees beside her, clutching at her. She tried to lift her chin, to raise her lips to his.

"I . . . I am all right," she whispered painfully. "I am not hurt. Cheadle . . . he . . . he is . . ."

She felt Will stiffen against her, his arm tightening about her shoulders protectively when he spied Cheadle's fallen form.

"He is dead," she said. "He . . . I saw him ride past me, and I . . . I followed him."

"You shot him?"

She nodded against the warm shelter of his chest.

"With that little pocket flintlock of yours?" He sounded incredulous, and when she nodded again, he laughed softly. "I will be damned."

"I . . . I bloody told you," she croaked, looking up at him and managing a frown. "I told you I could handle a pistol."

He laughed softly, folding himself over her, embracing her fiercely. "I stand corrected, then," he said, kissing her hair. "By my breath, I will never doubt you again."

CHAPTER 19

CHARLOTTE AND WILL RODE IN UPON A grim scene at Beech Hill. As they approached, Charlotte could still smell the fading odor of gun smoke in the air. She saw bodies lying sprawled facedown and motionless in the road; Lord Essex's footman and driver had both been shot and killed as they had tried to flee. The carriage had slid to a clumsy halt at the side of the road, and listed precariously with its right wheels in the grass. She could see the soft glow of its coach lights when they drew near, and two additional bodies on the ground. Her heart seized in terror at the sight of them.

"Reilly!" she whimpered. Reilly and Lewis' abandoned horses wandered nearby, large shadows emerging from the fog. "Will, what has happened?"

A silhouette staggered in their direction, lumbering

out of the fog, and Charlotte heard the distinctive clack of a pistol hammer drawn back. "Hoah, there!" the man shouted out loudly, hoarsely.

"Lewis!" Will shouted back. "Lewis! It is us!"

At his cry, Charlotte realized the two other bodies in the road were Julian Stockley and Camden Iden. Like Cheadle, the two young men were dressed all in black. They had lost their tricornes, and the broad flaps of their greatcoat tails lay draped in the dirt, like the lifeless wings of felled crows.

Lewis lowered his gun at Will's shout. "Lord Essex has been shot," he said grimly. "We were too late."

"What?" Charlotte gasped. "No, oh, no!"

She swung her leg around and hopped from her saddle without even reining her horse to a complete halt. She stumbled clumsily to claim her footing and rushed to Lewis as Will dismounted behind her. "Is he dead?" she cried.

"Charlotte?" he asked, bewildered. He turned to his cousin. "Where is Cheadle?"

"Dead," Will said. "Where is the Earl?"

"He is here," Reilly said, and Charlotte whirled to find him kneeling beside the coach, holding someone in his arms.

"Reilly!" she cried.

"Charlotte?" he gasped. "What are you doing here?" His brows furrowed when he caught sight of Will. "Are you bloody mad? What is she doing here?"

"Apparently taking care of Edmond Cheadle for us," Lewis said. "Will says she shot him dead."

Charlotte knelt beside her brother. Lord Essex was unconscious, cradled against Reilly's chest. His coat was stained with blood; he had been shot in the gut, and Reilly had his hand pressed firmly over the wound to try and slow the blood loss.

"You shot Cheadle?" Reilly asked.

She nodded. "Is Lord Essex dying?" she whispered.

"I do not know," Reilly said, his stern expression softening. "We were too late, Charlotte. We managed to stop them, but they . . . they . . ."

Lord Essex moaned feebly, tucking his cheek against Reilly's shoulder. "We have to do something, Reilly," Charlotte said. "He cannot die. He . . . please, he cannot!"

"We can bring him to Theydon," Will said. Lewis leaned heavily against the younger man for support, limping awkwardly.

"Lewis, you have been hurt!" Charlotte said, and he shook his head, waving his pistol dismissively.

"A pellet through my boot," he said. "In the sole and out the top. I had not even reined my horse to a stop yet. Thank God it was Camden Iden who took the shot; the man cannot hold his arm steady to shave his own chin, much less level a pistol."

"Charlotte, come help Lewis," Will said. "Reilly,

let me take the Earl. You cannot carry him, not with your ribs."

"He needs a surgeon," Reilly said. "We need to get him to London."

"He will never make it back to London," Will said. He knelt before Reilly, putting his arms about Lord Essex's shoulders and beneath his knees. "Let me take him," he said. "Come on. We have to get to Theydon."

❋ ❋ ❋

Lord Essex managed to survive the horseback ride to Theydon Hall. Will deposited the unconscious Earl in his bed, and Reilly immediately set to work, pulling Lord Essex's cravat loose, opening his overlapping layers of coats.

"We need linens," he said, opening the Earl's shirt and clapping his hand over his wound. "Lewis, hurry now and collect as many as you can find. I need a sharp knife, or folding razor if you have it at hand. Will, have you a sewing kit?"

"Yes," Will said, hurrying to one of his traveling trunks. The top was covered with books and papers; he shoved them to the floor and threw back the lid, rummaging inside.

"Charlotte, go with Lewis," Reilly said. "Get me some water. Buckets, bowls, tea cups—whatever you can pour it into. Get it up here as fast as you can manage."

"What are you going to do?" Charlotte asked as Reilly held his hands firmly over Lord Essex's bare midriff.

"I am going to get that pellet out of him," Reilly said, meeting her gaze. "If I can get it out, we can stitch him up. We might have a hope he will survive."

"Reilly assisted the ship surgeon aboard the *Endurance*," Will said, rushing to the bedside, presenting Reilly with a sewing kit and a folding razor.

"Yes, we only lost four men out of the five he tended to," Lewis offered. "And the fourth died of scurvy—hardly his fault."

❋   ❋   ❋

Charlotte and Will waited in the corridor beyond the chamber while Reilly set to work on the Earl. "Lord Essex cannot die," Charlotte said, pacing back and forth. She turned to Will, her eyes filled with fear. "If he dies, then it will all still be just as James wanted. The others are dead—Camden, Julian, and Cheadle. There . . . Will, there is no one left who can say he was involved."

"I know," Will admitted somberly.

"If he dies, James will say you killed him," she said, "He will say the Black Trio murdered him, and he . . . he will see you hanged . . ."

Will pulled Charlotte into his arms and kissed her. "It will be all right," he consoled. "I promise you, Charlotte. I promise you."

She trembled, trying desperately not to weep. "I have to go back to Darton Hall," she said.

"What?"

"Will," she said, taking his face between her hands. "Please. I have to go back. We must act as if nothing has happened, as if everything is still as it was arranged. For now, James does not suspect anything is amiss. To his mind, everything is yet as he had planned it, and until we know if Lord Essex will survive . . . until we can think of something if he does not, we have to make sure James keeps thinking that way."

"But you . . . that means you will have to marry him," Will said, bereft. "He is a murderer, Charlotte. There are men dead at Beech Hill because of his word. We can go to your mother. We can tell her what happened. We can summon the sheriff and show him what James has done."

"Listen to me," Charlotte said. "There is no proof of it, any of it. It would be only our word against James'—and you, Lewis, and Reilly are the ones with Lord Essex's blood on your hands—the same three whom James claims he can prove are the Black Trio."

"Charlotte . . ." Will said. "No. Please, no. There must be another way. I nearly lost you to a marriage with him, and nearly so again tonight at Cheadle's hands. I will be damned if I will lose you again, not to that bastard."

"I will find some way," Charlotte said. "Please, I will try, but in the meantime, you must see this through. We . . . we have to see it through."

"Even if it means wedding him?" Will asked, his eyes filled with a bewildered pain that nearly saw her broken.

She could not bear to see him hanged. No punishment on earth—not even marrying James Houghton—would be as cruel or devastating as that. If she married James, Will would at least still draw breath, and as long as he lived, she had hope to be with him. "Yes," she said nodding. "Even if it means I must wed."

CHAPTER 20

WHILE LEWIS AND REILLY REMAINED AT Theydon Hall, tending to Lord Essex, Charlotte and Will rode for Darton Hall. They stole into the house and crept upstairs to her room. Will was desperate not to leave her; he held her hand, his fingers twined in hers as if he could not bear to turn loose of her. His eyes were sorrowful, his face filled with torment.

"Charlotte . . ." he whispered, distraught. She did not let him say any more, but stopped his words with her lips.

"Stay with me," she whispered. "Just for awhile . . . just once more. Be with me."

She led him to the bed, her fingers moving down the length of his shirt, unfastening the buttons. She kept her lips against his all the while, wanting to sear the sensation, his kiss, into her mind, hold it dear and fast.

His hands gripped her shirt collar and he jerked the shirt open, snapping buttons free of their moorings and sending them tumbling with a soft clatter on the floor. He tore the shirt open, and pulled her against him.

The warmth of his body welcomed her; as her breasts pressed against the lean, firm muscles outlining his chest, and as the plane of her belly touched the hard muscles of his abdomen—a proximity so intimate, it was as though all at once, they had melded into one form—she moaned softly, seized with longing and sorrow. Charlotte shrugged her arms from her sleeves, abandoning her shirt.

The back of her legs met the bed, and as she sat he knelt between her legs, letting his hands follow the contours of her hips, outer thighs, and calves. He removed her boots, sliding the sheaths of leather from her legs, and let his mouth travel upward, along the inseam of her breeches, his lips lingering on her inner thighs. He canted his head, lifting his chin slightly, and then his breath was against her most tender of places.

He turned his cheek after a long moment, tucking his face against her lap as might a distraught child seeking comfort. He captured her hips between his palms, and trembled against her. "I cannot lose you. Please, Charlotte. Please do not ask this of me. You will break me."

"You will never lose me," she said. "You have my

heart, Will. Always."

He kissed her then, pushing her back on the bed and lowering his body to hers. His hardened length pressed against her insistently.

Then his mouth abandoned hers for the length of her throat, his lips and tongue fluttering against her flesh, stoking the smoldering embers into flames. When he touched her breast, her already frantic breath quickened. He twirled a delicate pink nipple between gentle fingers while he brought his mouth to her other breast, his teeth nipping her flesh.

His hand moved again, fingertips brushing lightly down the contours of her stomach. He slid his hand beneath the waistband of her breeches, slipping through the downy thatch of golden curls now within his reach. Charlotte raised her hips as he pulled her breeches off. He was fully aroused now, his own breeches managing only just barely to contain the significant swell. He untied the waistcord, and she watched him lean over, removing his boots and pants.

He came to her, and she moved her thighs, opening her legs to welcome him. There was no hesitation between them, and when he entered her, swiftly, deeply, he caught the intake of her breath against his mouth. He moved within her, setting a powerful, poignant rhythm, as if each motion was to be his last, and he meant to cherish each.

"Open your eyes," he commanded quietly.

She had not even realized they were closed, her head thrown back as she reveled in his touch. She opened her eyes and blinked, her face flushed with eager heat.

"Look at me," Will whispered. He held her gaze as he began to move again, and her eyelids drifted downward. "Look at me, Charlotte."

His hips ground against her, and the friction of his motion left Charlotte gasping in helpless delight. More than this, there was something powerful as she locked gazes with him, something profoundly intimate, as if by looking into his eyes she offered him her heart and mind as well as her body. He held her gaze, his body moving more swiftly, driving him more deeply, but more than any touch or caress, she met his eyes and felt bound to him, a part of him.

He moved faster and deeper, stroking her, coaxing her, leaving her whimpering, writhing. "Look at me," he said, kissing her, catching her fluttering, helpless voice against his tongue as she clutched at his shoulders, tangling her fingers in his hair. "Look at me now, Charlotte," he whispered against her mouth. "Now," he breathed again, and she cried out, her hands closing into fists as he drove her to climax.

She arched her back as the crescendo of sensations crashed upon her, stripping her of her wits, leaving her straining for breath. The tightening of her body, inside and out, brought him simultaneously to his own release, and he cried out hoarsely.

He slumped against her, exhausted and spent, enfolding her in his warmth and strength. "I love you," she whispered.

"Say that again," he demanded gently.

Charlotte smiled. "I love you, Will."

He smiled, but his eyes were caught between joy and sudden sorrow. "I could never tire of hearing you say those words." He closed his eyes. "I do not want this night to ever end, Charlotte."

"It does not have to," she said, and he opened his eyes, puzzled. "Not yet, anyway. There is still some time before the dawn."

"Is there now?" he asked, and when she nodded, he laughed softly, kissing her. "Give me a moment," he said. "Let me recover and then we will make the most of it."

❋ ❋ ❋

When he left her, the sun was a dim glow upon the edge of the horizon. Charlotte wanted to beg him to remain. She pressed her lips together against a desperate plea for him to keep with her, to stay. When he leaned over her, dressed again, ready to go, his eyes were filled with sorrow. "Come with me," he said, kissing her. "Please come with me."

She thought of him hanging, of Will, Lewis, and Reilly all dangling side by side from the broad limbs of the Tyburn tree, their hands trussed before them, their legs jerking, feet thrumming as their bodies convulsed—the Tyburn jig, this gruesome parody of dance was called. Her eyes filled with tears when she touched his face.

"I cannot," she said. She hugged him, throwing her arms around his neck and burying her face in his tousled hair. She shuddered against him, and he held her tightly. More than any pleasure his hands or hips had ever brought to her, this was what she would remember the most, what would always be precious to her, no matter what the remnants of the day would bring - the warmth of his breath against her; the strength of his arms, his hands; the measure of his heartbeat; the fragrance of his skin and hair.

"I love you. I will always love you, and I will come for you. I will come for you," he said again. "If Lord Essex is dead, I will not let Roding have you."

"You cannot. Will, he will see you hanged!"

"I do not care," he said. "Let him do his worst. I would rather be dead than be without you, Charlotte. I . . . I would rather my breath be choked from me at Tyburn than to draw ten thousand more without you beside me."

"I love you," she said, kissing him. "He cannot take

that from us, no matter what he does. He cannot change that. He will never make me forget it. I love you."

When he was gone, she sat on the edge of her bed. She watched the sun rise with dazed, unhappy eyes. She covered her face with her hands and wept.

CHAPTER 21

"CHARLOTTE, DARLING, HOLD STILL," LADY Chelmsford said, leaning forward in her carriage seat toward Charlotte. She swiped the pad of her thumb against her tongue and moved as if to dab at Charlotte's cheek. "Look at those shadows beneath your eyes. Some powder should see it hidden. Audrey, tell me we have packed powder."

"Leave her alone, Maude," Lady Epping said, catching her sister's wrist before she could touch Charlotte's face.

"She looks positively ghastly," Lady Chelmsford said. "As if she has not seen a wink of sleep."

Lady Epping tightened her grip on Lady Chelmsford's arm. "I doubt there is a bride alive who finds rest before her wedding day," she said.

Lady Chelmsford relented. She folded her hands

in her lap, settling back against the coach bench beside Lord Epping. She sniffed primly, wrinkling her powder-caked nose. "Well, I suppose given the circumstances, it is understandable," she remarked. "These are certainly the most unconventional nuptials I have ever seen arranged. It has all come about so swiftly, and in such confusing fashion, I dare say I can scarcely recall whom Charlotte is supposed to meet before the archbishop."

Lord Roding, Charlotte thought to say, but she kept quiet. She was to marry Lord Roding that morning. There would be no preventing it. Reilly had not returned to Darton Hall. They had delayed their departure for Roding Castle for as long as possible, but there had been no sign of him. While this left Charlotte's family bewildered, Charlotte knew all too well what it surely meant. Lord Essex had not survived the night. He had succumbed to his blood loss at Theydon Hall, and so had any hope she might have held.

"I can only imagine the rumors that will whirl about the whole occasion," Lady Chelmsford said, sniffing again. "There has not been such a fuss in Essex in ages. You should steel yourself for it, Audrey. It will not lessen in the aftermath. People are fascinated by this entire confounding circumstance. Tongues will only wag the more when Reilly does not arrive in timely fashion for the ceremony. You mark me at that."

Lord Epping rolled his eyes and made a harrumphing

sound. He looked out of his window, deliberately trying to ignore Lady Chelmsford.

"You should have married him off two years ago, rather than let him traipse off to the Navy, Rodney," Lady Chelmsford told him, waggling an admonishing finger. " 'It will instill discipline in him,' you said. Discipline, ha!" She snorted. "That boy has done naught but run mad since his return from the sea. Up until all hours and unaccounted for all night; missing social engagements without any courteous excuse. Positively shameful. You have granted him far too many liberties, and an excess in freedom, and he is spoiled for it."

When Lord Epping did not so much as avert his gaze from the window to acknowledge her, her brows pinched and she swung toward Lady Epping. "Audrey, you have always possessed the reasoning your darling husband lacks. You should marry that boy off immediately. Surely you can appreciate the prudence of it. A proper wedding to a girl of good breeding will tame the willful nature within him. Look what such a prospect has done for Charlotte."

She flapped her hand demonstratively at Charlotte, and at this, Lord Epping had enough. He turned to Lady Chelmsford. "Why are you still among us?" he asked. "Do you not have a home and affairs of your own in London that bear your attention?"

Lady Chelmsford sputtered, expecting rescue from

her sister. "Well, I never . . . !" she gasped.

"Yes, well, do not punish the rest of us for your shortcomings," Lord Epping muttered, crossing his arms over his chest and returning his surly gaze to the passing countryside.

❋ ❋ ❋

"Reilly will be here," Lady Epping told Charlotte, dabbing powder gently beneath her eyes. "Do not fret for it, lamb. He adores you. He would not miss the occasion of your wedding."

They had arrived to a massive crowd at Roding Castle. Lord and Lady Essex had invited more than three hundred for the wedding ceremonies, and the grounds surrounding the ruined Norman tower and adjacent, sprawling house were crammed with coaches. Lady Epping and Charlotte had retreated within the house to a quiet antechamber on the second floor to prepare. Charlotte had changed into her wedding gown while maids plaited and bundled her hair, adorning her blond locks with flowers.

She and her mother had been surprised to find themselves alone in the room; of Lady Margaret, Lady Essex and their own preparations, there had been no sign, although Margaret's wedding dress, an elaborate and somewhat horrendous sacque-styled contraption, hung upon a dressmaker's iron stand in the corner.

In waiting for Reilly, they had been nearly tardy in their arrival at the castle. It seemed peculiar that Lady Margaret, who called the house her home, would be even later still. The maids were gone; Charlotte was dressed and powdered, practically ready, and yet Margaret had not arrived. Had she not been so distracted by her own misery and melancholy, Charlotte might have been concerned.

"If I know your brother, he is here already," Lady Epping said, smiling as she set aside the small tin of powder. "And has been since the dawn, reacquainting himself with old friends."

Charlotte returned her mother's smile, unwilling to debate the matter. Lady Epping was perfectly aware of her unhappiness. She could see this plainly in her mother's eyes, in her repeated, forced attempts to make Charlotte smile.

"Here, darling," Lady Epping said, and she fumbled around in a satin traveling bag. She pulled something out and Charlotte was surprised when she offered a small flask. "It is brandy. Take a swig, but be careful not to dribble on your dress. It will help ease your nerves."

Charlotte's nerves were dulled enough with heartbreak, but she figured she might better endure the torment of her marriage ceremony if she was appropriately addled on brandy. She pressed the lip of the flask to her mouth and tilted her head back, gulping fervently.

Her eyes smarted as she swallowed, and the pleasant heat of the brandy singed her nose and throat. "Hoah . . ." she said, blinking. "That is splendid stuff, Mother."

"Yes, from your father's secret stash," Lady Epping said, and they snickered.

The door to the chamber flew open in a wide arc, slamming sharply against the wall. Margaret rushed in, heralded by a loud and plaintive wail, followed by her mother and a bevy of nervous, scuttling handmaids.

"How could he do this?" Margaret cried. She wore only her cinched corset, pannier frame and stockings; she was nude from the waist down beneath her pannier and apparently felt no need for modesty. She whirled to her mother, balling her hands into fists. "I told you this would happen! I told you he would bloody find some excuse—his business in London, or what have you! I told you, Mother! How could he do this to me?"

Lady Essex glanced sidelong at Charlotte and her mother, visibly mortified by her daughter's histrionics. "My lord must have been detained," she said in awkward explanation. "He has kept busy in London these past months. We expected his arrival last night, but I . . . I am certain he is underway and nearly here, only slightly delayed." She approached her daughter, her hands outstretched in supplication. "I am certain he is nearly here," she soothed. "He would not miss this blessed occasion."

"He promised me!" Margaret yowled. She flounced

down onto a chair, clapped her hands over her face and wailed. "He promised he would be here! He is ruining my wedding! I knew he would manage somehow! I told you he would!"

"Is all well, Mother?" James asked, appearing upon the threshold. Margaret shrieked, drawing her legs together, her hands darting for her exposed groin.

"Get out of here!" she yelled.

James looked around the room, looking anxious and pale. When he saw Charlotte, he relaxed visibly, the nervousness draining from his face and form.

"James, darling, go downstairs this instant," Lady Essex ordered, stepping in front of Margaret and flapping her hands to shoo him. "Have shame! You are not meant to see the brides. It will prove poor fortune!"

"Forgive me, Mother," James said, still looking at Charlotte. "I heard shouting. I was concerned."

"Tell me Father has arrived," Margaret cried, leaning over to peer around her mother's skirt. "Tell me he is downstairs and dressed appropriately, not stinking of road grime and lack of sleep! Tell me he is, James!"

"Father is yet absent?" James said, feigning complete and innocent surprise. "But he was due last night."

"Yes, well, I am certain he will be with us shortly," Lady Essex said. "Go downstairs and see if you might not greet him upon his arrival."

"Yes, my lady," James said, nodding. He glanced at

Charlotte again, letting his gaze draw along the length of her form. "Forgive my intrusion."

"Pardon me, my lord," Charlotte said as he moved to close the door. He paused, his brow raised in sudden, suspicious curiosity. "Have Lords Stapleford and Hallingbury arrived yet?"

James held her gaze for a long moment. She could almost see the wheels turning inside of his skull as he tried to decipher the inference of her inquiry simply from her eyes, the set of her mouth, the tone of her voice. "Why, no, darling," he said. "They have not."

"Would you send word when they do?" Charlotte asked sweetly. "Your man . . . Mr. Cheadle, is it? Would you have him announce them that I might offer welcome? They are both such dears."

At the mention of Cheadle, the color drained from James' face. He understood that she knew; if this revelation had been lost to him a moment ago, it was starkly clear now. Charlotte held his gaze evenly, again watching the cogworks of his mind shifting and whirling.

Lady Epping did not understand, however, and she glanced at Charlotte, puzzled. "I do not think that will be necessary, darling," she said. "I dare say Lady Essex is right. It is poor fortune for any man to see the brides before the ceremony. You may speak with them at your leisure later this afternoon, if it should please you."

James' brow raised slightly, as if to challenge Charlotte.

Her moment of causing him uncertainty had passed with a new realization: she was at Roding Castle. No matter what she might suspect or have learned, she was still there, and would still marry him. She did not know enough to prevent the marriage or escape, and thus, it proved of little consequence. Charlotte could see this plainly in his face, and her momentary triumph was snuffed.

"Forgive my intrusion, ladies." He bowed courteously and drew the door closed behind him.

CHAPTER 22

HE IS NOT COMING, CHARLOTTE REALIZED with dismay as her father drew her hand gently from his elbow and presented her to James.

Up until that moment, she had harbored some fleeting hope Will would come for her. He had promised he would, and while the reasonable portion of her mind had known fully well it was an impossible risk for him—one that would likely see him, Lewis, and Reilly side by side dangling from Tyburn—the rest of her had longed for it with almost despair. She had kept shooting anxious glances toward the door of her dressing chamber, hoping that at any moment, Will would come bursting through to snatch her in his arms and haul her away.

She had scanned the foyer as she and Lady Epping descended the stairs from the second floor to meet her father. *He will come for me,* she had thought. *He promised me he would. He promised me.*

She had drained her mother's flask dry by that point, and her mind felt sufficiently numb with brandy. She had bussed her mother's cheek when they parted company at the foot of the stairs. Lord Epping had been waiting, his arm crooked in invitation to escort her.

"You look lovely, lamb," Lord Epping told her in a hush as they walked along a narrow corridor cleaved through the crowded ballroom. She heard quartets of musicians arranged throughout the vaulted chamber playing a harmonic blend of stringed instruments and winds. Everyone watched them, a sea of powdered faces, starched shoulders, and piled wigs. Everyone smiled and whispered and leaned together, and their visages had all blended together to Charlotte's eyes, none of them familiar or comforting. She felt caught in a dream, or as if she tried to walk forward while submerged in deep water.

He will come for me, she had thought, even as she caught sight of James ahead of her, standing with the Archbishop of Colchester, who would join them. *He promised he would.*

"I am sorry for all of this fuss," Lord Epping had said.

"It is all right, Father," she had replied.

He had met her gaze and took her hand, offering her a squeeze. "I love you, Charlotte."

"I love you, too."

It was not until the moment when Lord Epping drew her hand from his sleeve, tucking it into the nook of James' elbow that the full, dismaying realization struck her headlong and brutally.

He is not coming.

Lord Epping stepped away from her, abandoning her to the altar as from behind them, Frederick Cuthbert led Margaret toward the Archbishop. Charlotte looked up at James, and found him watching her, his mouth unfurled in a thin smile. "You would take my breath," he said in an undertone.

"Good," she snapped back. "Drop dead, then."

James chuckled. "I am going to enjoy this," he said, his lips scarcely moving, his words little more than fluttering air. "We may have to forego the ball my mother has planned to follow the ceremony. I am stiffening already just thinking about having you all to myself . . . every inch of you . . . at last."

He lifted her hand to his mouth and bussed her knuckles. The tip of his tongue slid slowly, suggestively between her fingers; a subtle gesture no one but Charlotte noticed. When she snatched her hand away from him, however, everyone around them saw and a curious murmur stirred in the crowd behind them.

"Do you know how a man breaks a willful horse, Charlotte?" he asked. "He rides it hard and often. A woman is no different."

The ceremony began, and the crowd behind them fell obligingly silent. Charlotte did not hear the Archbishop speaking; his voice droned on rhythmically in her mind without the benefit of any discernible words. She looked down at her hand, draped over James' sleeve and imagined his repulsive tongue sliding over those places where only hours earlier, Will's mouth and hands had brushed with love and stirred such pleasure. She shuddered, feeling tears sting her eyes.

Margaret and Frederick exchanged their vows first, and then the Archbishop turned his attention to Charlotte and James. She looked up at the clergyman, her eyes filled with sorrow as he recited the vows aloud for James, pausing after lengthy passages to allow for James' recitation. When Charlotte's turn came, she was mute.

A ripple of awkward whispers filled the room at her silence. The Archbishop raised his brow expectantly at her. "My lady, your response?" he said in encouragement.

James' hand closed tightly atop hers. "Darling," he said, his mouth spread in a humorless smile. "Do recite your vows."

She glanced at him and he held her gaze. "It is far too late for protest," he whispered, still smiling. "And I think it has been made clear to you what shall come to pass if you try."

"Bastard," Charlotte snapped, loud enough for the Archbishop to hear. He took an uncertain, stumbling step backward.

"Say the words, Charlotte," James ordered. He still smiled, but there was no cheer in his eyes; she could see bright rage glittering there. His hand crushed against hers, and she blinked against a flood of sudden, helpless tears.

"Say them," he hissed.

"All right," she conceded. She looked back at the Archbishop, who regarded her with bewildered concern apparent in his face. She struggled to smile. "I . . . forgive me," she said. "Might you repeat them, please, sir, as I . . . the vows have slipped from my mind."

"Of course, my lady," the Archbishop said, smiling again, but looking perplexed. He offered the vows again. As he spoke, a new murmur stirred through the crowd, growing louder and more sharp. Charlotte heard people shuffling in confusion. The Archbishop's gaze traveled beyond her shoulder, and his voice faltered, fading. Charlotte turned to look over her shoulder and her mouth spread in a joyous grin.

"Father!" Margaret cried, pulling away from Frederick, and hurrying toward the rear of the ballroom. Lord Essex was making his way along the opened aisle among the guests, leaning heavily against Reilly. He was ghastly pale and his shuffling steps were weak and weary.

"Father!" Margaret cried again, and Lady Essex ducked out from the throng, following her daughter.

"My lord!" she cried, aghast. "My lord, what has

happened to you?"

Lewis and Will strode boldly up the aisle behind Reilly and the Earl, with Lewis swinging a walking cane broadly to aid his injured gait. At the sight of Will—whom all believed to be Kenley Fairfax, Charlotte's former betrothed—a new and even more tremendous surge of voices filled the room, echoing off the ceiling and filling the air with a cacophonous din.

"Will!" Charlotte cried, shoving her way through the crowd in his direction. She felt James' hand close roughly about her arm, jerking her back. She staggered and nearly fell. She fell gracelessly against the Archbishop, who caught her clumsily.

"My lady!" he exclaimed.

"How dare you, Theydon, you rot bastard!" James roared, silencing the crowd. "How dare you drag your wretched carcass here into my home and sully the occasion of my wedding!"

He charged forward, balling his hands into fists. "What have you done to my father?" he bellowed. "By my breath, Theydon, if you have harmed him in any way out of petty, vengeful spite toward me, I will—"

Lewis snapped his cane up in a sharp arc just as James drew within steps of Will. The brass tip of the cane caught James beneath the shelf of his chin, giving him pause. "You will do nothing but step back and stand down, Roding," Lewis said in a low voice.

James met his gaze. "I will enjoy watching you hang, Woodside," he seethed. He turned to his father, and then looked about the crowd, raising his voice. "Here is treachery!" he shouted. "And surely the reason for my father's delay!"

He grabbed Lord Essex by the sleeve and shoved Reilly aside. "Get your rot hands off my father—remove your hand, you bastard!" he barked. "These men are the Black Trio bandits who have been tormenting and trespassing upon our highways!"

Another startled din arose at this proclamation. Will, Lewis, and Reilly drew close to one another, nearly shoulder to shoulder.

"My man, Cheadle, found evidence to prove this," James declared. "He was a thief-taker proper in London before coming into my service. Such assertions were well within his realm of expertise to make! I dispatched Cheadle myself last evening to meet my father's coach at the Essex border and see him safely northward to Dunmow. I cannot tell you of my heart's horror when neither arrived at Roding in time for my vows!"

James spared his father a feigned, doting look. "Or my relief that one at least, and most beloved to me, has made it."

He glared at Will, making a great show of supporting Lord Essex's waning strength, sheltering him in a clumsy embrace. "What offense have you dared see upon my father, Theydon?" he shouted. "What have you done to Edmond Cheadle? I will see the lot of you strung from Tyburn! Someone ride to Epping at once and see the sheriff brought to me!"

"That will not be necessary, Lord Roding, as I am already in attendance," Howard Linford said, walking from the rear of the ballroom. His clothes were still rumpled and his hair yet askew. He seemed to have found no need to shave that morning, but there was a light in his eyes Charlotte had not noticed upon their introduction; a glimmer of bright intellect. "Fortunately, your father saw fit to send for me first to meet him here."

James appeared as if he had been belted upside the head at the sight of the sheriff. "Splendid, then," he said, his voice shaky all at once with uncertainty. "Splendid, sir. Arrest these men!" He jabbed his forefinger at Will, Lewis, and Reilly each in turn. "They are scoundrels and highwaymen! They have accosted my father and my bride! God above only knows what they have done to Edmond Cheadle!"

"She . . . is not your bride yet," Lord Essex said, raising his head. "And . . . and by my breath, the dear lass never shall be."

His voice was frail and weary, his strength obviously waning, but there was fury aglow in his eyes as he forcibly wrenched himself loose of James' grasp. The crowd reacted, drawing back in startled surprise.

"You . . . my lord, you are delirious," James said to his father. "Overwrought, obviously injured. You . . . you do not know what you are saying. What have these bastards done to you?"

"They have saved my life," Lord Essex said. "The life you would have seen taken for nothing more than shameful greed. I am humbled by them, and might only hope to spend the rest of those days you would have seen stolen in offering my gratitude to them."

James stared at his father in horror. He turned to Charlotte, his eyes blazing with furious indignation, and then he whirled, glaring at Reilly, Lewis, and Will. "That is preposterous!" he cried. "How dare you twist my father's mind and turn him against me? What madness have you filled him with to make him believe such ludicrous fabrications and blatant falsehoods?"

"I could declare the reasons here, Lord Roding," Linford said, conspicuously drumming his fingertips against the butt of a pistol he carried tucked down the front of his breeches. The sight of the gun alarmed the crowd, and they recoiled, murmuring in frightened confusion. "Here," Linford said. "Before God, the Archbishop and all of your good neighbors and fellows. Or we could retire to an antechamber, that you might be enlightened with a modicum of privacy, sir, and the maintenance of at least some measure of dignity."

James whirled in a circle, sputtering. He faced the

sheriff again, his face flushed, his eyes ablaze, his hands curled in tight, shaking fists. Linford did not cow a bit; he continued tapping his pistol butt patiently. "It is your choice, my lord," he said. "Either way, you are coach-bound for Newgate by noon."

CHAPTER 23

CHARLOTTE BROKE AWAY FROM THE ARCH-bishop and raced toward Will, shouldering her way through the crowd as Linford escorted James from the ballroom. James accompanied him willingly, with no irons placed upon him, but his face remained infused with outraged color. He glanced over his shoulder as he and the sheriff ducked into the foyer, and he did not miss Charlotte leaping into Will's arms.

She laughed, kissing Will, trying to remember not to cry out his name in her overwhelming joy, reminding herself that among society, he was Kenley Fairfax. "You came for me!" she cried, pressing her mouth against his and kissing him deeply.

Will held her tightly against him, lifting her off of

her feet and spinning her in a circle. She was torn between laughter and tears as he set her gently aground once more. "I will always come for you," he said, smiling broadly at her, letting the tip of his nose brush hers. "I will never leave you again. Never, Charlotte. I swear to you."

The crowd swarmed about them, and they lost sight of Reilly and Lewis. Will caught her hand and began to move, shoving a path through the throng toward the foyer. "Where are we going?" she cried out, laughing.

They stumbled into the foyer, and Will broke into a run, still clasping her hand and forcing her to snatch her skirts in her fist lest she trip as she matched his pace. "Wait!" she laughed. "What about Reilly and Lewis? Lord Essex?"

"They will speak with the sheriff," Will called back, grinning broadly as they dashed down a corridor. He looked ahead of him, pausing long enough to open doors here and there, finally settling on a vacant parlor. He swept Charlotte inside, both of them laughing. He was against her immediately, punting the door closed behind them with his boot heel, drawing her near, kissing her mouth, her throat.

"Will . . ." Charlotte said, touching his shoulders and giggling. "Will, the windows . . . people will see . . ."

Will glanced at the broad windows flanking the room. The grounds beyond were swarming with displaced wedding guests, and more than a few had taken inadvertent notice of the couple through the glass. Charlotte peeped over her shoulder, feeling color rise in her cheeks as Will's hand slipped over her breast, as his lips tugged lightly, playfully against her ear. "Let them see," he said.

He raised his head and smiled at her. The people beyond the glass faded, as did the muted voices through the windows and walls. All at once, in that moment, there was only Will, and nothing else mattered in the whole of the world.

"Yes," Charlotte agreed. "Bloody let them." She eagerly accepted his kiss, opening her mouth, drawing his tongue against hers. She felt something hard poke above her pannier, and she glanced down, seeing the brass-capped butt of a pistol tucked into his pocket.

"Expecting trouble, Lord Theydon?" she asked.

He followed her gaze and laughed, slipping the pistol out of his greatcoat "I would not see you marry that rot, even if I had to shoot someone to prevent it," he said.

Charlotte laughed and kissed him again. She would never grow tired of this, she decided; she would never weary of his mouth, his touch, his fragrance. "I love you," she said, her lips on his, lifting in tandem to match his smile.

The door to the parlor flew open behind them, banging into the wall with a sharp, startling report. Charlotte's head jerked up at the sound; Will whirled, and between them, they had less than a second to realize James loomed upon the threshold, his face twisted with rage. Somehow, he had come to grasp a pistol in his fist—a pistol he leveled with murderous intent at Charlotte.

Will shoved himself protectively in front of Charlotte. She caught a blur of motion as his arm swung upward, his pistol raising in his hand; sunlight winked off of brass, and then overlapping, thunderous booms shuddered the glass panes in the windows, nearly deafening her. A blinding flash of dazzling sparks and a sudden, choking cloud of smoke filled the narrow confines of the room. Will slammed hard against her, knocking her backward and off her feet. She crashed to the ground in a tangle of petticoats, and Will fell atop her, pinning her to the floor.

"Will!" she screamed, her eyes smarting with tears from the smoke. She struggled to sit up, choking and coughing. Will did not move; he lay sprawled and motionless against her, and she screamed in horror, clutching at him.

"Will!" she cried. She could not see much for the smoke, but she felt a rip in his coat above his breast; the ragged edges of the pierced fabric still smoldered, and were crisp against her fingertips. "No, no!"

He had been shot; shot through the heart. "No!" she shrieked, as the smoke waned and the burned, tattered pellet hole came into her view. "No, Will! Answer me! Answer me!"

Charlotte seized him by the lapels, shaking him furiously. "Answer me!" she cried. "Will, do not leave me! You promised you would not! You promised me!"

She felt something brush her face, and she recoiled with a start. Will uttered a low moan, and then touched her face again, brushing his fingers against her cheek. "I . . . I am not going anywhere . . ." he groaned.

Charlotte cried out happily, and clutched at him. "I thought you were dead!" she cried. "The pellet caught you in the chest . . . your heart, and I . . . I thought . . ."

She helped him sit up. He moved slowly, grimacing and coughing to clear his lungs of smoke. He reached beneath the flap of his greatcoat lapel, and pulled his silver snuff box from the inside breast pocket. Charlotte blinked at it, stunned; the round from James' pistol had struck it squarely and it had crimped at the forceful impact, nearly crumpling inward on itself.

She looked at Will and they both stared at one another, trembling with mutual shock. "I . . . I should thank your father for his kindly advice on where to stow this," Will said, shakily.

Howard Linford charged through the parlor doorway with a clamor of heavy boot stomps. His hair was a frazzled halo about his head. "Hoah!" he cried.

"Hoah!" Will yelled, jerking himself in front of

Charlotte.

"Hoah!" Reilly and Lewis hollered, their voices overlapping as they, too, rushed through the doorway, holding pistols and knocking roughly into Linford. The three men danced and staggered before reclaiming their respective footing.

"What in the bloody hell is going on?" Lewis yelled. He looked down at his feet, and his eyes widened. "Hullo . . ."

Charlotte followed his gaze and realized for the first time that James lay sprawled and still on the rug. "James!" she gasped, shying against Will. "Is . . . is he . . . ?"

Linford squatted, balancing his weight on his toes. He reached down, running his fingertips along James' neck. He glanced at Charlotte and Will. "Quite so, yes," he said. "Squarely, even. He has a space where his nose ought rightly to be, and is not anymore."

As the sheriff leveled his sharp gaze at Will, Charlotte scrambled to her feet in alarm. "He attacked us, Mr. Linford," she said, stepping in front of Will. "He attacked us—he burst through the door with a pistol in hand and he shot at us! Will was only . . . I . . . I mean Kenley was defending himself, and me! Look at Kenley's snuff box, sir. He would have been killed if he had not kept it in his breast pocket!"

She snatched the snuff box from Will and marched toward Linford, holding it out in her palm. Linford studied the box for a long moment. He glanced at Charotte, his brow raised, and then at Will. "I know he shot at you," he said. "It was my gun he used. Gave me a shove and a clubbing for good measure."

The corner of Linford's mouth hooked in a wry smile. "Of course, my wife might have told him that was useless. He hit my head—to hear her tell of it, there is naught but rocks rattling around up there anyway."

ℭHAPTER 24

April, 1749

CHARLOTTE KNELT ON THE GROUND BE
neath the parlor window of Theydon Hall. She reached
beside her, slipping her hands into a large canvas sack she
had stuffed full of dried pine needles, and pulled out a
large pile. She pressed the mulch around the base of a
small boxwood she had transplanted from Epping For
est to the yard. She had trimmed its wide limbs back
close to the trunk, hoping this measure, and the warmth
of the new spring sunshine, might coax it into settling
comfortably in its new home.

She had lined the entire front of the house with the
small shrubs, interspersing bulbs and perennial seed
lings between them. It would look lovely when it al

came into bloom; by the beginning of summer, the gray stones and stern angles of Theydon Hall would be well complemented by a bright array of colorful flowers.

The windows on the whole of the first floor, and most of the second had been filled with new glass panes. Work on reconstructing and repairing the roof was nearly completed; they had needed to pause in their efforts during the winter, but had resumed them in full once the colder months had passed. She could hear the sounds of the carpenters and tilers at work three storeys stories above her, and lifted her head toward the noise, smiling. Lewis and Will were up there somewhere, both hard at work since the dawn helping to lay and set new peg tiles in place atop fresh rafter beams.

With James' death, so too, had the legend of the Black Trio died. Howard Linford had announced publicly that Edmond Cheadle, Camden Iden and Julian Stockley were to blame for every one of the Trio's notorious robberies, with James as the instigator behind it all and standing in during Charlotte's robbery to offer pretense against any seeming culpability in the crimes. The events at Roding Castle had swept any suspicions or rumors to the contrary aside, and life had moved forward without Reilly, Lewis, or Will ever doubted in their accounts.

Charlotte did not even hear the soft creaking of rope when Will lowered himself swiftly, gracefully from the roof. She did not hear his quiet footsteps, his boots in the new vernal grass behind her, and when he leaned over her shoulder, drawing his arms about her and nuzzling her ear, she jumped, laughing aloud, clinging to his arms.

"You yob," she said, grinning as she rose to her feet and turned to face him. "You gave me a fright. You will make me drop this baby right here in the yard."

"It takes hours of conscientious pushing, shoving, and pain to birth a baby. You cannot just spread your legs and drop it," Will replied, leaning his forehead against hers. "Your sister told me that."

His hands moved, falling gently to her growing belly. Such a softness always came upon him when he did this, and he would flush with fondness. "And hullo to you, little Lord Theydon," he said, bending down to kiss the swell of her abdomen.

"How do you know it is a lord?" she asked, playfully, tousling his dark hair with her fingertips. "It could well be a 'my lady,' and here already, she is not even born yet, and you are offering her offense."

If anyone in the Essex County social circles had taken notice of the fact Charlotte's pregnancy seemed to come about within a very narrow timeframe—only weeks following her wedding to Kenley Fairfax, Baron Theydon, in early November—neither Charlotte nor Will were the wiser for it. In fact, neither of them had set foot into a banquet hall or ballroom since they left

Roding Castle. They had wed gratefully, willingly and gladly, and neither of them had thought of much else but each other, the promise of their child, and their home in the months that followed.

"Oh, it will be a lord," he said, glancing up at her. "God would never suffer me so to endure even a miniature version of you—one is aplenty."

Charlotte laughed, slapping at him. He had anticipated this response, counted on it, actually, and caught her hands with his own, drawing her against him. "I could never know any greater blessing than that," he added softly.

They both heard the sounds of distant hoof beats along the drive leading toward the house. Will turned, and Charlotte moved beside him, both of them curious and puzzled as they caught sight of a carriage approaching, followed in line by three large, laden buckboards.

"Are you expecting more lumber delivered?" Charlotte asked, shielding her eyes from the sun's glare.

"No," Will replied. "Anyone to pay call for you?"

"No, Caroline is not due until Thursday," Charlotte said. She frowned thoughtfully. "That looks like Father's coach."

"Company is coming," Lewis called from aloft. He swung down from the eaves, his boots swinging wildly in the air as he swooped toward the ground, clinging to the rope. He landed heavily, his face glossy with sweat.

"A coach and three wagons coming up the way."

"We know," Charlotte said. "I think it is my mother and father."

Lewis arched his brow at Will, taking into account his cousin's rather disheveled appearance. Will was dressed for labor in old, stained and faded breeches; muddy boots; a patched and decidedly threadbare shirt with half the buttons missing, so it lay open to nearly his navel. Will's hair was askew in madcap tufts and curls framing his head and clinging to his cheeks with sweat. There was dirt smudged on his face, crusted beneath his fingernails.

"Sweet God," Lewis remarked, turning his gaze to the roof again. "I think I shall head aloft again, and miss the ensuing fun."

The Epping carriage drew up in front of the house, the horses reined to a halt. Will glanced at Charlotte, clearly horrified. She rose onto her tiptoes, kissing the angle of his jaw. "You look lovely, and smell even better," she said. "Do not fret."

"Your mother is going to devour me," Will groaned, as Charlotte took him by the hand and dragged him toward the coach.

The footman had already propped open the door, and Lord Epping disembarked, smiling broadly to see them. "Hullo!" he cried, opening his arms wide.

"Father, hullo," Charlotte said, accepting his embrace "What a surprise!" She glanced behind the coach, toward the buckboards. The wagons were filled with heavy loads of furniture. She spied chairs, a buffet; a pair of highboys, a large wardrobe, a matching set of carved head- and footboards to a bed, several writing desks and more. She turned to her father, bewildered. "What is all of this?"

"Obviously if someone did not intercede on your behalf, darling, you would raise that baby in empty rooms with only its echo against the ceilings for décor," Lady Epping said, as the footman helped her exit the coach. "Look at you, dressed like a peasant and dusted in dirt. What have you been doing?"

"Planting boxwood, Mother," Charlotte said proudly. "I transplanted it myself from the forest. It will look divine when it blooms along the outer wall, do you not think?"

Lady Epping turned her gaze to Will. Lord Epping had extended a fond greeting to the young man, clasping hands with him heartily, but under Lady Epping's scrutiny, Will's bright expression faltered. "How . . . how do you fare, my lady?" he asked, lowering his face politely to his toes.

"I am well, Lord Theydon, thank you," she replied. "I thought since my daughter was with child, and thus fairly well confined to the grounds here, I might save her the trouble of shopping and offer you these furnishings, if they would please you."

"I . . . thank you, my lady," he said. "That . . . that is kind of you. I . . . I have been meaning to bring Charlotte to London before she grows too uncomfortable for the trip, but I . . . we were hoping to have the roof finished, and the glass replaced in the third floor . . ."

"They all belonged to Charlotte's grandmother," Lady Epping said. "My mother, Lord Theydon. Charlotte should enjoy a certain fondness to keep them."

"That is very gracious, my lady," Will said, completely flabbergasted by her generosity.

"I am certain they are a bit antiquated for your tastes, but they are functional yet, and not repulsive to the eye," Lady Epping said, waving her hand dismissively. "I thought perhaps you might offer me a proper tour of your home. I am certain I can offer some suggestions for pleasing placement."

"I . . . hoah, well, I . . . of course, my lady," he stammered. "I . . . I would be pleased to, and . . . and delighted besides, and . . ." He glanced down at himself and struggled against a dismayed groan. "I will change first, my lady," he said. "And . . . and wash a bit . . . make myself more presentable."

"Nonsense," Lady Epping said. "You have been working. There is no shame or offense offered when a man presents himself in a state wrought of decent labor. You can escort me as you are, Lord Theydon."

"Of course, my lady," Will said. He offered his elbow to Lady Epping when she held out her hand expectantly.

"Charlotte, darling, why do you not survey the wagon contents?" she called over her shoulder as Will led her toward the front steps. "If there is anything that does not suit your fancy, tell your father, and we can bring it back to Darton."

"Yes, Mother," Charlotte said, as confounded as her husband. Will gave her one last fleeting glance and then he and Lady Epping entered the house.

"What in the bloody world has gotten into her?" Charlotte asked, turning to her father. "She is not going to hurt him, is she?"

"I should think not," Lord Epping replied. "She has been in rather good humor about this visit all morning. Excited, even, I dare say."

"I thought that was on my account," someone said, and Charlotte's eyes widened in new surprise as Reilly stepped down from the coach.

"Reilly!" she cried, hurrying toward him, hugging his neck fiercely. "What are you doing in Epping parish? You are supposed to be shipboard and two months out on the Atlantic!"

"I have been land-laid, and two months in London," Reilly replied, kissing her cheek. "I have missed too much being out to sea, and now my little lamb sister is about to drop her baby. I would rather keep to England, all things being equal."

"They let you resign from the Navy?" Charlotte asked.

"King George himself granted me an honorable discharge," Reilly said, smiling. "Thanks to the gracious intervention of Kenward Houghton, the Earl of Essex, I suspect."

"Splendid, Reilly!" Charlotte cried, hugging him again. She turned her head toward the roof and shouted over his shoulder. "Lewis! Lewis, look who is here!"

Lewis' head appeared over one of the peaks. "By my breath, they will let anything wash ashore these days!" he cried out, laughing. Again, he went hurtling off the rooftop for the pulley lines. He swung downward, laughing all the way. "You bloody bastard! I thought you were doomed to chase rum-runners and privateers south of the Caribbean!"

As Lewis and Reilly exchanged fond embraces, Lord Epping took Charlotte by the hand and led her to the buckboards. "I think Reilly has taken a lass for himself," he remarked once they had drawn a safe distance out of Reilly's earshot.

"Really?" Charlotte asked, feigning surprise. Reilly had not yet broached the subject of Meghan with their parents. He would eventually; it was fairly well unavoidable, but she did not blame him for his reservations.

Lord Epping nodded, seeming pleased by the notion. "I do not know whom, but I suspect she is someone rather dear in his regard," he said. "He has made mention to me a time or two, only in passing, mind you, but enough to see it plainly in his face. He is smitten." He looked momentarily thoughtful. "Though I do not know why he would hesitate to tell your mother."

Charlotte raised a dubious brow. "Why, I cannot imagine either."

Lord Epping glanced at her, and the corner of his mouth hooked. They both laughed.

"Come on, Father," Charlotte said, trying to steer him toward the house. "I will have Una or one of the maids fix a pot of tea. I cannot dare leave Kenley alone with Mother too long."

"She wants to like him," Lord Epping said. "Truly, I think she does."

"Despite herself," Charlotte added, and he laughed again.

"She is trying, at any rate," he said. "And there is a good enough place to begin, do you not think?"

Charlotte smiled at her father as they stood in the comfortable shade of Theydon Hall, the home she and Will were making together. She leaned toward him to kiss his cheek, and felt the baby stir lightly, moving within her womb. She drew her hand against the swell of her belly and smiled at Lord Epping. "Yes, Father," she said. "I do believe that it is."

By Honor Bound

Helen A. Rosburg

Bound by fate. Bound by love. Bound by honor . . .

Honneure Mansart, orphaned child of a lowly servant, never dreamed that she would one day find herself at the glittering palace of Versailles as a servant to the young and lovely Marie Antoinette, future Queen of France. Nor could she have imagined the love of her life would turn out to be her beloved foster brother Phillipe, who also served the young princess. Their lives were golden.

But the young princess, Antoinette, has a mortal enemy in Madame du Barry, the aging king's mistress. And Honneure has a rival for Phillipe, a servant in du Barry's entourage. Together the women scheme to destroy both Antoinette and Honneure. Then Louis the XV dies, and his grandson inherits the throne. Marie Antoinette becomes the Queen of France.

Honneure and Phillipe, their lives inextricably entwined with those of the king and queen, find a second chance together. Yet as France's political climate overheats, sadness and tragedy stalk both couples once again . . . tragedy, and a terrible secret that might lead Honneure to the guillotine in the footsteps of her queen.

ISBN#097436391X
ISBN#9780974363912
Gold Imprint
US $6.99 / CDN $8.99
Available Now
www.helenrosburg.com

Helen A. Rosburg

Call of the Trumpet

Shattered when his Bedouin wife dies in childbirth, Francoise Villier, wealthy and prominent Frenchman, flees the African desert—the horses and the people—he has come to love so dearly. He takes with him only his infant daughter, Cecile, faithful Bedouin servant, Jali, and a magnificent Arab mare. Before he leaves, however, he extracts a promise from one of the most powerful of the desert chieftains.

Years later, upon her father's death, Cecile must make a momentous decision: stay in the country that has spurned her, and her mother's heritage; or seek that very heritage in the heart of the awesome and terrible Sahara Desert. With only the aging but devoted Jali, her vast knowledge of the Arab horses her father bred, and enormous courage, Cecile finally embarks on the journey of a lifetime to find her foster father, the legendary Raga eben Haddal.

So begins a vital struggle to survive, not only physically, but mentally and spiritually as Cecile's European upbringing clashes with a Bedouin culture that seems brutal-and male oriented-on the surface. It is a struggle that will earn her a new name, Al Dhiba bint Sada-She-Wolf, daughter of Sada-and teach her about love and loyalty. And heartbreak.

ISBN#1933836148
ISBN#9781933836140
Jewel Imprint: Sapphire
US $6.99 / CDN $8.99
August 2007
www.helenrosburg.com

VANQUISHED
HOPE TARR

A devil's bargain.

"The photograph must be damning, indisputably so. I mean to see Caledonia Rivers not only ruined but vanquished. Vanquished, St. Claire, I'll settle for nothing less."

Known as The Maid of Mayfair for her unassailable virtue, unwavering resolve, and quiet dignity, suffragette leader, Caledonia — Callie — Rivers is the perfect counter for detractors' portrayal of the women as rabble rousers, lunatics, even whores. But a high-ranking enemy within the government will stop at nothing to ensure that the Parliamentary bill to grant the vote to females dies in the Commons — including ruining the reputation of the Movement's chief spokeswoman.

After a streak of disastrous luck at the gaming tables threatens to land him at the bottom of the Thames, photographer Hadrian St. Claire reluctantly agrees to seduce the beautiful suffragist leader and then use his camera to capture her fall from grace. Posing as the photographer commissioned to make her portrait for the upcoming march on Parliament, Hadrian infiltrates Callie's inner circle. But lovely, soft-spoken Callie hardly fits his mental image of a dowdy, man-hating spinster. And as the passion between them flares from spark to full-on flame, Hadrian is the one in danger of being vanquished.

ISBN#1932815759
ISBN#9781932815757
Jewel Imprint: Sapphire
US $6.99 / CDN $8.99
Available Now
www.hopetarr.com

ENSLAVED
HOPE TARR

Daisy Lake is only a memory to successful barrister Gavin Car-michael. But a memory he cannot forget. "Through thick and thin, forever and ever, come what may, we'll stay together . . ." is the pact the young orphans made over a decade ago, before the wide-eyed little girl was torn from his arms. Only a precious, painful memory . . . until Gavin walks into an East End supper club where the headlining act is the infamous nightingale of the Montmartre music halls, Delilah du Lac.

Overcome, Gavin storms on stage and carries her off, determined to save her from the lifestyle she has apparently embraced. But Daisy wants no part of him. She has only one desire: to act on a proper London stage.

It is a dream Gavin can make come true. He promises to employ every resource at his disposal to see she gets a part in the upcoming run of Shakespeare's "As You Like It" . . . provided she agrees to live with him for one month.

Daisy has slept with men for far less. And Gavin has matured into an exceedingly handsome man. But as their sensual games increase in intensity, Gavin is the one in danger of being . . .

ENSLAVED

ISBN#1933836121
ISBN#9781933836126
Jewel Imprint: Sapphire
US $6.99 / CDN $8.99
June 2007
www.hopetarr.com

A Knight's Vengeance

CATHERINE KEAN

A quest for revenge . . .

Geoffrey de Lanceau is a knight, the son of the man who once ruled Wode. His noble sire died, however, branded as a traitor. But never will Geoffrey believe his father betrayed their king, and swears vengeance against the man who brought his sire down in a siege to take over Wode.

A quest for love . . .

Lady Elizabeth Brackendale dreamed of marrying for love, but is promised by her father to a lecherous old baron. Then she is abducted and held for ransom by a scarred, tormented rogue who turns out to be the very knight who has sworn vengeance against her father.

A quest for truth . . .

The threads of deception sewn eighteen years ago bind the past and present. Only by Geoffrey and Elizabeth championing their forbidden love can the truth — and the lies — be revealed about . . .

A Knight's Vengeance.

ISBN#1932815481
ISBN#9781932815482
Jewel Imprint: Sapphire
US $6.99 / CDN $8.99
Available Now
www.catherinekean.com

My Lady's Treasure

CATHERINE KEAN

The Treasure of Love . . .

Facing the tall, brooding rider by the stormy lakeshore, Lady Faye Rivellaux clings to her goal—to rescue the kidnapped child she vowed to protect. At all costs, she must win back the little girl she loves as her own. When the stranger demands a ransom she can never pay, Faye offers him instead her one last hope—a gold cup.

Brant Meslarches is stunned to see the chalice. Worth a fortune, it's proof a lost cache of wealth from the legendary Celtic King Arthur does exist, as Brant's murdered brother believed. Brant can't return the little girl to the lady whose desperate beauty captivates him. Yet, now that he's seen Lady Faye, he can't let her escape his grasp; she is the key to his only means of redemption.

The last thing Faye wants is an alliance with a scarred knight tormented by secrets. But, she has no other way to rescue the child. Risking all, she joins Brant's quest. And finds some things are more valuable than gold.

ISBN#1932815783
ISBN#9781932815788
Jewel Imprint: Sapphire
US $6.99 / CDN $8.99
April 2007
www.catherinekean.com

catherine kean

Dance of Desire

Desperate to save her brother Rudd from being condemned as traitor, Lady Rexana Villeaux must dance in disguise at a feast fo the High Sheriff of Warringham. Her goal is to distract him s her servant can steal a damning missive from the sheriff's sola Dressed in the gauzy costume of a desert courtesan, dancin with all the passion and sensuality in her soul, she succeeds i her mission. And, at the same time, condemns herself.

Fane Linford, the banished son of an English earl, joine Richard's crusade only to find himself a captive in a hellis eastern prison. He survived the years of torment, it's rumore because of the love of a Saracen courtesan. The rumors are tru And when he sees Rexana dance . . .

Richard has promised Fane an English bride, yet he desire only one woman — the exotic dancer who tempted him. The he discovers the dancer's identity. And learns her brother is i his dungeon, accused of plotting against the throne. It is mor temptation than Fane can resist.

The last thing Rexana wants is marriage to the dark and broodin Sheriff of Warringham. But her brother is his prisoner, and the may be only one way to save him. Taking the greatest chance c her life, Rexana becomes the sheriff's bride. And learns that th Dance of Desire was only a beginning . . .

ISBN#193281535X
ISBN#9781932815351
Jewel Imprint: Sapphire
US $6.99 / CDN $8.99
Available Now
www.catherinekean.com

Cynthia Thomason

Gabriel's Angel

The year is 1871, and life at a remote lighthouse off the Georgia coast has become routine for Livvy Drummond. Then a wounded convict escapes from a passing prison ship and swims ashore. He threatens her . . . and collapses at her feet.

When Lieutenant Gabriel Hampton opens his eyes, he beholds an angel. An angel, moreover, who not only nurses him back to health, but senses the nobility beneath his rugged, feral appearance. Having escaped a life sentence, the result of an unjust court martial, he finds new life, and new love, in the hands of the lightkeeper's beautiful granddaughter.

Springtime on the remote island is nearly idyllic for Livvy and Gabe until circumstances tear them apart. Although Livvy is determined to help Gabe escape his hopeless future, secrets from her childhood threaten to destroy what she and Gabe have built — secrets that tragically link her to Gabe in a way neither would ever have dreamed. Will they be able to find their way back to each other? Or will the Civil War claim another two victims?

ISBN#1932815562
ISBN#9781932815566
Jewel Imprint: Sapphire
US $6.99 / CDN $8.99
Available Now
www.cynthiathomason.com

The Lighthorseman
Marjorie Jones

Dale Winters rode in the great charge at Beersheba in the final months of The Great War and has never forgiven himself for surviving. His younger brother did not. As a result, guilt-ridden, Dale gives up the passion in his life — horses. If his brother could no longer ride the animals he loved so much, then neither would he. A shattered man, Dale returns to his home in Western Australia.

Emily Castle, late of Arizona, inherited one-half of the Castle Winters Sheep Station in Western Australia when her Uncle Charles passed away. For years, through his letters, her uncle had regaled Emily with tales of the exploits of the boys he had fostered. With a heart full of hope and happiness, she moves to her new home and an inevitable meeting with the amazing and adventurous Dale Winters.

But the man who comes home from the war is not the one she envisioned in her dreams. Broken promises and a vow made to a dead man have stolen away his joy of life. Then Emily wagers her share of the station, and herself, on a horse race and becomes unable to ride. Will Dale learn, before it's too late, that some promises are meant to be broken?

ISBN#1932815457
ISBN#9781932815450
Jewel Imprint: Sapphire
US $6.99 / CDN $8.99
Available Now
www.marjoriejones.com

SUNBURST'S CITADEL

THERESE NICHOLS

Amid the exotic splendor of historic India comes a
sweeping tale of desire and duty . . .

Shamsi, a beautiful but penniless entertainer, is haunted
by a childhood tragedy that changed her life. She hides
behind silken veils, praying to escape the desires of
men. And keeps her secret close to her heart.

Lord Karim, military advisor to the emperor, is bound
to put duty above all else, even the desires of his heart.
Though he loves Shamsi, his soul-mate, she is destined
for another. The man Karim serves. It is not the only
obstacle to their union.

Shamsi is Hindu, a commoner. Karim is a Christian
nobleman. Shamsi is Rajput; Karim a Moghul. And he
hides a secret of his own.

Can love survive the truth? Or will the fire of their passion leave only ashes?

ISBN#1932815619
ISBN#9781932815610
Jewel Imprint: Sapphire
US $6.99 / CDN $8.99
Available Now

Saddle up and brace yourself for a hilarious ride . . .

LASSO
THE MOON

BY BETH CIOTTA

Motivated by a childhood promise, Paris Garrett travels to the wilds of Arizona Territory (1877) to seek fame as a stage actress. Never mind that she doesn't possess a lick of experience or that her true passion is songwriting. Before he died, her beloved papa encouraged her to reach for the stars. She promised to lasso the moon! She's already slipped free of her over-protective brothers. Nothing and no one, especially some badge-wearing Romeo, is going to rein her in or stand in her way.

Joshua Grant's life went from diamonds to dirt in less time than a rattler strikes. His uncle was killed, leaving him with an opera house he doesn't want, and forcing him to quit the law enforcement job he loved. The topper: In order to keep his sidewinder snake of a cousin from inheriting, he has to honor his uncle's will and marry within two weeks. Life can't get much worse, and then he falls for an eccentric, spitfire songwriter with a mysterious past and a passel of troublesome admirers. Marrying Paris is about as smart as kissing a coyote, but that's exactly what he intends to do–whether she likes it or not.

Together they could realize their dreams.

That's if they don't drive each other crazy first!

ISBN#1932815287
ISBN#9781932815283
Jewel Imprint: Sapphire
US $6.99 / CDN $8.99
Available Now
www.bethciotta.com

ROMANCING
THE WEST
BY BETH CIOTTA

Emily McBride is in a pickle. The preacher's daughter secretly writes scandalous romantic adventures. But someone's uncovered her secret talent and threatens to expose her double life. Her small town friends and the man of her dreams will never speak to her again. Worse, she's growing fond of her new friend, a literary poet, who would surely be horrified by her novels.

When the Peacemaker Alliance recruits lawman Seth Wright, he's ready, willing, and able to kick ruthless desperado butt for the covert government agency. His enthusiasm wanes, however, when his first assignment takes him to California to propose marriage to Miss Emily McBride on behalf of his boss, and deliver her back to Arizona Territory. He's a lawman, not a courier. Worse, the small town librarian mistakes him for a dandified poet! Before he sets her straight, she confesses she's mixed up in something tawdry. With two unwanted suitors hounding her, the woman needs protection. So Seth assumes the fancy pants identity to room in her house without compromising her reputation.

Seth's good intentions take a monumental twist when he develops genuine feelings for the passionate book lover. She's not what she seems. More jolting, neither is he.

ISBN#1932815929
ISBN#9781932815924
Jewel Imprint: Sapphire
US $6.99 / CDN $8.99
July 2007
www.bethciotta.com

For more information

about other great titles from

Medallion Press, visit

www.medallionpress.com